PUCK *of the* IRISH

A Vipers Sin Bin Novel

K. D. MILLER

ISBN: 979-8-9887609-5-5

Cover by: Y'all That Graphic

✹ Created with Vellum

For all the book dragons out there who, like me, indulge in the cardinal sin of loving a blonde MMC (::gasp!::) - this one is for you.

Our blonde-haired, blue-eyed, dirty-talking, thirst trap expert, star Center of the Seattle Vipers thanks you wholeheartedly for your service 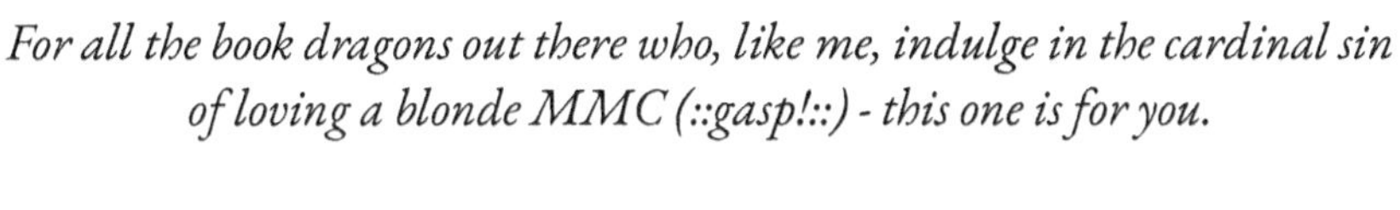

Contents

Chapter 1 — 1

Chapter 2 — 7

Chapter 3 — 15

Chapter 4 — 23

Chapter 5 — 31

Chapter 6 — 39

Chapter 7 — 47

Chapter 8 — 53

Chapter 9 — 61

Chapter 10 — 75

Chapter 11 — 83

Chapter 12 — 95

Chapter 13 — 105

Chapter 14 — 121

Chapter 15 — 129

Chapter 16 — 143

Chapter 17 — 151

Chapter 18 — 163

Chapter 19 — 175

Chapter 20 — 185

Chapter 21 — 193

Chapter 22 — 201

Chapter 23 — 215

Chapter 24 — 221

Chapter 25 — 229

Chapter 26 — 235

Acknowledgments — 241

Also by K.D. Miller — 243

One

NAT

"I'd say go for the salad fork."

I tear my gaze up from the table to see Anthony Rizzo striding over. Star center for the Seattle Vipers hockey team, social media thirst-trap expert, and all-around playboy, he's definitely not someone I thought I'd see here tonight. I blink in surprise but quirk a brow in question as he slides into the chair beside me. My other tablemates are all up schmoozing or dancing or throwing money around. I'm biding my time, hidden in the corner, until I can get the hell out of here.

"You looked like you were wondering which piece of cutlery you should use to gouge your eyes out. My vote is the salad fork," he clarifies as he leans back to lounge casually in the chair, giving me one of those slow, slightly crooked smiles of his that melts the panties off of anyone within a six-block radius. He looks too handsome for his own good. I mean, he *always* does—six-foot-four, blonde hair, blue eyes, abs for days and pearly whites that would make a dentist cream his jeans—but damn if the man can't wear the absolute hell out of a tux. I've seen him in suits before, of course. In fact, the first time I officially met the man he was in a suit for a social media photo shoot. I may or may not have done something incredibly embarrassing, but he thankfully didn't notice and I've managed to act like a normal human since then. Well, mostly. I can't be held responsible for what happens when Jell-o shots are involved.

"I would also suggest only gouging out one eye. Then you can have a patch. Ya know, do the whole sexy pirate thing."

"I'm not sure that works for girls," I point out.

"Oh you'd be surprised…" I snort, unable to help myself. He always makes me laugh, even when I'm in a shit mood.

"What are you doing here?" I ask, running my finger along the rim of my wine glass. He signals to a server for a drink, flashing her a winning smile when she delivers it and making the girl blush deeply. I'm not immune to his charms by any means, but we've managed to keep things friendly and professional since we met a couple of months back —we're kind of coworkers in a sense, and that can get all kinds of messy and complicated. Not only that, but he's a notorious one-and-done kind of guy, a new puck bunny on his arm every night, and while that's completely fine with me since I'm not so sure I want a relationship right now anyway, I would admittedly just hate to be one among so many, just a name on a long, long, *long*, list.

So, we've flirted, I've fantasized, he's eye-fucked, but that's the extent of it. We've hung out plenty of times, our rowdy little group of a handful of players, my boss, Hattie, our other marketing colleague, Bobby, and myself (dubbing ourselves the Vipers Sin Bin) doing trivia nights and bar crawls and barbecues, and while there have been a few *almost* moments between us, we've never crossed the line.

But fuck if I don't want to steamroll right over it tonight. I don't want to be here, I've already been given yet another lecture about my life choices, I've had the perfect amount of wine, and Rizzo is looking *too. damn. good.*

"I don't strike you as the philanthropic type?" he asks, feigning hurt. I know he actually does a lot for local charities and Make-a-Wish, and is always one to volunteer for events at the arena. That's the problem with Anthony Rizzo: on the surface, he's just a classic fuckboy—but in real-ity, he isn't one at all. Oh he gets laid six ways from Sunday by too many women to count, don't get me wrong, but he isn't actually a dickhead about it. He doesn't act like a jerk, isn't chauvinistic or gross, doesn't lead girls on or make empty promises just to get some.

He's actually a really good guy.

Which makes him dangerous. It would be extremely easy to fall for Rizzo, and that would be probably the dumbest decision I've ever made in a string of very questionable ones.

"You don't strike me as the attending galas for philanthropic causes type," I clarify.

He shrugs. "I came as a favor to a friend. It's for a good cause, the food is always top notch at a Harrington Foundation event, especially ones at the Celeste, there's an open bar, and, most importantly, I look fucking *fantastic* in a tux," he says with a wink and I roll my eyes, but smile. "So, I figured why not. The bigger question is what are *you* doing here, Nat?" He still lounges casually, like he doesn't have a care in the world, but he's searching my face in that way he has that most people don't notice. Rizzo sees far more than he lets on. He's happy to play the dumb jock (though he actually graduated top of his class from Cornell), or the eye candy that doesn't take much of anything seriously, but there's much more to him. I hate that I've noticed it. I hate that it makes him all the more interesting. I hate that it makes me like him even more.

Liking Anthony Rizzo only leads to heartache and awkward days at the office. Not a good idea. A casual hookup, on the other hand...*No. Still not a good idea*, I remind myself.

"I came as a favor to a friend," I say, repeating his answer. It's sort of a version of the truth if you stand back and squint really hard.

He arches a brow. "Is that so?"

I take a long sip of my wine, giving him a challenging look. He's tried to get into personal life questions in the past—not in a creepy or annoying way, just in a let's-get-to-know-each-other-because-we-all-hang-out-and-my-best-friend-is-probably-in-love-with-your-best-friend way—but I haven't given up much. My personal life is...complicated, so I prefer to keep it vague.

"Are you having a good time at least? You look amazing, by the way," he adds, letting his gaze drift downward over my tight black gown, lingering a bit where the slit cuts high up on my thigh, before slowly skating back upwards over my chest and throat, and finally meeting my eyes. His baby blues dance with a sultry playfulness that makes my pulse race. One of those *almost* moments is brewing, I can feel it, and right now, I don't want to stop at almost. *Bad idea, bad idea, bad idea...*

"Thanks," I say, trying not to sound breathless. "But I can't say that I'm having a good time, no."

"No?"

I shake my head. "These things are always a pain. A lot of money gets raised for great causes, so that part is good, but the rest of it is just tiresome. A bunch of rich people throwing around money and looking down their noses at everyone, comparing whose summer house in the Hamptons is bigger or who has the newest yacht." His eyes narrow a bit.

"Do you make a habit of attending charity galas? Even though you apparently hate them?"

Shit. I take another sip of wine, trying to come up with an answer when I see Erin heading my way, a determined—and slightly terrified— look on her face. Double shit.

"Do you wanna get out of here?" I ask quickly. Rizzo's brows go skyward and I roll my eyes. "Not like that, Thirst Trap," I say and he huffs out a laugh at my nickname for him. "But do you want to grab a drink somewhere that's...not here?"

"I suppose I can be persuaded to do that. I'm ready to get this bowtie off anyway," he says, standing and offering me his hand. I grin and glance around.

"Here, this way." I tug him into the shadows on the edge of the room and duck behind the stage to slip out of the side door. I've become a pro at sneaking out of these things without being noticed or stopped.

"Why do I get the feeling that was an escape of sorts?" he asks.

"Maybe it was," I tell him with a sly grin, the usual playful ease that we always have settling into place. Another problematic thing about Anthony Rizzo? I always have fun and feel like the most authentic version of myself with him—which is crazy, really, because I'm honestly not sure even I know who myself is these days. I'm slowly figuring it out, and taking the job with the Vipers has been a huge help in that regard, but I'm still not completely sure who Natalie Morgan is. So how the fuck does Rizzo make me somehow know exactly who I am whenever I'm with him?

Sure, at first, I was a little starstruck and completely distracted by the

Rizzo-ness of him. I've been following hockey my whole life, but especially the Vipers being Seattle born and bred, so meeting him was like meeting a celebrity. But once that initial jolt wore off and we started hanging out with our little group, things were just easy.

And dangerous.

And stupid.

Yet here I am, possibly making the dumbest decision of my life...and I can't help but smile at the gorgeous man in the tux standing beside me as he offers me his arm.

"Hmm, how about that drink then, Houdini?"

Two

RIZZO

"Jewel thief?" I ask over our second round of drinks. We ended up at one of my favorite spots just around the corner from the event, a small, almost hole-in-the-wall Irish pub called Delaney's where I can almost always come and not be bombarded. All the regulars and staff know me by now and don't think much of my appearances anymore. The owner, Sean, actually grew up not too far from my mom, so I'd immediately loved the place and they've had more than one Face-Time chat while I sat at the bar, reminiscing over childhood haunts and finding all the people they knew in common. Small world and all that.

Nat grins and damn does she have a great smile. She's beautiful, not just hot or sexy—though she's those things too—but really fucking *beautiful*. Don't ask me to explain the differences, but they exist, I promise you.

Whether she's done up to the nines, like she is tonight, or in leggings and a hoodie hanging out at Shep's place watching a game while we cook out, she's gorgeous, plain and simple. Just because I know better than to fuck around with anyone within the organization doesn't mean I haven't noticed...or thought about her in ways that I really shouldn't an embarrassingly large number of times. I tell myself that it's just that whole it-being-forbidden-makes-it-hotter thing that keeps Nat on my mind, but that's only half true, really. There's something about the girl that caught my eye the second I met her. I've even slowed my man-whoring as Shep calls it since Nat came along. I'm not ashamed of the way I live my life by any means, but for some reason...I don't know, I don't want Nat to think of me as just the hockey playing fuck boy who can't keep it in my pants. What the fuck is that about? I try not to read anything into it, but I can't ignore it completely no matter how hard I try.

But it doesn't matter either way. Nothing can happen between us like that.

She watches me over the rim of her glass, her gray eyes as mesmerizing as always. I don't think I've ever met anyone that has eyes like that. They're like gray marble, but with so much depth I sometimes feel like she's seeing way too much. Shep always says I do that to him, see more than he's trying to show everyone, so I guess Nat and I have that in common, but it makes me nervous when she looks at me that way. I like to dish out but not take it, apparently.

We sit close together at a small two-top table in the back corner beneath a glowing Guinness sign. She brushes my arm when she reaches for a fry and it sends a small jolt through me. And then I realize that this is the first time just the two of us have hung out. Sure, we end up chatting in a corner together when the group hangs out more often than not, or team up for Wii nights or cornhole, but everyone else is still there to keep us both in check—because with the way we click and the looks she gives me when she thinks I'm not watching, I know damn well that it isn't just me that's feeling it.

But now, there's no buffer, no one to make sure we don't do something stupid. There's just me, and Nat, and my good-decision-making brain slowly fucking off and letting the other one located a little farther south take over...

I clear my throat and meet her gaze, waiting for an answer.

"Nope, try again."

"Hmm. Witness protection?" I snap and point at her, eyes lighting up. "I know! You turned state's evidence and put a big mafia boss in prison for life and now he's out for revenge and you saw one of his henchmen in the gala?" She giggles and I can't help but grin.

"You watch too much *Law & Order*. Plus to turn state's evidence, I would have to be a criminal myself." She quirks a brow.

"I could see you doing all sorts of nefarious activities, Natalie." Her lips curl upwards and she shrugs a shoulder.

"Fair."

I take another drink and try to figure out the absolute mystery that is Nat Morgan. She has a way of answering personal questions yet not *actually* answering them, and somehow you don't really notice it until hours later. It's an art, really. Very impressive.

I know that she's from Seattle and went to Yale, which I actually only know because Hattie—or Mac, as we all call her—made a comment about being surrounded by all the Ivy Leaguers giving her a complex, and worked on the East Coast after graduation for a few years. I know she came back this way about a year ago after her mom died and that she's not very close to her dad who's a realtor or something. I know she's way overqualified for her job as an assistant but seems content in it for now. I know she loves Kona Big Waves and cheese fries, and is an absolute menace when it comes to hustling guys at the pool table. I may or may not have been a victim myself and had to cough up three hundred bucks to the little con woman one of the first few times we all hung out. I will admit it's kind of hot watching her do it to other poor souls though. Don't ask me to explain.

But that's about it. I don't know much past surface-level stuff like favorite sports teams and that she likes to do Karaoke when she drinks (and can actually carry a pretty good tune). But I want to know. I want to know more about her, the *real* her that I get the feeling she's hiding from the world for who knows what reason.

"Well, it's gotta be an ex then," I say, leaning back in my chair.

She hikes a shoulder. "I was avoiding someone, yeah. Aaron." A stupid fucking jolt of annoyance and jealousy spikes in my chest. Who the hell is this Aaron guy? Then I frown, shocked at my response. I don't fucking do jealousy, especially not with someone I'm not even dating. Not that I date at all. Whatever. Bottom line is that Nat can have as many ex-boyfriends as she wants. Why should that chap my ass?

...But what if he's the kind of ex that Hattie—or Mac as we all call her—has? I don't know much, but I know enough, and if this Aaron guy is even half as bad as Mac's ex, then maybe I need to go back to the gala and have a little chat with him. I'm typically pretty easy going off the ice, but when the situation calls for it, I'm not at all afraid to get my knuckles bloody.

"He's not like...stalking you, right?" I ask, not wanting to jump into her personal business if I'm not wanted there, but needing an answer at the same time. Her brow furrows for a moment but then amusement sparks in her gray eyes and her lips curl into a soft smile.

"Why? Would you go back and rough him up if I said yes?"

"Hell yeah I would. That shit doesn't fly," I answer automatically. Her brows rise in surprise and I know what she's thinking, so I push on. "Look, I may be a playboy, so I know what you're thinking, but I'm the kind that respects women, fucking *worships* them, and guys who don't understand respect need to be taught some manners."

Something shifts then, just a fraction, but it might as well be a fucking mile with the sudden heaviness in the small space between us. Her gaze seems to darken, shifting to my lips for a moment before pulling back up to meet my eyes.

"Worships them, huh?" she asks softly, and suddenly we're talking about something else entirely. I hadn't meant it to go that direction, exactly, but, well, it's true. I lean forward, throwing my rules to the wind and deciding that we're both fucking adults. If we want to hook up, we can do it and still manage to be normal around each other, I'm sure. *Unless she wants more...*I tell that voice to shut the fuck up. I'll deal with that later. She knows how I operate and it's not like my reputation is a secret or anything. She knows what she's getting into if she decides to make the decision.

And my God, do I need to her to make it so badly I think I might die if she doesn't.

"All night long, usually," I say, voice pitched low and laced with all the promises she can imagine. She swallows hard and our gazes stay locked for an endless, agonizing, perfect moment. I don't look away. I don't flinch. I hold her stare and let her see that I'm completely on board if she is.

Finally, her lips curl and one light brow arches in challenge.

"Prove it, Thirst Trap."

Fuck, is this really happening?

I don't think I've ever called for a check faster or louder than I had the moment the words were out of her mouth. She giggled and I grinned, deciding not to even wait for the check, just throwing a couple of hundreds down on the table and grabbing Nat's hand. I tug her from the chair, and thankfully have enough blood still flowing to the big brain to remember to put my jacket over her shoulders before pulling her out into the cold night. There's still a lot of snow left from the big storm we got a few days ago—which had apparently stranded Mac at Shep's place for a couple of days. The fact that they managed to keep their stupid *just friends* act in place through that is pretty fucking impressive, I'm not gonna lie, but it's obvious how they both feel. At least to me. But maybe it's just because I know Shep so well. Nat hasn't come out and said she knows that Mac is in love with Shep too, but she's hinted. One of these days the two of them will figure it out, I'm sure. If not, I know they'll regret it...

I turn to ask Nat what the plan is, but before I get a word out, her hands are knotted in my shirt and she's tugging me down towards her. Her lips slam to mine and my eyes fly wide in surprise before sliding closed in sheer bliss. I glide my palms along her cheeks, cradling her face and tangling the tips of my fingers into her hair as I tilt my head and deepen the kiss, coaxing her lips open between my own. I gently suck on her full bottom lip and she moans quietly, tightening her grip on my shirt. I move one hand to her hip, pulling her against me as I walk us backwards, pressing her against the side of the building.

Fuck.

I could get way too used to kissing Natalie Morgan. I love kissing. I could honestly make out for hours and be perfectly content, so I do it often, but I can't remember the last time a kiss felt like this. It's hot and electric and there's a deeper connection there that I don't want to think about too much right now. It starts slow and deep, but there's so much promise here, something entirely combustible that can burn us both to the ground if we let it. And fuck do I want to let it.

She starts matching me thrust for thrust, our tongues rolling and tangling, the kiss spiraling out of control in a matter of heartbeats. She isn't timid or reserved. She's giving as good as she's getting, demanding what she wants as we figure each other out, and fuck if it doesn't turn me on to no end. I'm happy with just about anything in the bedroom and have a reputation for trying almost everything you can think of at least once, so I've had a wide variety of bed partners. But a girl who doesn't back down, who pushes me back and takes what she needs and matches me, *that's* my sweet spot. That gets me harder than fucking steel and begging for more. That can bring me to my knees.

And this makes Nat far more dangerous than I initially thought she was.

She slides one hand to my pants, curling her fingers inside the waistband and using her grip to yank me forward, pressing our bodies more firmly together.

"Fuck, Nat," I rasp against her lips. She rocks her hips against mine and bites gently against my lower lip, pulling it between her teeth in a way that's got a direct line to my fucking cock. I'm hard as hell and ready to fuck her right here in the middle of downtown. No one would notice, right? "You keep that up and everything I said about respecting women is going to sound like total bullshit when I take you right here against this wall." I can feel her smile against my lips.

"Is that a promise?"

"Dear God, woman," I groan, nipping at her bottom lip in retaliation and palming her ass, using my grip to wrench her hard against me. "See what you're doing to me?" I ask when she gasps quietly. I should probably take things slow but I get the feeling that slow isn't what she wants. We'll just ignore the fact that I'm not sure I could even if I wanted to. She's driving me absolutely crazy in the best possible way. Every touch of her lips, every lap of her tongue, every rock of her hips. She knows *exactly* what she's doing and God if it isn't sexy as hell.

She laughs and I force myself to step away. If we're doing this, we're doing it fucking right.

And I have things to prove...

Three

NAT

"Let's go to my place," Rizzo says, sounding desperate and...a little nervous? I have no idea where he lives, but unless it's within a block, I'm going to combust before we get there. That kiss broke the dam. No, it didn't break it, it fucking *demolished* it into splinters. It's not like I'd doubted his skill or anything. I mean, he's got a different girl in his bed every other night for a reason, right? And even though he's good about not mixing business with pleasure, there are still enough regulars at the games that I've heard the rumors of his expertise. *God-like* has been used within my hearing more than once.

But even the rumors hadn't prepared me or done him justice. The man's lips are soft and perfect and if the way he uses his tongue for this is any indication of how he might use it in other areas...a shudder rolls through me at the mere thought, my toes curling and my stomach clenching in anticipation.

Well, I'm good and fucked, that's for sure.

"I hope it isn't far," I say, trying not to sound breathless and desperate but, well, I *am* breathless and desperate. I need him to keep kissing me. I need to rip his clothes off and touch those abs he's so fond of posting all over the internet. Maybe lick them a bit. I need him to make this one night worth the stupidity of going down this road with him.

It'll be fine. We're adults. Everything will be fine. We'll scratch this itch and then it'll be done, no harm, no penalty, back to friends in the morning.

I could tell him that I have a penthouse suite back at the Celeste, but I'm not ready to answer the questions that will inevitably come up if we head there, so I resign myself to keeping it in my pants until we get to his place.

"Do we need an Uber? I definitely shouldn't be driving—not that I'm not fully capable of making decisions, mind you," I add hastily, making sure he doesn't think I'm too drunk to know what I'm doing. Despite what his reputation might make you think, I know Rizzo would be the kind of guy who would call this night before it even begins if he thought I wasn't in the right state of mind. "But I shouldn't be driving."

"Good to know." He smiles at me and heat floods my stomach. That thing should be registered as a lethal weapon. "I've got a car with a driver waiting back at the Celeste. Come on." He holds out his hand and we make a run for it, grinning like idiots.

"Ahh!" I cry when I hit a bit of ice and skid a little bit, clutching onto to Rizzo for dear life so I don't go down hard on my ass.

"Gonna let a little ice take you out, Nat?" he teases. "So disappointing. I expected more from a member of the Sin Bin," he tsks. "We might have to revoke your membership."

"Ok, first off, Hattie can't even skate at all, so there's that. And I skate just fine, thank you. You try doing it in six-inch heels—hey!" I squeal as he lifts me up and throws me over his shoulder. I break out into a laughing fit as he makes his way quickly down the sidewalk, not having any trouble navigating the patches of ice dotted here and there. I grip the bottom of his jacket to steady myself and take a moment to admire the view.

"Ya know, you've got a pretty nice ass, there Thirst Trap," I observe and he laughs loudly, jostling me in his caveman carry.

"Of course it is. Have you seen me? *Everything* is nice." I snort. "Yours ain't so bad either," he says, stopping in front of the hotel doors and lowering me down, slowly sliding my body against his. Once I'm on my feet, he uses one finger to lift my chin up to meet his gaze. *Why the fuck is that so sexy?* "And the sight of it in this dress tonight. Mmm, mmm, *mmmm*, Natalie Morgan. You chose violence when you chose this little number."

My lips part on a soft inhale and his gaze dips down, those blue eyes looking...hungry. I shiver and I'm not entirely convinced it's because of the weather. He seems to shake himself and grabs my hand, pulling me around to the side of the building where several sleek black cars wait. Rizzo signals to one and it pulls up to the curb. He opens the door for me and I mentally give him a few points.

"Well, look at you."

"I am nothing if not a gentleman, Nat."

As I step towards the car, I brush his chest and whisper, "God, I hope not..."

He makes a low groaning sound and I laugh as I duck down and scooch across the seat to make room for him to slip in beside me.

"Where to, sir?"

Rizzo hesitates for a heartbeat and then tells the driver, "My place, Jerry."

"Yes, sir."

Rizzo slides closer to me but I push him away. He gives me a *what gives?* look.

"Nope. You stay over there. If you don't, Jerry is going to get one hell of a show—or possibly need therapy." The driver chuckles lightly and Rizzo tries to hide his smile.

"You're probably right," he agrees as he presses himself as far away from me as he can.

It's the longest ride of my life despite it only being ten minutes, tops, and I keep my hands clenched into fists in my lap the entire time to keep myself from reaching for him. I laugh when I glance over to see him doing the same thing, his jaw ticking like crazy with effort of holding himself back.

"You know this is torture, right?" he whispers.

"Oh I am *well* aware..."

"We're almost there," he assures me. "Still plenty of time for you to escape though, if you want." I grin at him.

"I think I've met my escape quota for the evening, thanks."

"Thank fucking God," he murmurs.

A few seconds later, Jerry pulls up outside of a soaring high rise apartment building.

"Wow, fancy."

Rizzo helps me out of the car and waves goodbye to Jerry before offering me his arm. I huff out a laugh but take it and we head inside. He nods to a younger guy sitting at the security desk, a spark of surprise flashing in his honey-brown eyes.

"I don't know if you know this or not, but I'm kind of a big-time star hockey player…" I roll my eyes and whack him playfully in the stomach as we reach the elevators. Everything is very sleek and modern and obviously it costs a pretty penny to live here. I'm weirdly grateful that he doesn't live in the building across the street instead of this one. That one is a Harrington property.

He reaches out and swipes a black card through the keypad and I know that must mean he has one of the top floor apartments, the kind you need special access to get to. I arch a brow at him.

"Penthouse?"

"Penthouse," he confirms, grinning, but then he leans down and kisses me softly on my neck, just below my ear, making me shudder. He moves to whisper in my ear, "that's *a lot* of floors to pass and keep my hands to myself, Nat…" I swallow hard and turn my head towards him. Our faces are so close that I can see the rings of gold around his irises, the blue dark and burning. Our lips are so agonizingly close again that I can feel his breath tickling my skin and would only need to lean a fraction of an inch to be in heaven again.

"Who says you have to?" I breathe, my entire body suddenly taut as a bowstring, practically quivering for his touch. I *need* it. I need Rizzo in a way that I've never needed anyone. *What the hell is wrong with me?* I feel like I'm coming out of my skin, like if I don't have his hands on me soon, I might go crazy. It's like I'm literally *craving* him.

"You are trouble," he says, chuckling low and leaning in just enough that I can feel the briefest contact of his lips against mine, but then he pulls away without actually kissing me, grinning. I want to pout. I want to scream. I want to jump his bones right here in the lobby in front of God and the security cameras. He winks and shifts to stand beside me, waiting patiently and innocently for the elevator, and I narrow my eyes at him. The bastard knows *exactly* what he's doing.

Well, two can play at that game.

My lips curl as I think about what's about to go down. I take off his jacket and drape it over my arm, shaking out my hair. He eyes me, his Spidey sense tingling, I'm sure. I make a show of righting the small diamond pendant at my throat before slowly trailing my fingers down my neck, gently running the tips over the top swells over my breasts.

"Natalie," he warns and I can't help but laugh lightly. This is going to be fun. I would say it's the wine lowering my inhibitions, but really, I think it's Rizz. I always feel so free with him, reckless in the best way. The elevator doors finally slide open and we step inside, both turning to face the front keeping a tiny bit of space between us. Already the air around us is thick and heavy with promise. As soon as the doors close, he reaches for me but I dance away, dropping his jacket and putting my back against one wall. He moves to follow, but I stop him with my six-inch-heel on his chest. He arches a brow, but looks entirely intrigued, the intrigue turning to something hotter and more dangerous as his gaze skates upward from my ankle, up my calf and leg, over my fully exposed thigh. His chest rises and falls quicker as I trace my finger up that same thigh, shifting when I get higher so that my finger tip whispers along the inside of my thigh, higher, and higher...

"*Nat?*" he breathes, half question, half plea. His pupils expand, the black starting to block out that beautiful blue.

I know we don't have much time, even going to the eightieth floor —and I just really hope this building doesn't have those insanely fast elevators that shoot you up a million stories in a matter of seconds—so I don't waste any time. I hold his gaze, bite my lip, and slide a finger past my thong.

"Jesus fucking Christ," he chokes out, gripping my ankle with one hand, running his other up my calf as he watches raptly while I pump, gasping quietly. I'm half shocked I'm doing this, but wholly don't care. It's hot and it's sexy and it's *Rizzo*. I know he'd never judge me for anything, especially right now when he looks like he would follow me straight into hell itself if I asked him to. It just feels right with him, like I don't have to be afraid or self-conscious. I don't know if it's because we're friends and I already feel comfortable with him, or because I know this is just a meaningless one-off, so I don't have to worry about pulling punches or doing the whole *play it coy at first so I don't scare him away* thing, but either way, I don't feel even a tiny bit of shame as I delve my finger over and over, rocking my hips slowly, holding his gaze all the while.

"Tell me," he grunts, voice low and hoarse. "Tell me that you're wet, Nat. Tell me you're wet for me." His words make me shiver and I love that he's vocal, already knowing that we're going to get along just fine in this department.

"Soaking," I pant.

"*Fuck*." He reaches down and runs a hand over his bulge, his erection straining his tuxedo pants and making my eyes widen. He smirks when he sees my eager stare, but before we can do anything more, the elevator slows and the bell dings. He steps away and lowers my foot gently to the ground as I withdraw my hand, but as I reach down to pick up his jacket, he grabs my wrist. I watch in aroused fascination as he guides my hand to his lips and sucks gently on my finger.

"Oh my God," I whisper, my entire body shuddering like a thousand little shocks are going through it. He releases my finger and gives me a sexy smile.

"You taste fucking amazing, Nat. But I'm going to need seconds. Possibly thirds. *Now*."

Four

RIZZO

WE SOMEHOW MAKE IT TO THE END OF THE HALLWAY TO MY door. I still can't quite believe I brought her here, but worrying about that is *way* down on my priority list right now. Watching her on the elevator had been about the sexiest thing I've ever seen in my fucking life, and I've seen more than my fair share of sexy things. And that teasing little taste of her on her own finger? *Mercy*. I need more. So much fucking more.

I manage to get the door unlocked with her lips fused to mine, and I'm honestly pretty impressed with myself. I walk her backwards into the foyer, my hands roving over her waist and hips and ass as the kiss burns hotter and hotter. I toss my jacket to the floor and I kick off my shoes, turning to press her against the closest wall.

"Rizz," she breathes. "This is so stupid...mmmm," she moans as I kiss along her jaw and down her throat.

"Completely stupid," I agree before running her earlobe between my teeth. She gasps and bucks her hips and I smile, loving the reactions I can wring from her. My cock throbs at the thought of all the ways I plan to do just that all night long. She pushes me away and I frown as I step back, wondering if she's changed her mind, but the look in her eyes is like a hunter on the prowl. It's fucking *hungry*.

She glances up and down my body and I think I know what she wants. I give her a slow, wicked smile as I take another step away, then another, putting more distance between us. Our gazes hold and we're both breathing hard. The space that is pretty damn large suddenly seems so fucking small. I slowly remove one cufflink, then the other, setting them on the entry table. She never takes her eyes off of me, watching raptly with lips parted, chest rising and falling quickly, hair in messy tangles. *Fucking sexy as hell.*

I unbutton my shirt, going slow and loving how it feels to have her eyes on me like this. When the fabric parts completely and I tug it off, tossing it to the floor, she inhales sharply and shakes her head.

"Jesus, Rizz," she whispers. "How are you even real?"

I huff out a small laugh at that, practically getting high off of the admiration and desire in her eyes, the way she takes her time to appreciate every inch of skin on display. Her hips arch subtly away from the wall and her teeth dig into her bottom lip in a way that makes me want to bite it myself. I unbuckle my belt with one hand and whip it from the loops in one quick pull, wrapping it around my other wrist as I tug it loose, and she blinks rapidly, shock and absolute arousal clear on her face.

"Why in the hell was that so sexy??"

I grin. I may or may not have practiced that move for an embarrassingly long time, but seeing her reaction is worth every second. I stand there, watching. Waiting. I cross my arms over my chest and give her a look.

"What are you waiting for?" she asks, voice a little raspy.

"I need you to tell me yes, Nat. I need you to tell me this is what you want. I'm not moving from this spot until you say it."

She eyes me for what feels like an eternity and then says the word that nearly brings me to my knees.

"*Yes.*"

I cross to her in two long strides, tunneling my hands into her hair and kissing her hard. She runs her palms over my stomach and up my chest, making my muscles jump in response. God, I love her hands on me.

"Can I tell you how glad I am that your thirst traps aren't CGI?" she asks against my lips, moving her hands all over, like she can't quite touch enough of me. I laugh as I pull her away from the wall and walk her backwards towards the dining table, our kissing never stopping, our tongues never slowing.

"Was there really any doubt? I'm offended, I think." She chuckles and wraps her hands around my neck, running her nails gently through the hair at my nape.

"You better make this worth it, Rizzo," she whispers as we reach the table. I unzip her dress, skating my fingertips along her spine as I do. She shivers and my pulse races when I don't run into anything along the way —no bra. Which means in about six seconds, I'm going to be in heaven.

"I plan to," I say, biting at her lip as she steps out of her heels. I tug the straps of her dress down her shoulders and it whispers down her body like a silk waterfall, pooling at her feet. I grip her hips and lift her onto the table, making her gasp in surprise. I take a moment to appreciate the absolute beauty that is Nat topless, and *dear God.* I put my palms on the tabletop on either side of her hips and lean in to kiss her again, hardly able to go a few seconds without my lips on hers, and she widens her knees, making room for my hips between her thighs. I trail kisses along her jaw and down the column of her throat, over her collarbone.

She moans quietly and tangles her hands in my hair, unabashedly guiding my mouth where she wants it. I obey, happy to give her anything and everything she needs. I hadn't been lying before: I absolutely love giving women all the attention. Of course I love getting off too, I'm not a fucking saint, but getting them off first—more than once —is like crack. I think it's the whole being too competitive thing. I always have been, both on and off the ice, so I wasn't really surprised when it ended up bleeding over into the bedroom too. I feel the need to be the best in everything, and the best don't leave their women unsatisfied. They leave them with jelly for legs, hardly able to breathe and with their voices hoarse from screams of ecstasy.

So, yeah, absolutely worshiping a beautiful woman until she can barely stand? That's my idea of a good fucking time.

I flick my tongue over one tight nipple, making her groan loudly and dig her nails into my scalp. I trail one hand downward while I close my lips around her, sucking hard, and tunnel my fingers beneath the tiny piece of lace pretending to be a thong. She doesn't hesitate for a second, just spreads her legs wider, begging for me to touch her, and I give her what she wants, quickly slipping a finger inside.

"Fuck, Nat," I moan around her nipple, pulling back to stare at her while I pump my finger slowly, building her up and up. "Still soaked for me."

"More," she breathes, rocking her hips and gripping my waist, looking nearly mindless already. I smile at her, holding her gaze while I add another finger, thrusting and curling them to hit that little hidden spot. "*Ah God*, don't stop."

"Lay back," I say quietly, leaning in to nip gently at her lower lip. I pull back and her eyes go wide, the tiniest bit of hesitation finally settling in. She swallows hard.

"Are you...I mean, you don't have to...I know a lot of guys don't like —" I silence her with a hard kiss and another thrust of my fingers.

"I'm not a lot of guys, Nat. Let's get that straight right now. When I said I want to worship every inch of you all night long, I wasn't kidding." Her breath hitches.

"You...you didn't exactly *say* that..." she tries to point out, though the end of the sentences trails off as I increase my rhythm and her eyes slide closed in distracted bliss.

"It was heavily implied," I say with a grin and her lips curl at the corners. She opens her eyes again, studying me to see if I'm bullshitting I'm guessing. I grab her hand with my free one and move her palm over my aching cock. I'm harder than I've ever been. She gasps quietly and starts to move her hand on her own, stroking and making me lose all my concentration for a long moment. Finally I remember what I was doing.

"Does this convince you?" I ask, putting my hand over hers, moving in time with her. "Thinking about my tongue on you is making me fucking hard as stone, Nat. That taste of you in the elevator nearly brought me to my knees. I want more. I *need* more. Believe me when I say that if I didn't want to, I wouldn't. I'm stubborn as fuck." She huffs out a laugh, but her pupils are blown wide and she looks like she might die from anticipation. I grin at her, knowing I'm about to get exactly what I want. I remove my hand, my fingers fucking soaked, and I try to suppress the shudder of pleasure that sends through me.

"Lay. Back," I tell her again as I slide to my knees in front of the table, hooking my fingers in the sides of her thong as I go and tugging it down. She shimmies enough to help me out and soon it's somewhere on the floor behind me. She obeys, laying back on the table, but she presses up on her elbows to watch as I stare at her, rubbing a hand over my mouth. *Fucking hell.* Bare. Wet. Open and practically quivering.

"Jesus Christ, Nat."

"Rizzo," she breathes. "Please..."

"Oh baby, no need to beg." With that, I lean in, throw her thighs over my shoulders, and fucking feast. I alternate long, languid laps of my tongue, enjoying the taste and heat of her, with faster thrusts and flicks, driving her higher and higher. She collapses back on the table after the first touch of my tongue, crying out something unintelligible, her back bowing off the surface as I do as promised and worship the goddess before me. She's fucking beautiful and sexy and hot and somehow even adorable at the same time with all the little noises she makes, the way her hands move restlessly from the table to her eyes, to her hair, to reach for my head, then back to dig into the table again, like she can't quite decide what to do or how to stay sane.

"God you taste so fucking good, Nat." She whimpers and rolls her hips, begging for more.

"Don't stop. Right there...ah God, I'm close, Rizz, please..." I don't dare stop, giving her exactly what she needs and reaching down to palm my erection as she explodes on my tongue. She cries out, thighs clenching tightly around me, and I slow things down the tiniest bit as her orgasm rocks through her. But I don't stop, because I'm not nearly done.

"Rizzo, I can't..."

"Oh you fucking can, Nat. I promise you can." I change rhythm as the last of the shudders and spasms finally calm, but soon enough I'm building her up and up and up, again and again, adding my fingers and gently sucking her clit.

"Oh my God...fuck, Rizz!" she screams as another orgasm rips through her. I grin as she writhes and whimpers. My forehead and chest are both beaded with sweat and my cock is nearly fucking bursting. She sits up and pushes me away for real this time.

"As amazing as that was, don't you fucking dare try to do that again right now, Thirst Trap," she snaps. I give her a look that's half pout, half disgruntled—I could get her to go at least three more times, easy. She crooks her finger at me and I rise from the floor. She leans in and runs her hands over my chest and down my stomach, before unbuttoning my pants and quickly shoving her hand. I choke out a sound that's honestly a little embarrassing as she wraps her palm around my shaft. She leans in and kisses me, not seeming to mind tasting herself on my lips. It's kind of fucking hot, actually.

"I need you to fuck me, Rizzo. I need you to fuck me right now, *hard*."

"Yes ma'am," I pant with a grin. I gently grip her wrist, making her remove her hand so I can get out of these clothes. I shove my pants and briefs down and step out while she stares. I'm not shy. Hell, you might even call me arrogant. I know that I look good—and work damn hard to stay that way, mind you—and I know that I'm no slouch in this department either, so I let her look as much as she wants. Her breasts rise and fall in quick bursts as she pants, licking her bottom lip as she reaches out to grip me again. It's heaven. It's agony. I'll never get enough of this. I reach out and slide one hand in her hair as she strokes, my eyes sliding closed.

"Ah, fuck, Nat. I love your hands on me." I open my eyes and look down to watch as she moves. The sight of my cock in her fist...hell, I could come just like this.

"Ya know," she whispers as she strokes, and I watch raptly, one hand still firmly in her hair. "I expected bigger." It takes me a second before I realize what she's said and I snap my head up to find her grinning a sultry, flirty little smile that makes my chest twist. She laughs lightly and I shake my head.

"Ooh baby, you'll regret that one." She digs her teeth into her bottom lip, that sexy challenge in her eyes.

"Promise?" she breathes and fuck if this isn't the most fun I've had in months.

I grip her hips and lift her from the table, setting her on her feet but quickly turning her so her back is to my chest. I wrap one arm around her breasts and reach the other hand down to rub her clit. She moans loudly, leaning her head back against my chest.

I whisper in her ear, "Do you want me to bend you over this table and fuck you until you can't take anymore, Natalie?" She inhales sharply but wiggles her ass against my cock in answer. "Say it," I tell her. She turns her head slightly, wrapping one hand around the back of my head and kissing me deeply.

"I want you to bend me over this table and *try* to last long enough to make me tap out," she says against my lips and *fuck me* if that little challenge isn't sexy. She smiles and pulls back enough to meet my gaze, quirking a brow as if to say *bring it on*.

"Oh, challenge accepted, baby. Challenge fucking accepted."

Five

NAT

I MAY HAVE BITTEN OFF MORE THAN I COULD CHEW, BUT IT'S the best mistake I've ever made. It might just be the best night of sex of my entire life. Ok, not *might*. It is. Hands down, bar none, all other competitors in the fucking dust. Rizz did, in fact, last long enough to make me tap out, taking me hard from behind bent over that table. I'd come two more times before I'd nearly collapsed, the only thing holding me up his body pinning me to the edge of the table. After that he moved us to the couch, somehow still going strong, but bless him, he slowed it down and wrung one more orgasm out of me before he finally joined me over the edge.

I'll give credit where credit is due: Anthony Rizzo just might be a sex god disguised as a hockey player.

We're sprawled out on the living room floor now, recovering, though I've yet to come back down completely from the absolute high of this night. I can't quite believe it, not just because of the mind-blowing sex, but because I've actually crossed that line with Rizzo.

And it felt so fucking right and addictive that it scares me.

I finally get the strength to sit up and Rizzo tugs a blanket from a stack beneath the coffee table and tosses it to me before grabbing a remote. He presses a button and the fireplace roars to life. I wrap the blanket around my shoulders but he's content to remain completely uncovered on the thick rug. I'm not complaining one bit. If this is my one night with him, I'll gladly take every second to admire that body of his, to commit every detail to memory to replay over and over in my head for the rest of eternity. I feel bad for whatever guy comes next, honestly, because I can't promise that Rizzo won't be the one I'm thinking of for a long, long time.

The thought spooks me a bit, so I get up and wander around the room to really look at the space for the first time. I spy an old hoodie lying on the back of the couch, so I snatch it up and pull it on. I inhale deeply and shiver—whatever cologne Rizzo wears smells *damn* good.

"Help yourself," he says with a laugh and I smile at him over my shoulder.

The place is huge, fully open-concept with the kitchen, dining, and living room space all in one giant room, really, but each area is well defined. The ceilings are high with exposed metal beams and the back wall is made up entirely of glass doors that open out onto an impressive balcony and an absolutely stunning view of Seattle.

"Not too shabby, Thirst Trap," I say, nodding to the lights outside. He hikes a shoulder, watching me from his spot on the floor.

"The view is killer, for sure, and it's a nice place, but not really my style, honestly."

"Really?"

"Yeah, it came fully furnished and that was fine with me—I didn't have the time or desire to have to worry about decorating and shit, so it worked out great—but now that I've been here for a while, I realize how not-me it is."

I look around again and agree that it doesn't feel very Rizzo to me, there's absolutely none of his personality anywhere. Everything is very... I don't know what to call it. Industrial-modern? All sleek lines and dark metal. It's gorgeous but a little cold, honestly, and there's basically no personal touches at all, he's right. No knickknacks or neon signs or movie posters—but I do spy one small area near the back of the room that has a cluster of framed photos on the wall.

"I'm actually moving soon," he calls as I wander closer to get a better look at the pictures.

"Where to?" I ask over my shoulder as I take in the pics. They're all of Rizzo and a woman who I'm assuming is his mom, with beautiful deep-red hair and the same blue eyes as her son. One in front of an old castle, one on a cliff side overlooking a gray ocean, another in front of a gorgeous church. Some of the backgrounds look vaguely familiar but I can't quite place them—until I see the Guinness Storehouse sign.

"Are these all in Ireland?" I ask as he saunters up behind me. He places a quick kiss on my neck, almost as if out of habit and I can't say that I hate it.

"To Shep's neighborhood, actually," he says, answering the first question. "I close in a few days and should be all moved in before Christmas. And, yeah, my mom and I go to Ireland every few years. It's kind of our thing."

I turn to look at him, glancing down at the pendant hanging from the chain around his neck that he always wears, and really look at it for the first time: St. Christopher but set atop what I realize now is a Celtic knot. I arch a brow.

"An Italian who's obsessed with Ireland?"

He laughs and shakes his head, running his thumb almost absently over the pendant.

"Not a drop of Italian in me. Or, well, there's probably some drops, let's be real—I should probably do one of those ancestry DNA test things to find out—but my family is like ninety-five percent Irish, at least on the side that I care about." He pulls his gaze away from the pictures to look at me, searching my eyes for...what, I don't know, but then he lets out a long breath.

"Rizzo is actually my stepdad's last name. He adopted me when I was thirteen and I love the man completely. He's my dad in all the ways that matter, and I was all too happy to take his name and be his son, but, yeah, my mom is Irish. Like, born and raised in Cork until she was eleven and they moved to the U.S. My grandparents ended up moving back after my mom went to college and all the rest of the relatives on that side are still there."

"Wow, really?"

"Yep. Why do you think St. Patrick's Day is my favorite holiday?" he asks with a smirk.

I roll my eyes. "Because they have green beer and the puck bunnies are even drunker than usual?"

He chuckles and takes my hand, tugging me back to the couch. He grabs the blanket from the floor and we settle in together, not exactly cuddling but...pretty damn close. *What the fuck is happening right now?*

"Growing up, St. Patrick's Day was this huge deal to me. I dunno, I guess I thought the holiday was *just* for us because in my little five-year-old brain, us being Irish was like a *big* deal. We were extra special and so St. Patrick's Day was just for me and mom, and everyone else who celebrated was actually celebrating us, like it was our fucking birthday or something." He laughs and shakes his head, and I can't help but smile, imagining a tiny Rizzo. It's...adorable, actually. And sweet. *And damn it do* not *make me like you even more, Anthony Rizzo...*

He continues on. "Mom would make shamrock cookies and green Kool Aid, and we'd have our own little St. Patrick's Day Parade in our tiny living room with decorations that we made out of construction paper. We'd call my grandparents who would always send a box of treats, and do lots of other very not-even-remotely Irish things, but mom was happy to do whatever made me happy. They're some of the best memories I have. I loved everything about it. Still do." He gives me one of his crooked, sexy grins. "The green beer and inebriated ladies are just extra perks now."

I snort. "Your mom didn't want to move back home after college?"

"Well, I kind of came along and then things got complicated," he says, smiling, but there's a hint of hurt there.

"Ah, gotcha." I want to ask about his dad, suddenly so damn curious about this man, this side of him that I never knew existed, but that feels like too much, especially coming from me. Instead I ask about the pictures again. "So, the trips?"

"Well, growing up we didn't have a lot of money—which incidentally is how I ended up playing hockey in the first place. My mom worked two jobs, sometimes three, just to make ends meet, and our downstairs neighbor would babysit me more or less for free. Hank was one of the best men I've ever known. He didn't have to help out a single mom like that, ya know?" I suspected dad was out of the picture, but hearing it confirmed makes me want to know the whole story. "He ran the ice rink which thankfully was within walking distance of our apartment complex, and he would watch me there and let me skate for free. I helped him around the place, cleaning up and sharpening skates once I got old enough to do it without slicing my own finger off. He was a former hockey star turned coach, and I guess saw something in me. He gave me my first hand-me-down stick and pads, taught me the basics, and there was no turning back after that." He smiles fondly at the memories and I can't help but smile back, hearing how such an amazing life and career got started.

"Sounds like we all owe a lot to Hank."

He nods his head. "We really, really do. I don't know where the hell I would have ended up without him. He was the one who pushed me to keep my grades up when all I wanted to do was be on the ice to make sure I'd be eligible for scholarships, and when that time came, he helped my parents do so much research, finding me every damn dime they could. He even reached out to old teammates and players to get me seen by coaches from the best schools. I never would have gone to Cornell without him, let alone be drafted. Never would have met Shep, never would have..." He looks at me with one of those rare serious, intense stares, but quickly continues on, "moved to Seattle. He passed about five years ago now, but he got to see me play in the big leagues and even bring home a couple of titles, and that's all I could have ever wanted."

"I'm sure he was proud of you." He nods, a sad smile on his face.

"I know he was. He and Ray—that's my stepdad—were the best two father figures a kid could ask for." He clears his throat before continuing on, "Anyway, back to the trips. So, yeah, mom and I didn't exactly have the spare funds that would allow for vacations to visit my grandparents in Ireland back in the day. Even after she married Ray, we weren't just swimming in cash or anything. My grandparents were able to come here a handful of times over the years, but it was hard for them too—they were both teachers before they retired, so not exactly lucrative careers. So, once I signed and started making the tiniest bit of real money, the first thing I did was take mom home. Then it just became our tradition. Ray comes sometimes too, but he likes to give me and mom our time together usually." He shrugs and I shake my head.

"What?" he asks, running his hands over my legs.

"You are...surprisingly wholesome beneath that playboy exterior of yours." It isn't exactly what I want to say, but we aren't going there.

His lips quirk. "Ok, all that was bullshit. I really just like the green beer and drunk chicks."

I smack him in the chest and he laughs, scooping me up and twisting us so quickly that I yelp and giggle in surprise before he settles over me. He leans in and kisses me in a way that makes my breath hitch, my entire body suddenly on fire all over again. I reach down and grip his cock, not as shocked as I should be that he's hard again. The man has some impressive stamina and rebound, that's for damn sure. He groans quietly and I bite gently on his lower lip.

"I believe you promised all night long...and it's only two a.m..."

With that, he makes good on his promise.

Six

RIZZO

I'M DOZING OFF WHEN NAT LEANS IN AND KISSES ME SOFTLY on the lips. I pry my eyes open and frown.

She's dressed and standing beside the couch instead of snuggled up next to me naked in all her glory.

"What are you doing?" I ask, sitting up, blinking away the confusion. I shouldn't want her to stay, especially not here, but...well, I don't like the idea of her leaving either.

"I gotta go," she says and then smirks. "Thanks for all the orgasms." She says it so casually, like that's all tonight was. Which, I mean, is what it was *supposed* to be. Just one night of fun to scratch that forbidden itch we've both been skirting around for almost two months now. But I thought...Well, I don't even fucking know what I thought. And now she's leaving me.

Talk about the tables turning. Heading out after a great night of sex is *my* M.O. I'm not the one left behind, and I honestly don't know how to feel about it right now. It's kind of...intriguing? Maybe a little attractive, even...but it's also frustrating. *And I don't want her to fucking leave...*

"Nat, wait, I—" She kisses me again.

"Don't ruin it," she whispers. She steps away and I let her, dropping my hand from her waist with a ridiculous effort. Her phone buzzes and she checks the screen. "My ride is here...See ya, Thirst Trap." I watch her walk towards the door, hips swaying and heels in her hand. "I'm stealing this, by the way," she calls after her shoulder, pointing to my old Cornell Hockey hoodie she's got pulled on over her dress. I huff out a laugh, not at all upset that she's keeping it. Hell, I actually kind of like it, like a little piece of me is marking her as mine somehow.

Which is insanely fucking stupid and not something I should like at all.

"Was it worth it?" I call out, remembering her plea when we started all this. *You better make this worth it, Rizzo.*

She turns at the door and grins.

"I give it a solid B+" She winks and heads out the door while I laugh at the sheer audacity of the lie.

As soon as the door clicks closed I run my hands through my hair, trying to process what in the hell had just happened. Her walking out, which is still a mind fuck, but also the entire night. We'd finally crossed that line and while I definitely think we can be normal at work and everything, there was something more than a fun night of orgasms going on here...wasn't there? Or fuck, was it just me? She'd left so casually, maybe it really was just a meaningless hook up to her.

It should be for me too. I don't do more than that, never really have. I dated a couple of girls in high school sort of seriously I guess, but other than that, it's all been casual and fun. So why does it feel like this was... more? Why am I already craving her again, and not just in the sexy way? I liked talking to her, I liked opening up in ways I rarely do. I can count on one hand the number of people who know about me and mom's St. Patrick's Day thing or our trips and what they mean, or about my childhood. So why had I told her all that?

I groan loudly and push all the thoughts away. It's too late—or early?—for this much thinking. I settle back in on the couch, not even bothering to head into the bedroom at this point, and try to get some sleep.

But damn it if the couch feels empty without Nat.

"Are you *sure* nothing happened during that little snowed-in adventure?" I ask Shep at the Skating with Santa Event a couple of days later. I haven't seen or talked to Nat since that night, but I'm not reading anything into that. We had practice, she has work and a life. It's fine. No matter what weird shit is going on in my head, the most important thing really is that things are cool between us. She's a good friend and I really love hanging out with her. I don't want that to be ruined. So, I've been scanning the rink every few minutes trying to catch a glimpse of her, but she hasn't gotten here yet.

He finishes lacing up his skates and gives me an exasperated look.

"Don't even start with me, you know damn well that it's a valid question."

He takes off his hat and runs a hand through his hair, tattooed knuckles on display. Girls seem to fucking love Shep's look, all tattooed biker bad-boy. We're polar opposites in that regard since I look more like the small town, All-American quarter back who dates the head cheerleader in some Hallmark movie, but he's my best friend on the planet. We've known each other since freshman year of college and have been together ever since. We got called up at the same time, played for the Kodiaks together, and then moved to the Vipers together too. I would literally take a bullet for the guy. He always jokes that he's my longest relationship and he's not actually wrong about that, which is probably a little sad, but whatever.

He exhales roughly. "Something...almost happened," he admits. My eyes go wide and he holds up his hands to halt my inquisition. "It didn't though. She was upset after telling me about her fucking ex—which, are you up for tracking a psycho down and putting him in the ground?"

"Do you really have to ask that? Who's car we taking?" His lips curl and he nods.

"Ok good. We'll circle back to that. Anyway, she had just told me about all that and she was upset and I didn't want to like, take advantage or whatever. She pulled away embarrassed before she actually kissed me, anyway, so I don't think she was ready to go down that road."

"You are both fucking idiots."

"You keep saying that," he sighs. "Anyway, how was that fundraiser thing you went to the other night?"

I normally don't keep secrets from Shep, but I'd kept my evening with Nat close to the vest. She isn't just some random chick that we'll never see again, so it doesn't feel right to tell anyone about our night, not unless she wants to.

"It was good," I say. Not a lie. "Great food. Good cause. I look like James Fucking Bond in a tux, so there's also that."

He chuckles and then Mac bounces over to the wall nearby, smiling widely at the two of us. I've grown incredibly fond of Hattie McNamara in her short time here. Not only is she a great girl (who my best friend just happens to be in love with even if he's too fucking stubborn to admit it yet), but she's gotten asses in seats at games like we haven't had in years. There had been serious talk about the Vipers being sold and moved to Jersey before Mac came along and started to turn shit around. *Jersey* for crying out loud. No thanks.

"Are y'all ready?" she asks in that adorable southern twang of hers.

"The real question is are *you* ready for what's happening afterwards?" Shep asks, leaning his forearms on the wall. Mac wrinkles her nose and I grin thinking about the walker we decorated for her. The whole team pitched in when Shep told us we were teaching our newest Viper to skate after the event.

"Don't remind me," she groans.

"Oh come on, Mac. It'll be fun, I promise. You can't be the only member of the Sin Bin who can't skate. It's illegal. And super embarrassing."

"Har har," she says with a roll of her eyes, but she's smiling, those sexy little dimples on full display, and I know that she's actually enjoying all these things Shep is doing to make her hate the holidays a little less. She glances at her watch. "Ok I'm gonna go get this show on the road. I'll be back in a bit." We watch as she heads up the stairs and out towards the main entrance where I imagine hundreds of kids are waiting to skate with Santa and a bunch of hockey players. I'm really looking forward to it, actually. I think it's going to be fun as hell, and I know I would have killed for something like this when I was younger, so I'm all too happy to help out.

A few minutes later, I see Nat directing some volunteers on the other side of the rink. *Welp, better pull off the band aid and get back to being friends.* I skate over, smiling widely and when she sees me coming, she thankfully returns it easily, though I do spy a faint blush across her high cheekbones. I slide to a stop at the wall just as she joins me there.

"Hey," I say casually.

"Hey back." She tucks a lock of hair behind her ear and I can't stop myself from shifting my gaze to her lips. God what I wouldn't give to kiss them again right now, to wrap my arms around her and pull her close...

"Stop looking at me like that," she scolds, but she's smiling and giving me a pointed look.

"Like what?" I ask innocently. She meets my gaze and gives me one of those sexy challenging looks I love so much.

"Like you've seen me naked and made me come too many times to keep track."

I huff out a laugh, surprised she's going the direct route instead of the ignore-the-elephant-in-the-corner one. I'm for it. If she can joke about our hook up, then that must mean she's ok with it, that she isn't regretting what happened. *But is she wanting another ground, like I am?* I haven't been able to stop thinking about her, about getting her back in my bed at the earliest opportunity.

But then I remember her walking away, the way I have with hundreds of one-night stands, and I think for her it really was just a one-time thing. Which is fine. Totally and completely fine. That's the smart move here, and I know it...but damn if I don't want to be smart right now. I want to be stupid as hell and turn this thing with Nat into...I don't know, a friends-with-benefits situation?

"Pretty sure it was seven, but who's counting?" I grin and nod towards the ice. "You skating or just supervising today?"

"Little of both. Since Hattie can't skate, I'll be on the ice keeping an eye on things and helping out."

"Well, after this afternoon, hopefully that won't be the case anymore." She grins at that.

"This is going to be so much fun. A small, evil part of me can't wait to watch her bust her ass. Payback for the pickle shots," she adds when I eye her and I wince, remembering the night Mac brought what she claimed were lime Skittle shots to the table only for us all to find out after downing them that they were dill pickle. Nat had had a...not very eloquent reaction, promptly puking into the bushes off the patio at the bar. We'd all died laughing, but apparently she's been secretly plotting her revenge.

"Wait until you see the surprise we made for her. It's going to be epic." We both laugh a bit and then she gets that calculating look in her eyes.

"We're good, right?"

"We're good," I assure her with my most winning smile. I'm still feeling some kind of way about the whole thing, but no matter what, I'm not going to let it mess things up, so I'll suck it up and deal with it. Whatever this is will pass, I'm sure of it.

"Good."

"Good," I repeat.

She holds my gaze and the gray seems to darken. I can't help but smirk when she darts a glance down at my lips.

"Are you sure you don't want an encore performance...?"

"Ok I'm going now, Thirst Trap," she says with a shaky laugh. "Behave yourself out there."

"I make no promises!" I call as she hurries up the nearest set of stairs. I watch her go, trying not to be super obvious about checking out her ass in those jeans as she jogs up, up, up. I finally tell myself to stop being a creep and pull my gaze away, slapping the top of the wall and skating over to meet up with a few of the other guys who just arrived.

"Jules! Howey! Get over here, I got a plan for later..." I run down my idea of teaching Mac to handle a puck and, with the help of the rest of the team, help her score a goal on Shep. They both grin when I finish.

"Oh, we're all over it, Rizz." Jules rubs his hands together like an evil villain from a movie and I laugh, punching him in the shoulder and setting off to skate some circles around the Man in Red himself.

Seven

NAT

"Hey, dad," I say, sliding into the seat across from him at our usual table. We meet for dinner at this roof-top restaurant every other Tuesday, as long as he's not traveling, and though lately the meetings have been more and more strained, we keep up the tradition.

Things with my dad have always been a little...complicated. Well, not always. When I was little, I was a complete and total daddy's girl. He was my hero and some of my favorite memories involved the two of us going on little adventures all over Seattle. Once I hit those lovely teenage years, though, things shifted. I do love him, but we butt heads constantly. Mom always said it was because we're too much alike, but neither one of us will admit to that out loud. He's just always had this idea of what my life should be, and I've always disagreed and pushed back—to a point. He pretty much always ended up getting his way in the end, but I made it as difficult as possible most of the time. At least until a year ago. It wasn't until I moved back here after mom died that I actually put my foot down and stopped going along with his plans completely. He's been...frustrated, is one way to put it. *Waiting for me to fall on my face and realize that he's right and I'm wrong and I need daddy to fix my life for me* is another.

"Hello, Natalie." A waiter comes over and fills my water glass and dad signals for another drink for himself. Macallan I'm assuming. He's in an impeccable suit, as always, his salt-and-pepper hair cropped short, his matching mustache and beard trimmed to perfection. We have the same gray eyes, the same cleft in our chin (though you can't see his, of course), and the same stubborn personality.

"You left early the other night," he observes as I dig into the bread. Of course Erin would have ratted me out when she found my table empty and no trace of me in the ballroom. I don't blame her. She's nice enough, but she's dad's lap dog and that means she'll always take his side over mine. My lips twitch remembering Rizzo thinking *Erin* was *Aaron*. The offer to have a little "chat" with the fictional ex-boyfriend stalking me through a fundraising gala was actually surprisingly hot for reasons I don't want to explore. I'll just blame the romance novels Hattie let me borrow last week.

"I was there, as promised, and stayed through dinner. I was tired," I lie with a shrug. "How did it turn out?"

"Enough raised to fund the construction of a whole new wing." I can't help but smile at that and he lets his iron façade soften a little bit, smiling back. In these rare moments, I can see how mom could have fallen for him all those years ago and I remember how close we used to be, how easy our relationship was.

"Mom would love that," I say, eyes watering a bit. Willow's House was named for her, after all, and was one of her most beloved projects. It's a children's hospital, mostly focusing on varieties of childhood cancers, but there are fully furnished apartments on-site available for the families to use so they can all be together during treatments.

"I think you're right." He and mom were madly in love, but they just couldn't be married to each other. It was the kind of love that burns too brightly I think. They were better as friends with, I learned as I got older, occasional benefits. Talk about scarring me for life when I walked into *that* on a Wednesday morning before school...and confusing the hell out of me. I know you can't blame your parents for all of your issues, but I think some of my relationship hang ups can definitely be laid on their doorstep. I've gotten over most of them over the years with the help of some therapy, but yeah, they really screwed me up for a while.

We talk about mostly trivial things over our meal—some of the foundation's new projects, trips he has coming up, how the guest bathroom shower needs to be replaced at my house—until he finally asks the inevitable question.

"Have you finished this little game, Natalie?" He says it in that tone that grates on my nerves like nails on a chalkboard, like he's talking to a petulant child who refuses to eat her broccoli. "It's been nearly a year. You're working as an assistant to something or another in a hockey organization." He makes it sound like it's the most ridiculous job he could fathom and my hackles rise even more. I love my fucking job. I love the people I work with and the work we do. It makes people happy, and more importantly, makes *me* happy. But he doesn't care about that. All he cares about is me following in his footsteps and re-joining the family business. He didn't see or care how miserable I was for the years I spent working for him in the New York office after graduation.

But after mom died, everything shifted. It was like losing her so suddenly just ripped away the blinders and I could finally see how unhappy and unfulfilling my life really was. I decided then that I was tired of settling for the life *he* wanted me to have. I wanted to do something on my own. I had no idea what, exactly, but I knew I didn't want to be in New York anymore. He was pissed as hell when I told him I was quitting and moving back to Seattle, but beneath the anger, he understood. Mom's death hit him extremely hard too, he just didn't let anyone see it.

So, he'd agreed to let me have this "sabbatical" as he calls it. I could do whatever I wanted job-wise, as long as I did *something*, until I got it out of my system and he wouldn't hound me. Who knew I'd find something I loved so much—and that turns out is the bane of his existence.

"You have a degree in business from Yale for God's sake, and you spend your time...what? Getting someone coffee? Asking hockey players what their favorite breakfast food is?" I grind my teeth, trying hard to keep myself in check and not make a scene.

"First off, I work for the Assistant Director for Media and Marketing for one of the top American Hockey League organizations. Second, I didn't want that fucking degree, dad. *You* did. I got it because...well, I don't really know why anymore, but I sure as shit didn't do it for myself. And third, I'm *happy* in this job. Doesn't that matter to you?"

"Of course I want you to be happy," he says, softening a fraction. I snort in obvious disagreement and he narrows his eyes. "But this isn't sustainable, Natalie. I know that you needed time to handle your mother's passing in your own way, and I've given you that time, but soon you're going to have to stop playing pretend and start your real life."

"And this isn't my real life?" I snap.

"Of course not," he scoffs.

"And that's enough for today." I push away from the table and toss my napkin on my plate. "I've got a lot of work to do for the job that you think is just so far beneath you, that I happen to fucking love."

"Natalie—" he says in an exasperated tone, but I cut him off.

"I'll see you in two weeks, dad. Love you."

He sighs but doesn't move to stop me. "I love you, too." As much as we verge on hating each other sometimes, as many times as I want to put my fist through a wall after these dinners with him, we always, *always* end our conversations with love. Deep down, we both do and we know how quickly things can change, how fast someone can be taken from this earth. I would never want our last words to each other to be anything but love, regardless of how mad I am at him.

I leave the restaurant, torn between fuming and hurt. And is stupid as it is, the one person I want to talk it through with is Rizzo. Not Hattie. Not Bobby. *Rizzo.*

Things have been...weird. I mean, not weird in the sense that we're being awkward around each other or anything, but I'm pretty sure he wants a round two. Which isn't exactly his M.O., so it's suspect...and I promised myself that it was a one off. One night to give in to temptation and that was it. Because I know that's for the best. Rizzo doesn't do relationships and even though I'm not sure I really do either, I don't think I can do the whole fuck buddies or friends-with-benefits thing with him. I would feel like a player in a batting line up or something, just one on the roster waiting for my turn at the plate, and as much as I tell myself that I'm not feeling things for Rizz, that it's all just hormones and his stupid god-like sex powers, I know it's a lie.

I can't go for round two...because I'll want a round three and a round four, and then suddenly I'm in love with him and he's breaking my heart or I'm breaking his and I have to quit my job and it's all awful.

So, even though we're friends, I'm going to ignore the desire to talk to him tonight and go home and drown my sorrows in some *Criminal Minds* and a glass of wine.

Maybe a whole damn bottle.

Eight

RIZZO

"So, I might have done something stupid," I say to Shep as we wave to the throngs of people lining the streets for the Christmas Parade from our spots on the Vipers float. I wasn't planning on spilling the beans about me and Nat, but it's been weighing on my mind nonstop. It's only been a few days but I feel like I'm going crazy. I need to talk about it and Shep is the person I talk to about everything.

"Might have?" he asks with a quirk of his brow.

"Ok, so there's no might about it. I slept with Nat. You know, Hattie's assistant?"

He groans and elbows me hard in the ribs. I let out a grunt of pain but the two of us keep our smiles plastered on our faces, waving to the kids like everything's fine.

"You fucking idiot."

"I know, I know."

"And?"

"And she told me it was a one-time thing," I say, trying to keep the incredulity and annoyance out of my voice. Shep turns to me, looking confused.

"Isn't that exactly how you like it?"

"No, no, no, you aren't listening. *She* told *me* it was a one off, not the other way around. When we were done, she got dressed, told me it was fun, kissed me, and then bolted."

Shep laughs loudly, slapping me on the back.

"She pulled a Rizzo on you."

"Yeah, she did. And fuck if it wasn't...hot?" I run my hand through my hair. It was hot in a weird, really messed up way. I'm always the one doing the walking out, always the one giving the bad news that it's a one-and-done thing. Her doing it is like this weird role reversal and challenge all built into one and I should probably talk to my therapist about this because there has to be something wrong with me.

"I don't know, man, maybe that's not the right word, but I haven't been able to stop thinking about her since. I'm desperate to get a round two. Like can barely enjoy my time with anyone else kind of desperate." Not barely. Can't. Period. I haven't been with anyone since that night with Nat, despite having ample opportunities, especially after the big win against Syracuse the other night. But I had zero desire to even try to go home with anyone. "What is wrong with me?" I groan.

"A lot," he answers, shaking his head, "a lot."

I spot a little girl in a 15 Vipers Jersey and point, grinning. "Hey! Someone give that girl two treat bags!" She smiles widely, waving like crazy when she sees me pointing at her, and turns to show me the back of her shirt where Rizzo is scrawled across her shoulders in sparkly teal letters. I wave at her and one of the teamsters gives her two treat bags. The little girl looks at her dad like she just won the lotto and it makes my chest feel all warm and fuzzy. She reminds me a bit of Ollie, actually.

Ollie is technically Shep's niece, but he's been raising her since she was four and officially adopted her last year. She's his daughter in all the ways that matter and watching him go from fellow man-whore to doting dad was honestly really fucking admirable. I gave him shit for it, of course, but he knows that I love that kid as much as he does, and was all too happy that he left all the puck bunnies for me in order to be a better father to her. Ollie is another reason I'm so thankful that Mac and Nat and Bobby have been able to turn things around for the Vipers —if the team left Seattle, I don't think Shep would follow and I'm honestly not sure if I would go somewhere without him at this point.

He and Ollie have become my family and I can't imagine my life without them.

"Maybe you're just growing up," Shep says, waving to what looks like an entire peewee hockey team.

"I've done no such thing!" I say, aghast. "Balls. Farts. Boobies. See— no grown-ups here." He laughs, shaking his head and I grin at him.

"I *mean*, maybe you're just getting tired of the game. Maybe you're ready for something more than one-night stands from puck bunnies who just fawn over your abs or fame."

"And chiseled jawline, don't forget the chiseled jawline. And massive coc—" I get a quick jab in the stomach, effectively cutting me off. We both laugh but then I sigh. That night with Nat had been...different. I mean, she came to my place for one, that was fucking novel. And yeah, her being the one to leave was kind of hot, that's true, but I also kind of hated it. I wanted her to stay. I wanted to fall asleep with her wrapped in my arms and wake up the same way. And wanting that was fucking terrifying. I have no idea what it even means. Do I want to...date her? Do I even know *how* to date someone?

"I don't know." Shep arches a brow and I know he can see right fucking through me. He's always been able to, from the first day we met. I roll my eyes. "Look, I'm not saying you're right, but...maybe you've got a point. *Maybe*," I emphasize when he gives me a triumphant smile. "But even if that's the case, there's no way that Nat will believe that I want more than just a hook up or fuck-buddies kind of thing."

"Well, sounds like you've got some work to do then, my friend." I groan and Shep grins, waving to the crowd like Miss Fucking America. We finally spot Mac, Nat, Ollie, and her grandparents and aunt, and everyone on the float goes crazy for Olls. The fact that this kid has an entire hockey team wrapped around her little finger is one of my favorite things about the Vipers. The way Shep looks at Mac, I honestly wonder how the fuck the entire crowd can't tell that he's in love with her. My friend has got it bad.

But they're both dancing around it, playing the whole "don't want to mess up the friendship" card. Which I get. I'd been worried about messing things up with Nat after we hooked up, and now even thinking about going again or trying for...more, makes me wonder *what if*. What if it doesn't work out and she ends up hating me? What if we can't stand to be in the same room as each other? What if she doesn't want more with me...but starts dating someone else? *Fuck*. The thought of her with some other guy while I have to stand by and watch? I suddenly want to punch something.

And to make things even more fucking confusing, as much as the idea of being with her for more than just mind-blowing sex makes something in my chest ache for it, it also scares the absolute shit out of me. Part of me is already running for the hills at the thought.

"Come onnn, don't bitch out on me! One more. Push it, ya posah!" Jules taunts encouragingly in his thick Boston accent while he spots me. I'm about to hit a personal record on bench and most of the guys are here cheering me on—or fucking with me.

"A hundred bucks says he can't do it," Howey says.

"I'll take that action," Mowser chimes in. "But make it two."

"Fuck...off..." I grit through clenched teeth psyching myself up to do the last rep.

"Come on, Rizz. You got this," Shep says from just over my right shoulder. I take a deep breath and lift the bar.

"Here we go, here we go! That's it, baby, yeah...yeah...YEAH!!" Jules roars when I push the bar back up with all my might, and everyone erupts when he helps me slam it back onto the rack. I sit up and get pummeled by the guys. I wipe the sweat from my brow and grin at Howey.

"Pay the fucking man." He rolls his eyes but gives me a fist bump. Everyone starts filing out of the gym, only having stuck around to see me try to break the record. Shep waits around though.

"You going tonight?"

"You know it. Can't believe you're gonna miss Jules and Howey trying to line dance." We both laugh at the thought. Mac had found a little country bar with a dance floor on the outskirts of the city, and her little Louisiana-bred heart had practically soared out of her chest. She immediately demanded that the Sin Bin take on the Tipsy Cowboy and we're always up for a challenge.

"I know, but I promised Olls a movie date."

"Buy her some extra popcorn from Uncle Rizzo."

"Will do. Please send me some video of this shit. Jules said he found boots. *And a hat.*"

"Oh this is going to be amazing." We both laugh and he slaps me on the shoulder before he heads out, leaving me alone in the gym. I lay back on the bench for a few minutes, feeling good about the new PR, thinking about seeing Nat tonight and mentally preparing to keep myself in check, and going through plays for tomorrow's game that's sure to be a bloodbath. I finally sigh and hoist myself up from the bench. I wipe it down and toss the rag in the bin before picking up my shirt and turning towards the door—

To find Nat standing there in a sports bra and skin tight leggings. Her eyes immediately dip to my bare chest, still slicked with sweat from my workout. I try to keep my eyes from roving over her stomach and hips. I don't want to be *that* guy at the gym but damn if it isn't nearly impossible.

I head her way and she watches me come, seeming to forcibly yank her gaze up from my torso, inhaling deeply and swallowing hard.

"Hey, Nat," I say casually, giving her my most winning smile.

"Hey, Rizzo," she replies, a little breathy before she clears her throat. "Uh...good workout?"

"Great, actually. Hit a new PR on bench. Howey lost two hundred bucks. Can't complain."

She huffs out a laugh and then glances around the room. I can see it the second she realizes we're alone. That palpable tension that always seems to show up between us snaps into place with an almost audible click. I know I shouldn't but I take a step towards her. She reaches out and rests a hand on my stomach. She doesn't push me away though, instead she splays her fingers, moving them gently over my skin, so I take another step closer. She moves back slowly as I move forward, her hand never leaving my stomach and burning me with her touch. If she minds me being all hot and sweaty, she doesn't show it. Her back hits the door frame and I leave just enough space between us to drive us both crazy.

She runs her hands up my stomach and chest before brushing her fingers over the pendant at my throat. My eyes slide closed. I know this is exactly what I told myself *not* to do, but I can't seem to stop. Despite my horndog reputation, I actually have incredible self-control when it comes to all things physical. But with Nat, all that control goes right out the fucking window.

"I've been replaying that night over and over, Nat. I can't get you out of my head..."

She shivers and I lean down, slowly sliding a hand to her nape, giving her time to tell me to stop. She doesn't.

"Rizz," she whispers and the word makes my cock jerk to attention.

"I miss kissing you," I tell her honestly, surprised by the words as they fly from my mouth without my permission. She licks her bottom lip and I take it as the invitation it is. She curls her hand around my hip and tugs me forward as I tilt my head and press my lips to hers. It's instant heat, like a match to a line of gasoline, and we both groan into the kiss, just waiting for that inevitable explosion. I gently roll my tongue against hers, just enjoying the feel of her again, loving the way she runs her hands over every inch of my exposed skin.

"We could go for seconds, Nat," I whisper between kisses. "Or thirds...or tenths..."

She makes a sexy little *mmm* sound, but then pulls away.

"We can't," she groans, though she leans in and kisses me softly one more time before pulling away for good, putting actual space between our faces. Our bodies are still close, her hands still lingering on my chest, and my hands are still resting on her neck, my thumbs tracing circles on her cheekbones. "One and done, that was the deal. No strings. No seconds." She says it with confidence, but almost like she's trying to convince herself. As much as I hate it, I nod and step away, trying to ignore the raging hardon I have now. I won't push it, no matter how badly I want her. She says one and done and I'll respect that.

"Ok," I say simply, holding her gaze. The gray is bright against her expanded pupils, her lips red and swollen from our kisses.

"Ok," she repeats, sounding a little stunned. We both stand there for a second a touch awkwardly and then bust out laughing. I'm glad we have this connection that lets us breeze through this stuff that could easily get dicey. *See, we can do this. It's fine.*

"I'll see you tonight," I tell her with a smile as I step aside and gesture for her to get on with her workout. "Hope your dancing shoes are ready," I add with a waggle of my eyebrows. She smiles, giving me one of those sexy challenging looks.

"Oh I'll be dancing circles around you, Thirst Trap. Don't you worry." I shrug one shoulder, unconcerned.

"Guess we'll see."

Nine

NAT

Fuck. Me.

Rizzo can dance. And I don't just mean he doesn't have two left feet. This. Man. Can. *Dance*.

I hadn't been banking on that when I'd issued my little challenge earlier—after another mind-melting kiss that should *not* have happened. I'd been *thisssss* close to saying fuck it and finding a storage closet somewhere, or hell, maybe even going at it right there on the gym floor, but somehow managed to rein myself in. Barely.

Despite the little slip up earlier, tonight has been an absolute blast. Hattie semi-successfully taught the whole group a handful of line dances, though Howey and Jules both still kind of look like fish flopping around on the deck of a boat half the time. Jules does actually look cute in his ten-gallon hat, I'll give him that, and he and Bobby keep bumping into each other and cracking up, so it seems like everyone is having a great time. Hattie is definitely in her element and I see many more nights at the Tipsy Cowboy in our future—especially because I can tell how much she wishes Shep was here too.

Rizzo, the sneaky bastard, can two-step like nobody's business. He'd held a hand out to Hattie in invitation as some fast-paced country song that I'd never heard came on. We both looked a little skeptical, but

Hattie had slid her hand into his and then the two of them started burning up the floor, spinning and twirling and moving like they should be on *Dancing with the Stars* or something. Hattie had grinned so big I was surprised her cheeks didn't hurt. I felt a little pang for my friend then, realizing how much she must miss home and doing things like this that she obviously loves.

She'd left for a new start and to get away from her psycho ex, not because she didn't love living in the south. I can't imagine having to give up everything I knew and loved for fear of my life and starting over completely. Sure, I'd lived on the East Coast for a while for school and work after graduation, but I always knew I could come home any time I wanted. Hattie doesn't have that luxury and it makes my heart hurt for her. I know she's happy here now, but it was definitely an adjustment for her at first. I hope nights like this make her feel a little less homesick.

I'd narrowed my eyes at Rizzo after that first dance with Hattie and he'd grinned like a jackass, clearly proud of himself for his big reveal. Of course, the girls have been all over him since the minute we walked in, but even more so after that little demonstration. *There really is just something about a man who can dance…*Most of them don't even seem to realize he's a professional athlete, just an insanely good-looking guy who can move his body in ways that should be illegal, and he's all too happy to spin them around the floor.

And I'm not jealous at all.

Despite the cold temps outside, Hattie and I had decided to lean all the way into the evening's theme and are clad in matching cut-offs, boots, and crop-tops. The look on Rizzo's face when he'd walked in had been priceless, and I hope that anyone else who noticed just chalked it up to Rizzo being Rizzo and flirting with anything with a pulse. Despite all the attention he's getting, I don't miss the way his gaze seems to find me no matter where I am in the bar, and that assuages a bit of the jealousy. Not that I had any to begin with. Whatever.

"Are you sure you don't need a ride?" Hattie calls, her cheeks flushed.

"I'm good!" I tell her. "I'm gonna grab a bottle of water and then I'm gonna head out. You go ahead."

"I'll make sure she gets home alright," Rizzo says, sliding up beside us. Hattie gives me a pointed look and I narrow my eyes at her. "I don't mean like that," he adds with an exaggerated roll of his eyes. "I mean, I'm sticking around for a bit longer, so I'll make sure she gets into her Uber safely on her way before I find someone to take me to bed or lose me forever!"

I look at him, torn between amusement of him being him...and irritation at the idea of him taking some random girl home.

"Did you just quote *Top Gun*?"

"Yes, ma'am, I did." I huff out a laugh, shaking my head. I turn back to Hattie, pulling her into a hug.

"I'm good, really. Go ahead. I'll see you tomorrow!"

She eyes me and then Rizzo, but lets it slide before whistling to Jules, Bobby, and Howey.

"Alright, y'all, let's mount up and ride out!" I wave to everyone as they make their way towards the exit and Rizzo leans his elbows on the high table.

"Did you have fun tonight?"

"A blast," I yell over the music. He leans in close to my ear.

"You gonna make me go the whole night without a dance, Nat?" He pulls back and quirks a brow in challenge, and I can't help but smile. I probably shouldn't but...fuck it. Not like either of us is dumb enough to hump each other in the middle of the dance floor...I don't think, anyway.

"Let's go, Thirst Trap." I grab his hand and tug him to the floor, throwing caution to the wind a bit now that our friends are gone. A new song starts up just as we find a clear spot and he reaches out and tugs me close. We start dancing, moving together as if we've done it a thousand times. It's a fast number, and we flash across the floor, spinning and turning and twirling, and soon I'm damn near giddy, laughing and smiling like an idiot.

When we come back together, I yell up at him, "Ok, spill it! Where the fuck did you learn to dance like this??" He smiles widely.

"I learned so I could impress a girl in high school. Transfer student from Tennessee!" he calls over *Flatliner* and I laugh out loud.

"Why am I not surprised?" He reaches up and tips the end of his hat to me with two fingers and I can't even begin to explain why it's sexy.

While Jules looked adorable in his hat, Rizzo looks like the male lead from a cowboy romance. In fact, he could probably model for one of the covers shirtless in that hat and it would sell a million copies. He shrugs and twirls me outward again.

"What about you, city girl? Why do you know how to two-step?" I'm not nearly as good as Hattie, but I can hold my own.

"College," I say with a shrug, as if that explains everything. He laughs and spins me again. His hands move all over me, leaving little licks of fire in their wake, but it isn't until the song fades into a slower one, Chris Stapleton singing about Tennessee Whiskey, that I realize *just* how close our bodies are, just how good it feels being like this with him. He swallows hard but arches a brow in question. I nod and he wraps an arm around my waist, pulling me close and making me shiver where his fingertips skim over my bare skin. We start to spin slowly, everything suddenly hot and heavy around us.

Of course the sexiest song known to man had to come on. I'm suddenly hyperaware of every spot that Rizzo is touching me, of the way his muscles move and flex beneath that tight white t-shirt; the way his tight jeans sit just right; the way he can't seem to stop looking at me like he wants to bend me over the bar...

"So, I think you should crack your shell just a tiny bit, Natalie Morgan," he finally says, low in my ear. It's like we're in some weird little bubble now, just the two of us out here on the floor even though we're surrounded by people.

"What do you mean?"

"I mean, I shared with you. I think you should share with me. It's only fair. It's what...friends do," he says, but I would swear he hesitates on the word *friends* for a second. He's got a point. I know I've kept walls up, but if this is *really* my life like I told dad it was, then I can't keep these people out forever. They are my friends, especially Rizzo.

So, I eye him and say, "You get three questions."

"Ten," he counters immediately.

"Five. For tonight," I clarify. He eyes me but finally nods.

"Alright, five it is. *For tonight,*" he repeats, letting me know that I've just opened up the door and he doesn't plan on ever letting me close it again. That should worry me, honestly, but it doesn't. If he figures out who my dad is—who I am—well, so be it. I'm tired of worrying about it. I mean, it isn't like he's a mobster or the President or something, I just didn't want his name and all the attention and expectations that come with it following me around—which is why I took mom's last name when I was fourteen, much to dad's chagrin.

"One: what exactly were you doing before you moved back to Seattle?"

"I was working in New York for a real estate acquisition and development company."

"That sounds...fancy?" I laugh and hike a shoulder. It was what it was. "Did you like New York?"

"I miss the pizza," I admit. "But I like Seattle more—that counts as your second question, by the way." He rolls his eyes and slowly spins me out away from him and then back tight into his body, skating his fingers up my spine and making my breath hitch.

"Siblings?"

"Nope, just me."

"Parents? I mean, I know your dad lives here and your mom passed, but..." He trails off, leaving the question open. He knows the very, very basics and he's asking for more. So, I take a deep breath and give him something real.

"My relationship with my dad is...complicated. It always has been. We butt heads a lot, but at the end of the day, we love each other. And mom died from a brain aneurysm. She went to bed one night and just... didn't wake up in the morning. She was gone. Just like that." I still don't think I've processed losing her completely, but each day is a little easier... until it's somehow worse than the day it happened. It's like a roller-coaster: ups and downs and twists and turns, and just when you think you're on a good beat, suddenly the damn thing shoots you backwards and your free-falling and wanting to puke.

"I'm so sorry, Nat." One day I'll tell him more about it. About her and our life and losing her, but tonight I just nod and give him one of those *it's-not-ok-but-it's-ok* smiles.

"Last question," I say quietly, running my hand up his chest and around the back of his neck, toying with the edges of his hair. He holds my stare, reaching up to lightly pinch my chin between his thumb and forefinger. I swallow hard, searching his eyes for something to keep me from falling, but all I find is a stronger desire to. *Stupid, stupid, stupid.* Wanting another round of mind-blowing sex is one thing. Falling for Anthony Rizzo is something else entirely.

"I really want to kiss you again," he says.

"That's not a question," I say, barely a whisper but he somehow hears me over the music. His lips curl up into a sexy smile and I hold my breath while I wait for him to lean down and kiss me. The song ends and he blinks, shaking himself.

"Come on, let's get you home." I nod, half hoping that he means that he's coming home *with* me, not just throwing me in an Uber. He leads me out to the parking lot and to his waiting Maserati and my pulse races. It's black and sleek and sexy, and I'd be lying if I said I wasn't excited to ride in it. He's got a big ass Range Rover too, and I think an old Mustang. The guy likes cars, that's for sure, and I idly wonder how much extra he pays for parking spaces for all of them in the garage beneath that fancy apartment building of his.

He opens the passenger door for me and I eye him.

"I had one beer when we first got here six hours ago and nothing but water since then. I promise I'm fine to drive." I nod, trusting him completely, and settle down into the soft leather seat. He starts her up and Hannah Montana—or technically Miley Cyrus, I guess—blares from the speakers, so loudly that I wince. He quickly twists the knob to lower the volume and I eye him.

"Uh, Ollie was in the car earlier..."

"Mmm hmm..."

He pulls out of the parking lot and we sit in silence for a few minutes, but then Rizzo starts to sing along quietly, giving me a sidelong glance, and I bust out laughing. I reach over and crank the music back up and then we're both signing it at the top of our lungs. We have a full karaoke party all the way through town, me giving him directions here and there to my place. Eventually, he pulls up outside the house and kills the music. My cheeks and belly hurt from smiling and laughing so hard, and he wipes tears from his eyes.

"Those are so not the words," he says, still laughing.

"They are too! *It doesn't make a difference if we're naked or not. That's what he says!*"

He clutches at his side.

"It doesn't make a difference if we *make it* or not. *Make it* or not." I grin, realizing that he's probably right now that he says it, but refusing to let him win.

"Nah, it's definitely naked. I will die on this hill." He smiles and shakes his head, muttering something about a loss cause. Eventually the laughter fades and he nods towards the big craftsman.

"Nice house."

"It's where I grew up, actually. I moved back in after...when I came back from New York." He nods in understanding and I lean back against the headrest, turning my face towards him. He's so handsome I could cry, but it's more than that.

"Why do you have to be so much fun?" I ask with a sigh.

"Fun is a bad thing?"

Fun is a...complicated thing that could lead to even more complicated things because I'm really, really starting to like Rizzo more than I should.

We sit there in the quiet, just looking at each other and it's a nice moment. There's that simmering heat just beneath the surface like there always is between us, but it's also an easy, companionable moment to just *be* with him. He's one of the few people that I can just sit with and not feel any pressure to fill a silence or act a certain way.

After a few minutes I realize I need to make a decision here. I can get out of the car, say goodnight, and stay on the smart path of one-and-done (with a few kissing indiscretions here and there, admittedly).

Or, I can invite him in and have another amazing night of sex, and set myself down the path to inevitable heartache. Just as I'm about to make the dumb decision and tell him to turn the car off, he takes a deep, almost shuddering breath, as if he's preparing for something unpleasant. Or scary. I tilt my head, immediately on alert.

"Will you have dinner with me?" he blurts. I blink in confusion, clearly mishearing him. "Not tonight, obviously," he says, waving towards the dash clock. "I mean...do you want to go out with me? On a... date?"

I stare at him incredulously. He's fucking with me, right?

"You don't date," I remind him slowly.

"Well, I've never climbed Mount Everest either, but I'm sure I could do it if I wanted to," he says almost defensively and I remember how competitive he is about literally *everything*. The Bop It Incident flashes through my mind and I almost laugh. Suffice it to say that he and Howey ended up rolling around on the floor trying to pummel each other, and the Bop It wound up sailing through a window and landing in a pile of snow.

"You're seriously...asking me out?"

"...Yes?" he says, though it comes out as question.

"Why?"

"I...don't know." Well that's a great answer. My face must say as much. "I didn't mean it like that, I just meant...I want another night with you, Nat. And I don't want it to just be a random hook up..." He only sounds half sure and bless his heart for trying, as Hattie would say, but I think even the *thought* of dating is giving him hives. I don't think I've ever seen Anthony Rizzo nervous about anything, even when he's playing for division titles or throwing down with three guys on the ice. But right now it looks like he might just puke or pass out or both.

"I don't think of you as just another booty call or one night stand, Nat. I want you to know that. So, I thought...dinner."

I huff out a small laugh. It's actually really sweet that he's trying to make sure I don't feel like I'm just one among the many, but that's still what I'll be. Having dinner first won't change the fact that he'll have another puck bunny tomorrow, and another the night after that, and another two or three when they go to Philly next week.

And that's totally fine. That's his life and it's one he enjoys. I'm not asking him to change that for me...not that I think he's capable of changing it, even if I did ask.

"Rizz, stop. Look, I appreciate you not wanting me to feel like a random hook up, but you don't have to do all that. It's ok. I know what this was. Is. Was." I can't keep it straight. "I'm not asking you to change anything or pretend to be something you aren't."

He eyes me, like he's trying to read if I'm serious or not. He gets that determined look in his eyes, like he has when he's on the ice: laser focused and seeing a thousand tiny details all at once, coming up with the perfect plan to make his way to the goal no matter who or what stands in his way.

"So, is that a no, then?"

"It's a..." I bite my lip, searching his eyes and wanting nothing more than to say yes, regardless of how fucking stupid it is. "It's an I'll think about it."

He smiles and nods and before I can stop myself, I'm across the seat and kissing him again. He makes a surprised noise, but quickly tangles a hand in my hair and kisses me back. Slowly. Deeply. Making my toes curl in my boots and my stomach flip. His lips force mine apart and his tongue delves into my mouth, stroking mine and gently demanding what he wants. I'm powerless not to give him anything and everything. I tilt my head, letting him control the kiss and steer it anywhere he wants. I toy with the hair at his nape and inhale sharply when his hand glides down my side, fingers skating over bare skin. I arch my hips upward, wishing this car had more damn room right about now.

"*Natalie*," he sighs in an amused, accusatory groan.

I pull away and curse against his lips. "Fuck. I'm sorry. I didn't mean to do that. I've gotta go." He chuckles lightly and I kiss him once more, quick and soft, before practically leaping from the car like it's on fire. I don't make smart choices when in confined spaces with Anthony Rizzo.

He leans across the seat and grins up at me.

"Night, Nat."

"Get some sleep, Thirst Trap," I say breathless. "You've got a big game tomorrow."

"Yes, ma'am." I laugh and shake my head before closing the car door. I wave him off, hopping from foot to foot to keep warm, but the car stays put. He rolls the window down.

"I'm not leaving until you get safely inside."

And he has to be a gentleman. *Of course he does.* The universe really hates me right now...but I'll have to thank his mother one day because she sure did raise a good one.

I roll my eyes but smile before turning and jogging across the lawn and up the front porch, freezing my butt off. *The outfit choice was still worth it*, I think with a grin, knowing damn well that Rizzo's eyes are glued to my ass right now. I might put a little extra swagger in my step because, well, I can't quite help teasing him.

I get the door open and wave as I step inside. He waves and finally drives off as I close the door and turn the lock. I lean my head against the cool wood.

"Stupid, stupid, stupid."

"Tell me not to sleep with Rizzo again," I beg Hattie. I'm sitting on the table in her office next to a big ass bouquet of flowers, wrestling with my life choices. I'd dreamed about Rizzo all night. Like *dreamed* dreamed. The kind of the dirty persuasion that leaves you sweaty and panting and wishing it was real when you wake up. And I've been on edge all day from it, freaking desperate for him. It's getting really out of hand.

"From what you told me, you didn't really do much sleepin' the first time around." I grab a notepad off the table and throw it at her. She ducks out of the way, laughing, and I love her so much but also want to strangle her right now.

"I'm serious!" I say kicking my feet in frustration. "I don't think I can hold out much longer. I swear me telling him it was a one-and-done somehow made him *more* interested. He's hinted at wanting another hook up since it happened," I hedge, not wanting to admit that I've already slipped with him more than once—just kissing, but still—"but now he's being weird—he asked me to dinner. Like a legit *dinner date.*"

Hattie arches her brows in surprise, clearly saying *how very un-Rizzo of him.*

"Right?! That's what I thought! I know it's just a means to an end, another night in the sack, but still."

"Well, what did you say?" she asks, not ready to just shrug it off, which only makes it worse. I don't need her to be thoughtful and understanding. I need her to tell me I'm an idiot and to move on with my life —*sans* Rizzo's dick.

"I told him...I'd think about it." I groan and put my head in my hands. "I'm not going to be able to hold out much longer. When I knew it would just be one night of fun and then we'd be adults and just see each other at work like normal, it didn't seem like that big a deal. I could handle that. But with him actively trying for another round?" I puff up my cheeks and let out a long, slow breath. "It's a completely different ballgame that I am not equipped to play. I mean, you've seen him! I do *not* think with my brain when he's around, I think with something else entirely and it very, *very* much wants me to accept his invitation. Actually, it just wants me to say fuck dinner all together and tell him to just take me to a hotel."

Hattie laughs, running the edge of her pen over her bottom lip and looking thoughtful.

"Well...would it really be so bad if it wasn't a one-and-done? I mean, plenty of people have steady fuck-buddies."

"Yes! Or, well, no. Maybe? I don't know! I was ok being a notch in his skyscraper-length bedpost for one really, *really* good night, but continually just being one in a rotation of countless women? I don't think I could do it." I pinch the bridge of my nose, not wanting to admit that the thought of it actually makes me want to scream. Thinking about Rizzo with other girls is becoming...frustrating. Which really isn't fair of me.

"Ugh, let's change the subject. Who sent you flowers? The parade float guy? He seemed *very* smitten with you."

"They aren't from the parade float guy, thank you very much," she says, coming over to the table and messing with the flowers. "Well, I guess they *could* be—I don't actually know who they're from. No name on the note—but I doubt it. Parade float guy actually got Bobby's number, though he did mention another girl he was dating recently, so I think he's an into-the-wine-not-the-label guy."

"Ooo" I say, excited for Bobby to finally have a date. He's been in a bit of a dry spell. "And?"

"Not a bad time, but no sparks from what I've been told."

"Well, hell, maybe I'll call float guy then. Maybe he'll get my mind off Rizzo and his giant co—"

"Ok, ok, come on, you," she cuts me off with a laugh. "Let's go grab Bobby and head down to the game." It's a big one tonight, sure to be a total gongshow, and I'm excited to get down there. Maybe watching Rizzo be an absolute menace on the ice will distract me from thoughts of him in other places...but I know deep down it'll just make me want him more. He's sexy when he plays, plain and simple. The cocky confidence, the buttery smooth way he flies over the ice, the way he handles the puck...It's hot, ok?

Hattie laces her arm through mine and we head out of her office. She leans in and adds in a low voice, "But, uh, explain exactly what you mean by *giant*..."

I huff out a laugh as Bobby joins us.

"What are we laughing about?"

"Hattie here wanted all the dirty details about a certain star center's, uh, equipment."

His brows fly upward but then his lips curl into a slow smile.

"Well, get on with it then. Share with the class, Natalie."

I probably shouldn't kiss and tell, but I give in and hold out my hands a good bit apart, palms facing each other to show them a measurement.

"You're shittin' me," Hattie says, eyes wide and mouth open in shock and horror—and definitely some intrigue.

"You know, I'd heard rumors, but having them confirmed by a reputable source..." I punch Bobby in the arm and he grins.

"Would you two hurry up? We're going to miss the best part of the entire night: pre-game stretching."

Ten

RIZZO

I don't know if I'm happy that Nat turned me down, annoyed that she turned me down, or horrified that I'd even asked her out at all. A combination of all three, I guess. I try to push thoughts of Nat and dating and everything else out of my head and focus on the upcoming game. This one is always a rough one. Once upon a time, a baby-faced Rizzo and Shep both got recruited by the Kodiaks out of college—and then proceeded to both leave them for the Vipers at the same time a few years later. Some of the guys decided to take it personally and ever since then have made a point to make this game as violent and bloody as possible. It's stupid really, but hockey players—all athletes actually—are nothing if not dramatic.

My phone buzzes and I pull it out, hoping to see a text from Nat, but smile all the same when I see it's from my mom. I open up the message and snort.

Mom: Good luck tonight! Go Vipers! 🏒 🐻 🥅

                  lol thanks, ma. Love you.

Mom: Light the lamp. Be safe. Love you. 🤍

"You ready?" Shep asks, punching me in the shoulder. I toss my phone in my locker and turn to face him.

"Hell yeah. I've got a good feeling about tonight."

He grins. "Does that have anything to do with you leaving the bar last night with Nat?"

"For the last time, nothing happened." Nothing much, anyway. Apparently Mac had spilled the beans that Nat and I were the last to leave the bar and was conjecturing her little southern heart out. "I drove her home. She went inside. I went to my place and passed out—alone. End of story." He gives me a skeptical look, but I'm saved from further conversation by coach calling for our attention. He gives us our pregame speech and then I put in my ear buds, cranking my Game Day Playlist and getting in the zone.

It's fucking go time.

The game is more brutal than usual, emotions running extra high for some reason. Fights break out every few minutes, the penalty box pretty much stays occupied, and I've already scattered Figgy's chicklets across the fucking ice. Well worth the time in the box for that one—Martin Figueroa was a prick a decade ago and he's an even bigger one now, getting in cheap shots and talking so much trash it's insane, and not just the typical stuff. Real vile, uncool shit. Not to mention there are rumors he doesn't like to take no for an answer from women, so honestly he deserves a lot worse than having his teeth knocked out.

It's back and forth all night, blueline to blueline and back again. Shep is doing damn work in the net to keep us up by four, but the game is intense as hell. Another fight breaks out and while they get it broken up, I skate by the glass where Nat, Mac, and Bobby are sitting. I smile at Nat and I swear she bites her fucking lip as she watches me go by. And now my cock is trying to join the game. *Damn this woman...*

I shake myself, focusing back on the game. If we can just hold them a bit longer, we'll be golden.

"Ah fuck!" I yell as a couple of Kodiaks make a break towards our goal. Jules and Roman are hot on their heels though, skating like bats out of hell, and I'm not far behind. Shep is ready, waiting with that intense, almost scary focus he has. He's like a big cat or a snake waiting to pounce on their prey, sitting so silent and still until the last possible second, and then it's all over.

And then someone goes down, causing a massive five-guy dog pile that careens towards Shep at top speed. I tense as they get closer, knowing it's going to be one hell of a collision. They slam into Shep and there's a tangle of bodies shoving the goal backwards across the ice. I wince at the hit, knowing that it has to hurt...but then I see a helmet fly across the ice and my heart clenches, sending spikes of fear through me.

It's Shep's helmet...and he's not moving.

No. No, no, no.

I skate faster than I've ever skated in my life, reaching him in a heart-beat and sliding on my knees on the ice, shoving a Kodiak violently to the side, not giving a shit if he's hurt too, which is probably fucked up of me but I don't care. The refs are trying to get us all back, telling us to give everyone breathing room, but fuck them.

"Shep? Shep!? Fuck, come on, Con, answer me." Nothing. He's out cold and there's a dark streak on the ice beneath him that I know is blood. My stomach lurches. Hockey is a brutal sport. Injuries are common and blood is par for the course, but seeing your best friend in the world down like this is different. I've seen guys never walk away from hits like this. I have the wherewithal not to touch or shake him, but I move my hands restlessly over him, uselessly trying to figure out something to do to help. "Connor, God damn it, you can't do this to us. *Come on...*"

Our athletic trainers finally make their way over and this time I let them force me back. Jules helps me up and I see that he has a nasty cut across his brow, blood pouring down his face.

"You need to get that looked at," I tell him, though the words sound like they're coming from someone else, far, far away. I shift my gaze back to Shep. I don't want to leave his side but I know I can't help him. But what I *can* do?

Beat the absolute shit out of Figgy.

The bastard was one of the ones in the dog pile and all I can see is red. If he did this on purpose...

I throw my gloves off and skate at him like a freight train, not slowing even a little before plowing into him and clocking him right in the jaw. My momentum propels us a few feet until he hits the glass. He manages to stay mostly upright, so I grip the front of his jersey and pull him back towards me, rearing back to give him another. This one catches him right in the eye and is going to leave a nice shiner. I get in one more shot before he's able to push me away, and it splits his skin on his cheek, maybe even cracks the bone. I grin at the sight of his blood, probably looking maniacal as fuck, but I don't care. Several other sets of hands finally pull me off of him completely, and whistles blow all over the place, but I don't give a flying fuck.

"What the—"

"Tell me you didn't fucking do it, you sorry sack of shit!!" I scream around Nowski as he tries to keep me from jumping at Figgy again and ripping his throat out. "Tell me it wasn't a cheap shot. I swear to fucking God, Figgy, I'll end you right here on the ice if you did this on purpose!!" Part of me knows I'm not being entirely rational right now, but I can't seem to listen to that part. I can only listen to the part that's roaring in rage to cover up the fear and panic. If I listen to those, I'll break down. No, the rage is much better.

"I didn't!! Fuck, Rizz, I wouldn't! I swear to God." He wipes blood from his lip and glares at me, but there's a hint of sympathy and worry in his eyes. "Jesus, I'm an asshole, but I wouldn't do that and you fucking know it."

"Rizzo, come on, man," Roman says from beside me, tugging at my arm to pull me back. Nowski remains in place between me and Figgy in case I try again I guess. I glare at Figgy for one more long second but finally throw up my hands and turn away. But what I see makes my whole body go numb. The medics are on the ice now and they're getting Shep strapped to a spine board. My heart roars loudly in my ears, my stomach feeling cold and hollow. He still isn't fucking moving. He could be paralyzed or fucking dead for all I know—

Then I remember Hattie. I whip around to where they're sitting and our eyes catch for half a heartbeat. Hers are wide and filled with absolute terror, and if I didn't know that she was in love with him before this moment, I sure as hell would know it now. That look...I shudder. I hope I never see that look again in my life.

And then she's gone, turning and sprinting up the stadium steps like a bat out of hell. I see Bobby but not Nat. Where is she? I suddenly need my eyes on her. To know she's ok or to calm me down or who the fuck knows why, but all I want in this moment is to see her. When I figure out that staring at the empty seat next to Bobby isn't going to make her magically appear, I cut my eyes back to Shep, still lifeless but now loaded up on the spine board and being carried off the ice. My heart feels like it's being squeezed by a giant fist and I know I need to fucking breathe but my brain and body don't seem to be communicating.

"Rizz. Hey, Rizzo, look at me, man." I force my gaze away from where they're hurrying down the tunnel that leads to the training and locker rooms on the ground floor, and find Howey staring at me. He puts a gloved hand on my chest and holds my gaze. "Rizzo, you gotta breathe, man, you're gonna pass out." I blink and nod, knowing he's right. I close my eyes and force my body to obey. It feels like it takes hours, but finally that fist around my heart loosens its grip enough that I can get some air into my lungs.

"He'll be alright. He's Shep, ya know?" Howey says, trying to smile but I can see the worry beneath it. "He's like fucking Superman. Nothing can keep him down for long."

I try to laugh but barely manage a grimace-like smile. Eventually everything settles back down and the game resumes. I do more time in the box for my attack on Figgy, and though I know we have to keep playing, it feels so wrong to be up here while Shep is...I swallow hard, forcing the thought away as I skirt around a couple of Kodiaks and manage to score another goal. We've still got the lead and though he's no Shep, Rosie is a hell of a goalie. We'll pull this out, I know it.

I look over again and still no Nat. No Bobby now, either. Maybe they're both comforting Mac somewhere. I skate back to the bench during a time out and find Jules back from getting his brow patched up.

"He's awake," he says quickly, smiling, and I swear I take the first full breath I have since it happened. It feels like hours ago, but I know it's only been a few minutes, really. "Awake and talking. They're taking him to the hospital to get checked out, of course, but he was alert and everything. Talked to Mac."

"She ok?"

He shakes his head. "She was shaken up real bad, man. I think she's alright now, but she almost passed out I think. Kasey got her squared away, but yeah, she took it hard." I nod in understanding and thank him for the update.

The time-out ends and now that I know Shep is ok—well, alive anyway—I'm ready to finish this.

"Let's fucking go," I tell Jules and we fist bump as he climbs over the wall and heads back towards the center line with me.

Eleven

NAT

The game is crazy, but going good so far. I mean, no one has been outright ejected and the Vipers are up, so for now, that's a big win. I'm on the hunt for drinks and cotton candy for the woman-child that is Hattie, and I wind my way through the crowd on the main concourse towards the concession stand where staff can get our goodies for free. Perks of the job and all that. The place is jam packed and while it's frustrating when you're really fucking thirsty, it's amazing. It means that all the things Hattie is doing—well, all of us, but she's the master-mind—are working. We're going to save the organization and keep their asses right here in Seattle.

Just as I make it to the east side of the concourse one of the front office guys, Joey, comes towards me. I wave and smile.

"Hey, Joey," I say when a family of eight finally passes and he can reach me.

"Hey, Nat, I was just heading down to the seats to find you."

"Oh," I say, brows flying up. "You were looking for me?" I figured he was just craving a beer and a hot dog. "What's up?"

"Um, some guy is looking for you?" My brow furrows.

"A guy?" Who the hell would be looking for me?

"Older guy. Seems...important. And a little scary. He has one of the VIP boxes filled with a bunch of rich looking people."

My heart thuds in my chest. Shit.

"Which box?"

"Four." I want to roll my eyes. Of course it's Box Four—the most expensive luxury box in the entire arena.

"Thanks," I mutter and rush off towards the Box, beer and cotton candy forgotten for the moment. I apparently need to go see my father.

When I enter the room I see dad over in the corner, laughing with a group of men with a glass of scotch in his hand. I walk over, trying to keep my temper in check. He has every right to be here, I remind myself, but it seems like an attack of some sort, or like he's checking up on me or something. I don't know. Maybe I'm paranoid and he just wanted to show some clients a good time. He has season tickets to the Wolves and the Rattlers, after all, so it isn't like hanging out at sporting events is strange for him, exactly, but he's never really been that big into hockey. It was one of the draws of this job—no real chance of running into him in the course of business, as it were.

He sees me approach and nods, telling the others to give him a moment, and comes over.

"What are you doing here?" I snap, a little more peevish than I intend.

"Well that's a lovely way to greet your father," he muses, but he smirks. He's clearly having a good time and isn't going to let my bad attitude get in the way.

"Sorry," I say, feeling a little bad. "Hi, dad."

"Hi, Natalie."

"Enjoying the game?"

He smiles. "I'd forgotten how entertaining these games could be, actually. I might just have to buy out this box permanently." Well, that would mean a lot of money to the organization, but I can't say that I love that idea. Having him here makes me feel uneasy.

"You wanted to see me?" I ask, glancing down at the rink to see Rizzo streaking across the ice. *Go, go, go.* I pull my gaze back to dad, waiting expectantly.

"I was here, so I figured I'd say hello, that's all."

I arch a brow. "That's all?"

"I may also have some news."

"There it is. Spill whatever it is you want to say dad, I need to get back to my friends."

"Lysander is moving to London to start up our international branch."

I stare at him blankly. "Uhh, tell him I said congratulations? And Pip Pip Cheerio?" His lips twitch at the corners.

"You will take his position," he says simply, as if that's the most obvious thing in the world. "You start after the first of the year to give you time to...wind things up here. It's already in the works."

"*In the works?*" I repeat. Audacity must be half off for the holidays because what in the actual fuck?? "I don't want Lysander's job, dad." Did he really call me here in the middle of the game to ask—no, he didn't even fucking *ask*. He *told* me that I'm coming back to work for him. "Why would you just assume that I would??"

"Natalie," he sighs, clearly exasperated. The crowd goes crazy and I glance sidelong and see some Kodiaks breaking away down the ice. *Shit!* I turn back to dad as he continues. "This has gone on long enough."

"Who are you to decide that?" I snap. Something is happening down on the ice, but I can't pull my gaze away from dad's, now starting to burn with anger. Well, let him be angry. *I'm* fucking pissed.

"I'm your father," he grits out, keeping his voice low as not to draw attention, though no one seems to really be paying us any regardless. Must be another big fight down there.

"That doesn't mean you get to dictate my entire life!" I grit out through clenched teeth, trying desperately to keep my temper in check. "I let you for a long time, but not anymore. I don't want to work for the company. I don't want to just be the girl in the corner office on the sixtieth floor who only has the job because of her daddy." He starts to interrupt, to say that I have an Ivy League education, that no one would dare think that, but we both know it's bullshit—no matter what education and accolades I have. I'll only ever be seen as his daughter who didn't have to work for her position. Having a different last name is helpful, but gossip travels fast up the corporate ladder. The way people looked at me in New York once word got out, like the only thing worse than having my daddy hand me this position on a silver platter would have been sleeping my way to the top. Either way, it fucking sucked.

"I want to forge my own path in whatever place I choose. I am *happy* here! I'm doing things that matter."

"Oh, coordinating reindeer tosses?" he says derisively, gesturing towards the flyer on the wall for the event happening after tonight's game. With four simple words he manages to make me feel two inches tall. I stare at him, not sure what the hell I want to say back. Part of me wants to tell him to fuck off. Part of me wants to cry and ask why he can't just be proud of me no matter what I do. Another part wants to punch him.

"Oh my god, I think he's really hurt," someone says quietly from one of the seats and that gets my attention. I realize now that the entire stadium has gone eerily quiet. Something is wrong. I jerk my head away from my toe-to-toe with dad, searching the rink down below. The goal is clear against the wall and medics are on the ice loading someone onto one of those boards. My heart clenches. *Oh God.* I run across the room, closer to one of the big screens that display the games up in these suites to get a better look. Who is it? What happened? *Oh God, not him...please...*

"Natalie?" dad says, stepping up beside me and putting a comforting hand on my shoulder. The animosity from moments ago has disappeared, and I want to throw my arms around him. For a second, he's just being my dad, concerned by something that's obviously upsetting to me. He has his moments, I'll give him that. That's why our relationship is so fucking frustrating, because in times like this, I'm reminded of how much I love the man, how alike we are and how if we could just shift a few edges a tiny bit, we'd fit together perfectly. He's a good dad, great even when he puts all the other bullshit aside, but he can only seem to do that sporadically, and it's in those times that the edges that need shifting seem like mountains that we'll never be able to move.

But for the moment, I appreciate his steady hand on my shoulder as I try to figure out what the hell is going on, to see which one of my friends might be hurt. My heart pounds loudly in my ears, over and over as the words echo through my mind. *Not him. Not him. Not him.*

And then the camera angle shifts as one of the medics moves out of the way and I see who it is.

"Oh God, Shep," I whisper, covering my mouth with a hand. The camera is focused in on him, on his unmoving body and my stomach twists. *Oh God. Where's Rizzo?* The cameraman isn't helping, staying focused on Shep, so I turn away from the screen and run to the front of the box, leaning out over the railing as my eyes dart over all of the players, trying to find 15...

And then I see him, beating the shit out of one of the guys on the other team. Was he the one responsible for whatever happened to Shep? Is that why Rizzo is going to town on the dude? I've seen him in plenty of game time fights, but this is different. This is...frantic and brutal. Eventually he's pulled off, and the medics get Shep off of the ice and down the tunnel. Everything feels slow and kind of unreal, and I feel cold and detached. I know I need to get myself together.

"Hattie," I whisper in horror. She's probably freaking out. Shep is... well, officially he's her best friend, but it's easy for anyone to see that she's completely falling for him.

"Natalie, are you alright?" dad asks when I turn to fly from the suite.

"Not really, dad. That's my friend down there on that spine board and one of my other friends needs me. I have to go."

"I'm sorry," he says. "About your friend. We'll, uh, discuss everything else later."

I shake my head, trying to focus but my head is a melee. Worry for Shep, worry for Hattie, fucking fury that dad even brought the job shit back up again right now, relief that Rizzo is ok, but worry for him too seeing his best friend hurt...and an intense urge to just throw myself into his arms. It's all too much.

"Fuck the job offer, dad. I decline."

With that, I bolt from the room and go to find Hattie.

Shep was awake and talking before they took him to the hospital, and that seems to be enough to let Hattie keep herself together through the rest of the game and the Reindeer Toss afterward. I ask if she wants me to handle it so she can go, but she insists that she stay. I think the distraction is the only thing keeping her sane, honestly, so I throw myself into the event beside her, letting all the crazy block out everything else for a while. I'm desperate to see Rizzo, to make sure he's alright and...I don't know, seeing Shep hurt like that just has me feeling like if I don't get my hands on Rizzo I might go crazy.

I offer to drive Hattie home when it's all said and done, but she says she's fine. I think she plans on camping out at the hospital, and I don't blame her. We say our goodbyes and she goes back up to her office to grab a few things and I wait in the wide hallway on the ground floor. I debate if I should try to find Rizzo or just text him later to check on him, but the decision is made for me when he rounds the corner.

His entire body seems to relax when he sees me and I immediately go to him and wrap my arms around his neck. He hugs me back and in this moment, there's nothing sexual or heated between us. It's just two friends being there for each other. He lets out a long, shuddering exhale and then pulls away.

"Are you alright?" I ask, searching those blue eyes that I'm quickly becoming all too familiar with.

"Yeah, I'm good, I just—" His phone rings and he gives me an apologetic look as he fishes it out of his pocket. "Oh I need to grab this, one sec." I nod, assuming he's going to walk away to take the call in private, but instead he tugs me out of the middle of the corridor towards the wall with him. A bunch of the other guys walk by and I nod and wave as they leave for the night, Rizzo doing that guy-head-jerk thing in farewell.

He slides the bar to answer what I see now is a FaceTime call. I take a small step away, not wanting to intrude as he holds the phone up in front of his face.

"Hey, ma." I blink in surprise, the shock on my face making him laugh lightly. He smiles widely, an easy, genuine smile that makes my heart melt a little.

"AJ!" she exclaims in a mix of relief and worry.

I arch a brow at him and mouth *AJ?*

He cuts his eyes at me over the top of the phone, eyes dancing with mischief.

"Oh God, honey, is Connor alright? We were watching the game on television and saw him get hurt and I was so, so worried."

"He's ok. Coach just heard from the hospital." I exhale roughly in relief and he reaches out and squeezes my hand, almost absently, and I glance around to see if anyone is watching us, but we're alone. "He's got a mild concussion and a cracked rib, but no internal bleeding or anything like that. He's got a couple of stitches for a cut on his head, but it's superficial—you know how much head wounds bleed even when they're minor. You remember the time I cracked my head on the workbench in the back of the rink with Hank? Looked like an episode of *CSI* back there, but it was totally fine, barely a scratch."

"Oh I remember it vividly, thank you very much," she says dryly and I can hear a small hint of her Irish accent. It's not thick after so many years here, I guess, but it's definitely there in the almost musical lilt. "Are you ok?"

"Yeah, ma, I'm fine, just a little banged up. You know how the Kodiak games always are." He leans one shoulder against the wall and I mirror his stance, facing him.

"No, I mean about Connor," she says. Rizzo's smile fades and I can see just how worried he'd been, how much Shep being hurt really rattled him. "I know seeing him hurt like that must have been hard."

"I'm alright now that I know he's alright."

"Give him and Ollie big love for me. Oh! Do you have a closing date yet?"

"Oh, yeah, actually." I eye him with interest. He'd mentioned moving out of his apartment that night we spent together, but I haven't asked him about it since. I've had other, dirtier things on my mind. I'm a bad friend. A bad, horny friend.

"Next week and she's all mine. You'll have to come visit after you get back from your trip."

"That sounds great, honey. Ok, I'll let you go—I'm sure you have… things to do after the game." She says it with a knowing smile in her voice and I bark out a laugh, quickly slapping a hand over my mouth to stifle it while Rizzo rolls his eyes.

"Who was that?" his mom asks.

"Your mom knows you're a slut?" I whisper, shocked.

"Shut it," he whispers back, before answering his mom. "That's my very rude friend, Nat." He shifts so that we're beside each other and tilts the phone so I'm on the screen now too. My brows fly up in surprise. Being on a FaceTime call with Rizzo's mom was not on my Bingo card, but here we are.

"Oh!" she breathes in surprise, blinking. "Well, hi there, rude friend Nat!" She gives me a warm smile and I can see so much of her in Rizzo.

"Hi, Mrs. Rizzo."

"Oh, call me Muriel, dear."

"Nice to meet you, Muriel," I say, smiling.

"Is that a *girl's* voice?" A man's head pops onto the screen in front of his mom's. He's got black hair with a few streaks of gray at his temples, deeply tanned skin, and glasses hanging around his neck. Rizzo's mom swats at him and he shifts back so he's a little farther from the screen, settling in beside her on the couch. Rizzo rolls his eyes.

"Dad, this is my friend, Nat. Nat, this is my dad, Ray."

"Hi, nice to meet you," I say with a small wave.

"Back at you, young lady. Are you keeping our boy there in line?"

"Well, I'm not a miracle worker."

They both bust out laughing and Rizzo tries to look disgruntled but he can't hide his smile.

"Hey, that was a great game, kid! Is Nat here your lucky charm?"

Rizzo scoffs. "As if I need luck."

"Ahh, I don't know, son, you've been even more impressive than usual the past few games," Ray says thoughtfully, rubbing his chin. I mean, he *has* seemed to be on fire lately, but that definitely can't have anything to do with me...The logical part of my brain knows that's true. The other part loves the idea that he's been absolutely tearing it up because of me somehow. It's so stupid.

"Now, Nat, are you one of the...what do they call them, hun?" he asks, turning to is wife. "Puck bunnies?" I snort and Rizzo coughs, nearly choking in surprise.

"Dad!" he groans, running his hand through his hair.

"What?" Ray asks, innocently. "Is that not the right phrase?" Muriel tries and fails to stop laughing, and Ray cringes. "Oh, is that something you're not suppose to call them to their face?"

"Oh my God, dad, please stop. Nat isn't a..." He pinches the bridge of his nose. "We're just friends," Rizzo says firmly. "She works for our media department."

"Oh! I love all the videos of the boys answering questions on the... oh what's that app called again? Clipper? They're so fun!" Muriel exclaims. I love that she calls them 'the boys' like she still sees Rizzo as a kid playing pee wee hockey with his friends. "Was that your idea? It's so creative!"

"It was a collaborative effort with my boss, Hattie," I say with a smile, a surge of pride warming my chest to have our work complimented. It may not seem like much to someone like my dad, but it means something to me. If what I'm a part of can bring a smile to someone's face, not just pad someone's already very padded wallet, then that makes me feel as if I'm doing something good in the world.

"Well, keep them coming, they make my whole day!" Rizzo smiles at me and I can't help but grin back. "Ok, honey, we'll let you go. You kids have a fun night. AJ, let me know how Connor is doing, ok?"

"I will."

"It was so nice to meet you, *Just A Friend* Nat." Muriel gives me a smile that says she's not sure she believes that for a second and my cheeks heat.

"You too."

"Love you. See you soon," Rizzo says, waving.

"Love you," they both echo in unison.

He hangs up and sighs.

"AJ?" I ask immediately.

"That would be my name."

"Uh...what?"

"I mean, pretty much only my mom and dad use it anymore, Shep every now and then, but it's what everyone called me growing up—before mom married Ray and he adopted me and I officially had a cool last name to go by instead." He grins and I huff out a laugh. "Anthony James. Anthony was the sperm donor's name and I think it was hard for mom to call me that after he left—which was when I was like two—so I just became AJ." He hikes a shoulder and I wonder how many people know this story, know this name. Does him sharing it with me...mean something? Or am I just being an idiot?

Probably the latter, I think with an inward roll of my eyes. I tilt my head, studying him.

"It suits you, actually." He eyes me and his lips curl up into one of those crooked, sexy smirks of his.

"Care to try screaming it while I lick your pu—" I clamp my hand over his mouth and look around again. We're still alone, thankfully, and when I pull my hand away, he's grinning like a lunatic.

"You are terrible," I say, laughing.

"I know," he says with a sigh. "I'm gonna grab Shep's stuff and check in with Sara to make sure she's good to keep Ollie the rest of the night, and then head to the hospital."

I frown, looking at my watch.

"Aren't visiting hours way over by now?" He gives me a pointed look. "But of course you think that won't matter because you're Anthony Fucking Rizzo."

"You're finally getting it, Nat."

"Tell him I'm glad he's ok. Text Hattie and let her know what the doctors said, ok?"

"Will do."

I lean up and kiss him softly on the cheek, forcing myself to behave.

"I'm really glad it wasn't you," I say quietly. "When I first saw...I wasn't sure..." I shake my head, trying to push past the memory of that moment of absolute terror when I thought it might have been him on the ice, unmoving. "I'm glad you're alright," I finish. Too many things seem to be flashing behind his eyes and before he can land on any one of them, before he can ask me what that means or pull me into his arms like I want him to so desperately, I tug gently on the front of his hoodie and then pat his chest before turning to walk away.

"The offer still stands!" he calls out when I make it halfway down the hall. I turn and walk backwards.

"Which offer? Dinner? Or screaming your name?" I ask, *really* hoping that everyone is actually gone like I think.

He laughs lightly. "Both."

"Good night, AJ," I say with a smirk.

Twelve

RIZZO

As expected, I sweet-talked and name-dropped my way into the hospital despite it being super late. Shep is fine, just like the doctors said, but I needed to see it with my own eyes. The adrenaline had been running so high when everything first happened, that it didn't hit me until later how scared I really was. I love Connor Shepherd like a brother and the thought of losing him, or of him being seriously hurt, kind of knocked my world off its axis.

Seeing Nat earlier had helped keep the worst of the panic and fear at bay for a time, and I don't want to look too hard into why that might be. My feelings for her are confusing at best and dangerous at worst. I still don't know that I could figure out how to date someone even if I wanted to, so the fear of commitment is compounded by the fear of failure, and it's honestly making my head hurt.

"Good evening, Mr. Rizzo," Jax, the security guard at the front desk of my building says when I stride through the lobby.

"Hey, Jax, how are you doing?"

"Good, sir, thanks. I saw the game—is Mr. Shepherd alright?"

"He is, yeah. Spending the night in the hospital, but he'll be just fine."

"Glad to hear it. Have a good evening, sir."

I nod and walk past the desk, but then stop and back up. On an absolute whim, I tell him to add Nat to my approved visitor list. I'm not holding out much hope, but...just in case. Jax gives me a surprised look but smiles and assures me that he'll take care of it.

When I get to my apartment, I toss my keys on the counter and run my fingers through my hair. I've got a few boxes started and they're strewn throughout the place. I really need to get this all done. A lot of this crap stays, of course, since it came with the apartment, but all my personal shit needs to be packed up.

"That's a problem for tomorrow me," I say, kicking a box out of the way as I make my way to my room. I'm exhausted but also keyed up, the conflicting feelings making me feel jittery and a little loopy. I decide a shower might help calm me down. I wince a little as the stream of water hits a sore spot on my shoulder—I'll have plenty of bruises after tonight's showdown—but I feel a bit better once I'm done. I'm just drying off when my phone buzzes on the counter. I arch a brow. It's almost 2:30 in the morning. Who the hell is texting me? Could be Shep but the meds were dragging him down pretty hard when I left, so I doubt it. I would guess a booty-call but none of those girls have this phone number—yes, ok, I'm that asshole that has a separate phone for random hook-up purposes. Sue me.

Then a spear of worry shoots through me thinking that it could be Sara and that something happened to Ollie. I snatch up the phone and my brows fly up when I see Nat's name on the screen.

> Nat: You still up?

> Yeah, actually. Just got out of the shower.

> Nat: Going to post more thirst traps? 😛

I laugh and decide to do just that since she brought it up—not to post, but just to send to her. I've become pretty damn good at taking mirror selfies, so I snap a quick shot, holding the towel in a *very* strategic spot to barely cover things...

I send it to her and wait, finishing toweling off and heading back to the bedroom. I pull on some sweatpants and flop down on the bed, grinning when she texts back.

Nat: I think that got me pregnant

I laugh out loud, running a hand through my wet hair.

Surprised you're awake

Nat: Couldn't sleep

The three little bubbles that say she's typing show up and disappear, over and over, and I smirk at the screen, having a feeling I might know what she's so worried about saying. I lean back against the headboard, turning the TV on to *Sportscenter* to catch some highlights of the game, and wait.

Nat: Thinking about that offer…

My lips curl. Do I be nice, or make her say it?
"Definitely make her say it," I say to the empty room.

About dinner? I was thinking Mexican…

Nat: I hate you.

I laugh again, completely unsurprised that she knew exactly what I was doing.

Tell me what you want, Nat.

I hold my breath as I watch the screen, waiting for the bubbles to pop up. Is she going to go there? It's probably a bad idea, but I don't care. This sounds like the perfect remedy for my state of confusion right now. Finally, another message comes through.

Nat: I want to see if the great AJ Rizzo can
make me come through the phone.

"Jesus Christ," I croak when I read the words, not fully prepared, but fuck, I'm down. I'm not even going to address the stupid little feeling her calling me AJ sends rippling through my chest, even through text. It's been a long time since I've done this. I don't really do much sexting with my hook-ups, more just get in, get off, get out, all in the flesh. I crack my neck, and pump myself up, like I'm about to play a game. I'm determined to get this right. She probably has crazy high expectations and I'll be damned if I let her down.

"Alright, you can do this, Rizz. Just tell her all the things you want to do to her..." I shudder at the thought. Ok, maybe this will be easier than I thought.

> Oh, you want to come, baby?

Nat: So bad.

I can picture her biting her lip, and I groan, already getting hard.

> I'm hard already just thinking about you, Nat.

Nat: Hmm I wish I was there to help with that.

> I'd let you, but not until I got my fill first. I want my tongue on that pretty little pussy of yours again so bad I can't stop thinking about it.

Nat: Oh God.

Nat: ...did you really like doing that?

> Fucking loved it. You taste so fucking good, Nat. I could eat you for hours if you'd let me.

I dig my heels into the mattress just imagining it. This isn't just bull-shit to throw out during sexting. It's one thousand percent true and I swear if I never get another taste of Natalie Morgan, I might die.

Nat: It felt so good.

Nat: I love your tongue on me.

> You like when I lick your pussy, Nat? When I roll my tongue all over, get you so fucking wet?

Nat: Mmmm

> When I spread your lips wide and lick you nice and slow…

> Press a finger inside and pump while I flick my tongue over your clit, over and over.

Nat: God, you're good at this

I smirk, glad that I haven't completely messed this up.

> Don't tap out on me yet…

Nat: Keep going.

> Tell me what you're doing.

> You aren't the only one who wants to come.

Nat: I'm rubbing my clit wishing it was your tongue.

"Fuckkkk," I groan, reaching down into my sweats to grip my cock. I pump my fist as I imagine Nat playing with herself.

> Are you wet?

Nat: Soaked.

> I wish I could taste it.

Nat: I want to taste YOU.

Ah fuck. We never got around to her going down on me that night and I'd be lying if I said I hadn't thought about it at least a thousand times since then.

> Oh baby I would give just about anything to see those pretty lips around my cock.

> Nat: Sucking you deep…

> Fuck.

The little minx is turning the tables, and I'm not mad about it at all. I pump my fist on my cock, wishing so fucking badly it was Natalie's instead.

> Nat: I'm so wet, Rizz. I want your cock in my mouth. I want your tongue on my pussy.

God, this woman…

> Finger yourself for me, baby. Pump them in and out. Tell me how it feels.

> Nat: Wet. Tight. Hot.

I nearly growl. I don't think I've ever been this turned on via fucking text.

> Nat: I wish you were fucking my mouth right now.

Oh God, the thought of it…I grit my teeth, refusing to go yet.

> I'm getting close, Nat. You've got me so hard right now. Imagining fucking your mouth while you look up at me from your knees…

I shudder violently.

> But I wouldn't let you finish me that way. I'd pull out and bend you over the bed, slamming hard into that hot, wet pussy.

Nat: Oh fuck.

I need to feel you come around my cock,
squeezing me so fucking tight.

I decide to take a risk and snap a pick of my cock in my hand and send it her way. I hold my breath while I wait for a response...and then nearly lose my shit when it's a picture of her fingering herself.

That's so fucking hot. God, come for me
baby. Come on your fingers and imagine
they're mine.

Nat: Keep stroking. I want to see it...Send
me a video...

Jesus Christ, this went way further than I thought it would, but I'm not shy by any means and it's Nat—I'd do anything for her. I frown, not wanting to look at that particular thought too closely.

So, I take a quick video, stroking nice and slow. I gnash my teeth to keep from actually coming, just the thought of Nat *wanting* to see this making me so turned on it's almost painful. I would give my left nut to be able to fuck her right now, to actually do all the things we're talking about.

Nat: Oh my God.

Nat: Holy shit that's so hot. God, I love
watching you...

Nat: Ah fuck. I just came so hard, Rizz.

Just thinking about it easily pushes me over the edge. I stroke myself a few more times and that's all she wrote. I come in a rush, hips arching off the bed as hot lashes of cum sear my stomach and chest. I lie there, panting for a few seconds before I can manage to text again.

So did I. Such a fucking mess.

Nat: ...prove it.

I grin, loving Nat's dirty side. I snap a pic and send it to her.

Nat: Mmm wish I was there to clean it up.

You're going to get me hard again already saying shit like that, Nat…

Nat: 😌🍆

Nat: Ok, I know I've said this before, but that's the last time. No more hooking up.

I don't think this technically counts as a hook-up…

Nat: Still. No more. That was my last drink. Straight to AA tomorrow.

I grin at the screen. *God I hope she's wrong.*

Good night, Nat

Nat: Night, AJ

Thirteen

NAT

"I thought I made my thoughts on the matter pretty fucking clear, dad."

"You were upset in the moment. So we're going to have the conversation again, Natalie. It's far past time for a serious discussion."

"I'm not doing this right now. I'm at work," I hiss, leaning around my computer to make sure no one's within hearing distance. "I'll talk to you more at dinner next week."

"Fine."

"Love you," I say through gritted teeth.

"Love you too."

We hang up and I ball my hands into fists, so annoyed that I'm shaking. I can't believe he's back to planning my entire life for me, like I don't get a say. I'm a fucking adult. I'm tired of him acting like I'm not, like I'm just some puppet that'll do whatever he wants me to do when he pulls the strings. I have a bad feeling that next week's dinner is going to end in a blow out, but I don't care.

A knock on my door draws my attention.

"Hey, Bobby, come on in."

He smiles and saunters in, sinking into one of the soft leather chairs beside my desk. He takes off his glasses and rubs his eyes and I arch a brow.

"Someone looks tired."

"I was up late," he says vaguely, but I narrow my eyes when his cheeks darken a bit.

"Bobby Tremblay, are you *blushing*??" He straightens and his light brown cheeks darken even more and my mouth pops open. "You are!! Spill it!"

"I am not! I just..." He rubs the back of his neck. "I kind of hooked up with someone last night. Someone I definitely shouldn't have."

I huff out a laugh. "Join the fucking club, my friend," I mutter.

"I'll be the treasurer," he says with a half-smile.

"How was it?" I ask eagerly, leaning in and wanting all the details. I've been trying to find someone to set him up with, but he shoots down all of my suggestions. Bobby is very picky, apparently.

"It was...amazing," he sighs with a smile. "Really fucking amazing." I squeal and he rolls his eyes. "Don't get all excited. It was just a casual thing."

"For now," I say with a grin and he can't help but smile at my enthusiasm.

"Are you still hooking up with a certain star Center with a rumored extra large...stick?" he asks, pointedly.

"No. Yes. No," I say shaking my head. "Definitely no." He gives me a look that says cut the bullshit, and I groan. "Ok, so we might have, uh, sexted last night? Is that still what it's called?"

Now he leans forward, golden eyes alight with interest.

"Was it hot? Ah hell, I bet it was hot. He looks like the kind of guy with a filthy mouth who knows all the right things to say."

"It was. He is." I put my head in my hands. "But that's the last time. I'm not letting anything happen again, text or otherwise."

"Sure, sure," he says breezily.

"I mean it!" He gives me a look that says he doesn't believe that for a second and I flip him off. My phone buzzes then and his brows raise up.

"Tell me it's him...please tell me it's him."

"I will stab you," I tell him, brandishing my letter opener. "And no, it's Hattie in the Sin Bin Chat..." He pats his pocket and then must realize he left his phone in his own office. "Ha! Look at this pic!"

I show Bobby the selfie of Hattie with a very disgruntled looking Shep in a wheelchair.

"Looks like he's headed home. She's taking the day, obviously. Wanna go by there later? Maybe bring them some food or something?"

"Sound like a plan," he says, rising from the chair and pushing his glasses up his nose. "I'm going to pretend to work but probably sleep at my desk with my eyes open. Holler if you need me."

"Hattie is rubbing off on you. You're going to be saying *y'all* and *bless your heart* soon." He laughs and waves as he leaves. I get through some emails and my phone buzzes again.

Rizzo: Hey

Don't even think about it

Rizzo: That was an innocent, completely platonic hey, thank you very much!

I'm watching you, Thirst Trap...

I shiver thinking about the picture he sent last night...the one I definitely saved immediately and have looked at no less than fifty times this morning. I know he's got a million across his various social media accounts, but none of them are quite this...thirst-inducing. And I'm not even talking about the X-rated ones. Those were also saved for, uh, research purposes.

Rizzo: 😇😇😇

Rizzo: Gonna go to Shep's later. You coming?

Yeah, me and Bobby were just saying we might bring them some food. I'll text Hattie and coordinate.

Rizzo: Sounds good. See you later.

I laugh and decide it's time for an early lunch. I need to find a dress for the organization Christmas party next week anyway, so maybe it'll be a long lunch, actually. I idly wonder what kind of dress might catch Rizzo's attention, but remind myself that it doesn't matter because last night was the last night.

End of story.

The story apparently isn't over.

We make out in the pantry at Shep's place that afternoon, jerking away when Howey almost walks in on us.

"Are there more paper plates in here?" he asks, completely oblivious, thank God.

"Uh, yeah, I think they're in that cabinet right there." I nod and Rizzo leans down to open it up and pull out a stack of plates.

"Sweet. Thanks."

"We have got to stop this," I hiss quietly as soon as Howey is out of earshot, and Rizzo laughs.

"You started it!" I give him a level look and he holds up his hands in surrender. "Ok, ok, so maybe I kind of started it when I tried to grab that bowl above your head and leaned my body up against yours..." I shudder at the memory, my hands already itching to pull him close to me again. What in the literal fuck is wrong with me? I can't get enough of him. I can't stop this pull between us. It's like we're magnets. Dangerous, stupid fucking magnets.

"Ok, I'm sorry. I'll be on my best behavior for the rest of the evening."

"You better," I warn.

We *might* end up sexting again that night, but the next morning I wake up feeling like death and hooking up is the furthest thing on my mind.

> Rizzo: Hey, you alright? Mac said you were sick.

> I feel awful. Are you ok?

Rizzo: Yeah, I'm fine. Immune system of a horse.

Do horses have good immune systems?

Rizzo: IDFK 😬 but "healthy as a horse" is a saying for a reason, isn't it? So, I'm going with yes, they have great immune systems.

Rizzo: Not the point. Focus, Morgan. Do you need anything?

I huff out a laugh.

No, I'm ok. Thanks.

An hour later, I hear my front door opening. Could be dad or Hattie—or someone breaking in, but at this point, they can take whatever they want. I don't care. I couldn't move to stop them even if I wanted to. To my utter surprise, it's Rizzo who strolls into the living room, several shopping bags hanging from his arms. I blink in surprise and am suddenly very aware of how disgusting I must look. My hair is in a dirty, messy bun. I'd had a fever on and off all night and morning, so at many points I was a sweaty pile of gross. No make up. Old sweats...and embarrassingly, his Cornell Hockey hoodie that I stole that very first night. I may or may not wear it almost every night.

"What are you doing here?" I moan, trying to sit up. It takes a couple of tries and the room sways when I first make it upright, but eventually it levels out.

"Nursing you back to health, obviously," he says from behind the couch, unpacking the bags and setting things on the counter. I turn to watch: at least eight different kinds of medicine, cough drops, candy, soup—chicken and stars, my favorite from when I was kid. My heart twists a little at the fact he remembered me telling him that one drunken night—Gatorades, orange juice, pretzels, and saltines.

"Jesus, Rizz," I breathe, sounding stuffy and horrible.

"Well, I didn't know exactly what was wrong, so I came prepared for anything. Where are your glasses and what are your symptoms? Also, I borrowed Mac's key, I did not pick the lock, in case you were wondering."

I huff out a laugh and point to the cabinet beside the fridge before giving him a rundown of what's wrong. He nods, rummages through all the medicine boxes, and selects a winner. He comes around and squats down in front of the couch, handing me first the glass and then the meds.

"You didn't have to do all this. What if I get you sick!" I protest, suddenly worried for his health. He arches a brow.

"You had your tongue down my throat yesterday afternoon. I'm pretty sure I would have already been compromised." I can't help but laugh at that, and he gestures for me to take the medicine. I roll my eyes but obey. The juice is cold and delicious and I'll admit that I was thirsty as hell but was just too tired to get up for myself before now.

"Thank you," I say after I drain nearly the entire glass. He takes it from me and sets it on the coffee table. His eyes dip to my—his—sweat-shirt and his lips curl upward, but he doesn't comment.

"Are you hot? Cold?"

"A little cold," I admit. He grabs another blanket from the ladder in the corner and settles it over me. "Thanks, Rizzo. This is...it was really nice of you."

"You'd do the same for me," he shrugs. "But I would expect you to be in a slutty nurse costume. Just for future reference." I can't help but laugh and he gives me that easy, sexy smile that I love so much. I expect him to leave then but instead he slides onto the couch and settles my pillow in his lap.

"You don't have to—"

"What are we watching?" he asks, cutting me off and giving me a look that says there will be no arguing. He pats the pillow and waits. I sigh but lie back down. He tugs the blanket up over my shoulder and rests his hand there. I really shouldn't be as happy as I am that he's here and I'm trying really hard not to read too much into this. It's just a friend helping a friend. Like he said, I would do the same for him, and if Shep hadn't just gotten out of the hospital, I'm sure Hattie would be the one here doing all of this for me.

"Sleep, Nat. I'll be here when you wake up."

And with that, I close my eyes and drift off in his lap.

"What the fuck am I doing?" I mutter to myself for the hundredth time as I walk down the sidewalk towards the high rise a few days later. "Stupid, stupid, stupid..."

Before I can talk myself out of it, I'm in the lobby and walking up to the security desk. *This is never going to work.*

"Can I help you, ma'am?" the young guy behind the desk asks. He's got light brown skin, is ridiculously toned, with a diamond stud in one ear and a tattoo curling up one side of his neck. I think he's the same one that was here the first time I was here, but can't be completely sure. I was admittedly pretty distracted that night.

"Hi," I say with a smile, putting on my best schmoozing voice. I learned from the best, and when I want something, I can usually get it. "I know this might sound a little crazy, but I'm actually here to see Anthony Rizzo. I'm a friend," I add, making sure he doesn't think I'm just a crazy fan...but then I realize of course a crazy fan would say that. "Seriously, we're friends. See—" I show him my phone. My background photo is the Sin Bin hanging out on Shep's back deck, and Rizzo has his arm thrown around both me and Bobby. The guy looks at the pic and nods, but I feel like I'm blowing this. I'm usually much better, but this whole thing with Rizzo has me all...flustered.

"So, anyway," I look around and lean in, "I was hoping to surprise him, and I know that it's probably against all kinds of rules but—"

"Are you Natalie Morgan, by chance?" he asks and I snap my mouth shut, blinking.

"Um, yes?"

"Here you go, you're all set." He slides a black key card to me across the marble counter and smiles, showing off pearly whites and one dimple.

"He was...expecting me?" I ask, frowning.

"You're on his approved visitor list," he says and understanding hits. He probably puts all his booty calls on the list for easy access. Got it. I decide not to think about that too hard before I lose my nerve. I pull my coat tighter around me and grab the card, smiling at the man.

"He's probably got a whole stack of these things back there, huh?" I say lightly.

He shakes his head. "No ma'am, just four—including Mr. Rizzo's parents."

"Oh," I say, surprised.

He smiles at me, like he knows something I don't, and I try not to look as confused as I am.

"Have a good evening, ma'am."

"Uh, thanks. You too."

I hurry to the elevators and use my card to access one of only two that will take me to the top floor. I tell myself to go right back down again a thousand times in the time it takes me to reach his floor, but I don't. I need to see him. I need to touch him. I need to kiss him until I can't breathe and I forget my own name and I can just pray that this will be the end of it. I'll stop wanting him so damned badly after one more night. There's so much we didn't get to do before, that's all, I tell myself. It's just...curiosity.

It definitely isn't the fact that I'm pretty sure I'm falling for him.

Before I lose my nerve, I march down the hall to his door and knock. I have no idea if he's even home...and then another, awful idea floats into my mind, one I should have fucking thought about before now: what if he has another girl in there already.

"Shit," I whisper, heat flooding my cheeks and my heart going triple time. I take a half step back, thinking this was a terrible idea and wondering how I could be so stupid, when the door finally opens. To my relief, he seems to be alone.

"Nat?" he asks, blue eyes full of surprise. My gaze travels down his body, and I wonder how he can possibly make something as casual as worn, holey jeans and a white t-shirt look so damn sexy. I yank my eyes back to his.

"Are you alone? Yes or no."

"Yes?" he asks, brow furrowed. I sigh in utter relief.

"Not one fucking word," I say sternly and his lips curl upward as I step forward and kiss him. He quickly wraps one arm around the small of my back, pulling me close. His other hand cups my cheek, the tips of his fingers tunneling in my hair. *God I love when he does that.* His lips quickly part mine, his tongue rolling and demanding. I push him backward into the apartment and he closes the door once I'm over the threshold, quickly pressing my body back against it, his lips never leaving mine. He moves closer, pushing the length of his body hard against mine, and I nearly whimper at the contact.

I'm officially off the wagon yet again. I'm not sure I'll ever beat this addiction to him.

"I thought you liked when I talk?" he whispers against my lips before biting my lower one. I gasp and arch my hips against him. "When I tell you all the things I want to do to you…"

"Shut up," I pant, pulling up on his shirt. He laughs and reaches back to tug it off over his head in that ridiculously sexy way guys do, and then my hands are on him, roving over every muscle and scar. He moans quietly as he traces kisses along my jaw and down my throat, reaching up to start unbuttoning my coat. I smile, wondering what he's going to think when he sees my insane little surprise.

He freezes when he gets the last button free and parts my coat to reveal nothing but a very sexy—and expensive—black, lacy lingerie set paired with my thigh-high, lace-up heeled boots.

"*Nat,*" he breathes, stepping back to let his gaze slowly scan my body. He scrubs a hand across his jaw. "Is it my birthday?" I giggle and let my coat slip from my arms, reaching up to pull the clip from my hair to let it tumble down my back in big, loose curls. I don't know what exactly had possessed me to enact this little plan, but I sure am glad I did. I don't think I've ever seen him so…enthralled. I lean back against the door and he continues to stare, his eyes drinking up every inch of me. I feel almost drunk from the pure desire in that look. He finally meets my gaze again and I barely stop a shiver.

"Surprised?" I ask in a voice that's incredibly sultry and I'm not entirely sure belongs to me. Rizzo brings out this insane, confident, carnal part of me that I never knew existed. And I fucking like it. I have no reservations or fears with him. I feel completely comfortable with him in ways I never knew you could feel with a person. I've dated plenty, but I was always worried about what they might think or do, of what picture I was supposed to portray for the outside world. But with him, I can just be me, in every possible way.

Fuck.

I really think this means...no. No, I'm not ruining this night with big feeling revelations.

"I hoped you'd come," he whispers. "I didn't think you would, but I fucking hoped. And my God. This..." He runs his eyes up and down me again. "This is possibly the sexiest thing that's ever happened in my life."

"Well, then you better thank me properly."

He slowly raises his gaze back to mine and a slow, sinful smile spreads across his face.

"Yes, ma'am."

Hours later, we're wrapped up in a blanket in his bed and I wonder how the fuck we ended up here again. Actually, I know exactly how we ended up here. I'm apparently basically just a horny teenager who can't control myself. Fantastic.

We did everything we talked about in those text messages and then some, and I don't think I can move at this point, let alone even think about going another round. He runs his fingers lightly up and down my spine and I don't know that I've ever felt so relaxed or content.

"You know you called me AJ?"

"Hmm?"

"Before, while we were...you kept saying AJ instead of Rizzo." I turn my head to look at him. "I liked it," he says quietly, almost like it's a confession. For whatever reason, ever since that phone call with his parents, he's been AJ in my head. It's like some secret that I only know and it makes me stupidly happy. I hadn't really realized I'd said it out loud though.

"Well, I guess I took you up on your offer then," I say with a sleepy grin. "To scream it while you did certain unholy things with that tongue of yours." He chuckles and my eyes start to feel heavy. I could absolutely fall asleep right here in his arms, in his bed, which is a terrible idea, so I force them open and push up onto my forearms, looking around the room.

"You ready for the big move?" I ask, spying all the boxes lining the walls.

"As I'll ever be, I guess. Movers come tomorrow actually. So, good timing. You might have surprised some other random person in lingerie and a trench coat if you'd waited until tomorrow night."

"That would have been one hell of a welcome to the building." He laughs lightly. "But you're excited? For the new house, I mean. Not so much the actual act of moving and unpacking, that part is never fun. The pictures are gorgeous." It's around the corner from Shep's place in their gated community, but out there *around the corner* means a couple of miles. Those lots are huge, each one ten plus acres, and the one he found is on the *plus* side of that for sure. The house isn't ostentatious or ridiculous, and I think it actually fits his personality much better than this place. It's like a modern hunting lodge, if that's a thing, with a pool house, separate four car garage for all his toys, and an apartment above that. He joked that it's going to be Ollie's place for when she gets older and wants to run away from Shep's house.

"Yeah, I really am. I love the house and I really love all the space. I haven't lived in a house in my entire adult life, can you believe that?"

"Really?"

"Yep. Went from the dorms in college to all apartments from there. They were just easier. No upkeep or anything to worry about." He sifts my hair through his fingers and I want to purr like a cat.

"So why now?"

He shrugs. "According to Shep, I'm *maturing*." He says it like it's the worst thing in the world and I snort. He smiles and sighs. "I think he's right though. Not completely, of course, but I don't know, I'm kind of tired of..." He waves his hand in the air, seeming to encompass the apartment but also his life in general. Does that include the random hook ups? I don't know that I can believe he'd ever be ready to be done with all of that...no matter how much I might want it to be true.

"Well, I should get a prize or something, shouldn't I?"

"For that miraculous blow job? Absolutely, baby. Prizes, trophies, medals. Sonnets written in your honor. Ships named for you. Ballads—"

I jab him in the side, making him jerk away with a cute little squeal that makes me tilt my head, momentarily distracted. I perk up and he looks worried.

"Are you *ticklish*, AJ?"

"Don't even think about it, Nat. I mean it," he warns, holding out his hands in an attempt to stop me from leaping on top of him. It doesn't work. I straddle him and grab his side again, and he starts laughing uncontrollably.

"St-stop...I...c-can't breathe...Nat!" I giggle and then he shifts, moving so that I'm pinned beneath him. "That was entirely uncalled for," he says, breathless.

"I will be telling the entire team your little secret," I tell him with a grin. He swoops down and kisses me and I'm once again reminded how much fucking fun I have with him.

"So why do you deserve a trophy?" he asks, smiling and shifting so that he's lying beside me, head dropped up on his upturned hand.

"I meant," I say eyeing him, "for being the last hook up in the apartment. The end of a very epic era." I say it lightly, teasing. I'm not jealous of his previous hook ups or anything—there would be no reason to be —but a small part of me wonders if he's comparing me to them all in the back of his head, or thinking about one of them when he's with me.

His expression turns a bit more serious. He reaches over and brushes my hair from my face, cupping my cheek.

"Nat, you're the only girl that's ever been here." I blink, brow furrowing.

"What?"

"I never bring girls here. We go to their place or a hotel or...well, I'm not above public spaces, we'll just say that. But not a single one has ever come to this apartment. It's why Jerry was so shocked that first night when I told him to drive *here*."

He stares at me with something I can't name—or maybe I can, but I'm scared to, scared to hope that it's what I think it is—and the weight of what he's saying really settles over me.

And suddenly, I need to leave. I don't think he can mean it the way I think he does, or the way I want him to, or the way he may even believe he does. I sit up and gently push his hand away. He frowns slightly and I search for my underwear, only to realize that it's still in the living room. We hadn't made it very far earlier before everything had been stripped off in a frenzy. I leap from the bed as if it's electrified, not really understanding the panic rising in my chest, the walls slowly closing around my heart.

"I should get going," I say, trying to keep my voice calm and even.

"It's late, Nat. Why don't you just—"

"I can't, AJ." I say, feeling like I might cry or like my heart might burst through my chest. "I don't know what this is, but you don't mean it, not really. I know you and I know that you don't want...this," I say gesturing between us. "Not for anything more than what we just did."

"That's not true," he says, sitting up and sounding upset.

"It is. You might think you want to try dating or whatever, but I know you'd end up regretting it and you'd resent me for being the one to make you do it and you'd probably end up cheating on me in the end and—"

"Wow, so now I'm a cheating asshole, too? Thanks for that." I can see the irritation setting over him, the relaxed contentment we were just sharing quickly fading. And I don't blame him. That was probably a low blow and I have no reason to believe he'd do that, but I don't know what the hell is going on or why I'm freaking out right now and saying shit that I shouldn't. I keep saying that he can't do monogamy or commitment, but hell, maybe it's *me*. Maybe I'm the one who can't handle this or is too scared to even try.

"And can you maybe stop telling me what *I* think or feel?" he adds, his voice harder than I've ever heard it. He rises from the bed and yanks up a pair of sweats from the floor, pulling them on. I head out into the living room, hating that I'm about to have to do the angry walk of shame in my stupid lingerie and coat, but here we are. It's not like I thought to bring a change of clothes with me when I came up with this brilliant plan.

I tug on my boyshorts and bra, looking around for my boots when he comes into the room behind me.

"Nat, what hell is going on? Why are you being like this?"

"I don't know," I mutter honestly, dropping to my knees beside the couch to tug out one boot from beneath it. He walks over and holds out the other one to me and I take it, tugging them both on and lacing them up. He isn't trying to stop me—not that I blame him. I'm acting like a mental case right now, even I can see it. I just completely flipped the switch for no real reason—but he watches with his arms crossed over his bare chest, jaw clenching and unclenching.

"Is it the other girls? I can be done with all that, Nat. I haven't hooked up with anyone else since our first night together anyway, hand to God. I haven't even *wanted* to."

"Let's just forget about it all, ok? We had fun, the sex was great, and we're still friends. Let's just quit while we're ahead. For real this time, Rizzo." He clenches his jaw.

"Back to Rizzo now?" He eyes me when I stand and pick up my coat, and shakes his head in irritation or annoyance or hurt—or a combination of all three. I don't answer, so he goes on. "That's really what you want?"

No.

"Yes."

He grinds his teeth but nods.

"Alright, if that's what you want. No more hook ups. Back to just being friends."

I finish buttoning my coat and toss my hair up into a messy bun. I hold his gaze and clench my hands into fists when the back of my nose burns with tears.

"It's for the best. Trust me."

"Whatever you say, Nat." The look on his face makes my chest twist painfully and a voice in the back of my head is screaming at me to knock it the fuck off and chill out, but I can't.

I sigh, knowing that I've ruined everything, but I hope after a couple of days, we'll be able to figure out how to just be friends again. I don't want to lose that. I *can't* lose that. I understand now why Hattie is so scared to tell Shep how she really feels. She's too afraid to take a chance and possibly lose her best friend, one of the most important people in her life.

And that's how I feel about AJ Rizzo. He's somehow become one of my favorite people on the planet in just a few short months. When I see some stupid gif or meme online, I immediately want to send it to him.

When I'm annoyed, he's the person I want to vent to. When I'm lounging around on a random Sunday afternoon, he's the one I want beside me on the couch, hogging the cover and stealing all the popcorn. When I'm sick, he's the one I want taking care of me, just like he had the other day. I squeeze my eyes shut and force all of the thoughts to quiet.

"Bye, Thirst Trap," I say quietly from the door, turning away quickly so he can't see the tears starting to fall.

Fourteen

RIZZO

"WHERE DO YOU WANT THIS ONE?" SHEP ASKS, POINTING TO another box. The movers delivered all my stuff and had offered to unpack everything for me, but I'd been in such a shit mood after that night with Nat, I'd declined and all but kicked them out. I'd tipped them all extremely well, so hopefully they weren't too disgruntled over my less than sunny disposition.

"I don't care," I say, rubbing my eyes and leaning my arms on the kitchen island.

"Dude, what is your deal? Are you having buyer's remorse or something?"

"What? No, it's not that. I love the house." I really do. It feels like home in a way that the apartment never did. I had to actually buy furniture, of course, but with Mac's help, it turned out to be fun and I got stuff I actually like. Part of me had wished it was Nat with me the entire time we were shopping, but I'd told that part to shut the fuck up and stop being stupid. I don't know why she'd flipped the script so effectively in a matter of seconds that night, but neither of us have been ready to go right back to being friends and acting like nothing happened yet. We will, of course. We're both adults and both of us are perfectly capable of moving on, but I, at least, need a little time first.

"Then I'm assuming it has to do with a certain blonde-haired, gray-eyed girl we know?"

I groan and he laughs, heading to the fridge and grabbing a couple of beers. He walks into the living room and slumps down into one of my new leather chairs, grimacing ever so slightly at his broken rib. He holds one of the bottles out into the air in my direction. I roll my eyes but head over and snatch the bottle before throwing myself dramatically into the other chair.

"So, what's up?"

"I don't even fucking know, man." I tell him about the other night, how everything had been great and then Nat just did a complete one-eighty. I really didn't think knowing she was the only woman to ever be in my apartment would be upsetting. Hell, I thought it would make her *happy*, actually. I really don't understand women for shit, apparently.

I take another long sip of beer, glancing around the living room and to the view out the back windows. All the hassle of moving is one thousand percent worth it for this, to finally feel like I'm where I belong. I'm ignoring the little voice in the back of my head saying that I wish I wasn't here alone...

"I thought *I* was the one who had a commitment phobia, but it sure as shit seems like she does too."

Shep takes his hat off and runs a hand through his hair before tugging it back on again, looking thoughtful.

"Maybe she just actually really likes you and is scared to let herself hope that maybe you mean this whole dating thing."

"But I do mean it!...I think?" I add, frowning. I mean, I do. I really do want to try for more with Nat, I think, but there's also a part of me that's terrified of it. "I've stopped fucking around with other chicks already since we started whatever the hell this is. That has to count for something, right?" Shep chuckles.

"For you? It absolutely should. I don't think you've ever gone more than a few days without some new chick riding your co—"

"Ok, ok, I get it, asshole," I cut in, throwing my bottle cap at him. He snatches out of the air with those annoying goalie reflexes—great on the ice, but when I want to ding him in the head with a bottle cap, they turn out to be a pain in the ass. He laughs at my annoyed expression and runs the fingers of his right hand over the tattooed knuckles of his left. *I really think I need a tattoo*...I shake myself. Now is not the time for distractions.

"But even more than that, I went over and took care of her when she was sick a few days after the Kodiak game." His brows rise at that. "When in the fucking history of me have I ever taken care of someone like that. Someone other than you. You don't count. I mean someone of the female persuasion."

"Never," he agrees.

"See! So, it should be obvious that I'm serious, right? That I'm really willing to give this a real shot?" I sigh heavily. "Or maybe it's not. Maybe I have to be an adult and come out and say it? But now I can't. I have to just leave it be then, right? She said she was done, so that's it."

Shep eyes me thoughtfully.

"I think you give her time to figure out what's going on and then see what happens. Maybe she'll surprise you. She might have a whole host of her own reasons why she flipped out, you don't know. She might have a psycho ex or something like Mac." I can see the fury in his eyes at the thought of Hattie's ex-boyfriend who is a real fucking piece of work. I thought I'd known enough before, but now I know so much more and would gladly put the bastard six feet under with a smile on my fucking face.

Does Nat have something in her past that's making her unsure about this whole thing? Maybe it has nothing to do with me at all. And now I feel like a conceited ass for assuming it was all about me. To be fair, it usually is, but every now and then, I do take a backseat.

Changing subjects, I ask Shep if he's ready for the Christmas party next week and in no uncertain terms, ask if he's ever going to get around to telling Mac how he feels. He ignores the question and I tell him he's an idiot, not for the first time.

"You remember we're all meeting up for drinks tomorrow, right? So you're going to have to play nice with Nat."

I roll my eyes. "As if I would be anything but perfectly cordial."

"Don't be cordial. Be yourself. Whatever y'all have going on, you better figure it out. The group isn't breaking up, alright?"

I snort. "Did you just say 'y'all'?"

He grins at me. "It rubs off on you, what can I say?"

Drinks are…fine. Nat and I both do an alarmingly great job of acting completely normal. We hug hello. We laugh. We play darts. We pick songs on the jukebox. No one would ever know that we're in the middle of a confusing ass post-hook-up situation.

"Look, Rizz, about the other night—"

I hold up my hand. "Water under the bridge. It's fine, Nat. Really. I get it. I won't push for more again, I promise." I give her a winning smile and make a cross over my heart to seal the vow. She doesn't look relieved like I think she will, and that gives me stupid hope that maybe she's not set on this whole being done thing either. Do I know if I want to be in an actual, adult relationship? Not completely. But do I know that I can't stop thinking about Nat and would give my left nut to touch her again? Abso-fucking-lutely. I have no idea where that leaves us, but really, it doesn't matter because I wasn't lying: I'm not trying again. She made the choice to be done. She'll have to be the one to choose otherwise.

But damn if I don't want her to choose otherwise.

She clears her expression and posts on a smile that doesn't reach her eyes. I get the feeling suddenly that she's very used to putting on a façade for people, to pretending to be fine when she's really not. But why? I feel like there's so much I still don't know about Natalie Morgan and wonder if she'll ever really let me in, whether as a friend or otherwise.

"Another round?" she asks brightly, gesturing to my empty bottle. I nod and she grabs the rest of the empties from the table, waltzing to the bar, nudging Jules in the shoulder on the way where he and Bobby are playing pool. I let out a long exhale, wondering how long it'll take before this whole thing gets easier.

My guess: fucking never.

The Christmas party is a special kind of torture. It's a good ass time, as always, but seeing Nat looking that fucking good and having to act like I don't notice or care is almost impossible. She's in a tight, deep crimson number and sky-high heels that I would love to have digging into my back right about now. I clear my throat and tear my gaze away from where she's dancing with Nowski and ask Mac to dance with me. She eyes Nat, but shrugs and accepts.

I twirl her around the floor and she laughs breezily. I dart a surreptitious glance at Nat to see if she's watching, to see if she's jealous like the teenage idiot I am deep down. She's watching, just like I hope, but quickly pulls her gaze away when our eyes meet. Mac doesn't miss the exchange and rolls her eyes, but remains silent. She has no room to talk.

I dance with Kasey, one of our trainers, and a couple of other girls, but all the while my gaze searches out Nat. It's very fucking inconvenient. We end up next to each other and partnerless somehow when the next song starts, and so I hold out my hand in invitation. We're friends after all. It's pretty much expected that we'd dance. She slides her hand into mine and I force the small shiver of pleasure away. We start to spin slowly, and I make sure to keep far more distance between us than the last time we danced. Memories of her in those cut offs and that tiny shirt seep in but I stop them in their tracks.

"Having fun?" I ask because if I don't say something, my lips will try to occupy themselves in other ways, no matter what I promised myself.

"Yeah, it's a nice party."

"They go all out every year. It's a great organization."

"It really is."

"Thank you, for helping to save it." She blinks in surprise. "I don't think I've ever said it, but I mean it. I don't know what I would have done if the team got sold, honestly."

"Oh," she says softly, her gaze holding mine before drifting slowly to my lips. "I'm glad you aren't going anywhere..." I feel it, that undeniable force between us, demanding and pulling and—

"Kiss!"

"Kiss! Kiss! Kiss!"

We both jump as if electrocuted, jerking our heads towards the commotion, only to realize that no one was yelling at *us*.

"Oh, shit," Nat breathes, and my chest squeezes uncomfortably as we watch Mac watch Emery (the surprise blind date Kasey brought for Shep) kiss him under the mistletoe. Mac looks like someone just punched her right in the stomach. She quickly bolts from the dance floor, but no one else seems to notice—they're all whooping and hollering and egging Shep on. I know without a doubt that he's not into it and I feel bad for the guy. Nat gives me a worried look and I nod, telling her I understand, and she rushes off to find Mac.

Shep pulls away and smiles at Emery, though it isn't a real one, and gives her an *excuse me for one second* gesture. He storms my way, looking shocked and upset and uncomfortable.

"Drink?" I ask, turning to fall into step beside my best friend and knowing exactly what's going through his mind. He saw Mac's face before she bolted. He knows how upset she is. He's thinking he might have just fucked everything up before it even got a chance to begin.

"Make it a double."

Mac does a great job of acting fine the rest of the night, but knowing her as well as I do, I can tell that she's actively avoiding Shep. Not that I blame her. I'm pretty much doing the same thing with Nat. As the night starts to shift from swanky, sophisticated Christmas party to Saturday night in the club, I see her preparing to make her exit and I head her way. I need a little break myself after watching Nat laugh with some tool from Accounting. Ok, I know that's not fair. He's probably a perfectly nice guy, but right now, I don't want to see him making Nat laugh like that, or watch her lay her hand on his arm so casually. I don't think that I've ever been jealous in my life, but right now, I'm beyond jealous of the dude. I grind my teeth, knowing I'm being absolutely ridiculous, so I bee-line for Mac. I need to get out of here for a while.

"You leaving?" I ask low in her ear and she jumps a little, making me grin. She swats at my chest but nods.

"I think I'm all partied out for the night." I follow her gaze as she watches Shep across the room talking to Howey and his wife, the two looking...off. I know they hit a rough patch not too long ago, but they've been trying to work out it out. I'm not sure how well it's going based on that body language—both of them look like even standing near each other is uncomfortable as hell—but props to them for trying I guess. Mac quickly pulls her eyes away and focuses back on me.

"Well, allow me to accompany you. I need to grab something from my room." I hold out my arm and she laughs before wrapping hers around it, and we head towards the doors.

"Is the thing you need to grab from your room your balls to just suck it up and go after Nat again already?" she murmurs quietly, leaning into me.

My mouth drops open. "I...I mean, it isn't...I tried...*She's* the one who..." I can't even get a handle on my thoughts to get a full sentence out, and Mac laughs.

"Figure it the fuck out, my friend," she says with a sympathetic pat on my chest.

"Back at you, Mac," I say pointedly. I know exactly how much she loves Shep, and exactly how much he loves her back. I know they're both scared but if they can't figure it out...well, what the fuck hope do *I* have with Nat?

"I wish I could," she mutters as we leave the ballroom. She gives me a hug bye before getting off the elevator on her floor. I didn't actually need anything from my room, but I don't really know that I feel like partying anymore either, so I head on up anyway. I walk in and yank off my tie, unbuttoning the top couple of buttons of my shirt before collapsing on the bed. I tuck my hands behind my head and stare at the ceiling. *Figure it the fuck out, my friend.*

"Easier said than done, Mac," I mutter, and let thoughts of Nat lull me into a restless sleep.

Fifteen

NAT

"You know you two are disgusting, right?" I tease Hattie as we watch Shep walk into the locker room—after a very public display of affection. The two of them have been in that early relationship stage ever since the Christmas party where they can't keep their hands off of each other and they're so cute that you want to puke just watching them. At least the night had ended well for someone.

I'd tried to ignore AJ—*Rizzo*, I remind myself for the hundredth time. AJ was a secret name for when things were maybe heading somewhere. Rizzo is the name for my platonic friend. I'd tried to ignore *Rizzo* and had failed. I'd tried to flirt with some new guy in Accounting that I can't even remember his name and that had felt terrible. I'd searched for Rizzo and when he was nowhere to be found, my heart had sank, thinking the worst and assuming he'd found someone else to take to his bed for the night. I'd gone to my room and admittedly cried myself to sleep. Not my finest moment. I still haven't figured out exactly why I freaked out so much that night as his apartment other than the intense fear of being hurt. I guess that's the answer, really, just a fear of getting my heartbroken. That's never actually happened before. I've had a few semi-serious boyfriends over the years, but *I'd* been the one to break things off every time...*ah shit*, I realize with a start. I'd dumped each of them when things started to shift into serious-serious.

Oh God, I really am the one with the commitment issues, not Rizzo.

And I'd freaked out because I knew without a doubt that I wouldn't be the one to walk away from Rizzo. If we started things, I'd be in the for the long haul and give him the power to break my heart. Not just break it, but fucking shatter it, because...I'm already in love with him. *Shit, shit, shit.* This is a lot to process all at once so I force all of these big revelations away and focus back on Hattie.

She grins at me and winks. "I know, I know...but ask me if I care."

I laugh and bump her shoulder. "I'm really happy for you, you know that right?"

"Thanks, Nat. It's felt like such a long time coming even though we've only known each other a few months, but," she sighs and runs her hand through her long brown hair, "it feels like I've known him forever. He's like my other half and I know how annoying and cliché that sounds." She wrinkles her nose, making us both laugh again. "But it's true. I can't help it."

"Oh, hey, Roman! Question time!" I call to the bruiser before he walks into the locker room. He grins and trots over.

"Eggnog – yum or yuck?" Hattie asks.

"Oh definitely yum. I could drink a gallon of the stuff—actually did once on a dare. It did *not* end well, but I still love it." He smiles when we both make disgusted faces, and gives us a little salute before heading off. We've made all of our questions this month holiday-centric, and they're getting great reactions on social media. Even Miss Grinch herself, Hattie MacNamara, has seemed to be leaning into all the holiday stuff more lately. I'll give the credit for that to Shep and all his planning to make her love Christmas after all this time of hating it. Granted, she definitely had cause—the girl has the absolute worst luck when it comes to December. She even got mugged by Santa once for fuck's sake!—but it's actually really sweet watching her heart grow three sizes because of Shep's love for the holiday. And her, of course. He hasn't actually said it yet, to my knowledge, but we all know it's true.

"So, uh, any new developments on the Rizzo front?"

"We are back to being friends with zero benefits...but it's not the same as before." I sigh, hating how things ended up. I knew this was a possibility when I crossed the line...and then crossed it again...and again...but I really thought we'd be alright. And, really, if it was *just* sex, I think we would be, but there's so much more than that between us.

"Is that what you really want?"

"I...have no idea," I say with a groan. "Part of me wants to give it a real try, but the other part is terrified to."

"I get that. You know how scared I was to go there with Connor, scared to lose what we had."

"But Shep wasn't allergic to monogamy." She huffs out a laugh and I can't help but join. "I just think that we'll try to be more, I'll fall completely in love with him, and then he'll decide he misses getting laid by a different girl every night. Then not only does my heart get broken, but we really will ruin any shred of friendship we have left. I can't imagine hanging out with the Sin Bin after that."

She looks thoughtful, but before she can respond, another group of players shows up and we get some more clips to add to our Eggnog Showdown video.

I don't want to be here, but I'd promised dad months ago I'd attend this fundraiser. It's a giant toy drive for underprivileged kids and those living at the group home, so I can't be *too* mad about being here, but I haven't spoken to him since the Kodiaks game save that one phone call and a few texts—he'd had go to out of town so we missed our scheduled dinner the following week—and I wouldn't put it past him to bring up the whole job thing again tonight.

"Oh, Natalie, you're here!" Erin exclaims, hurrying over with her tablet glued to her hand and her Bluetooth in her ear like always.

I hand off my gift donation to one attendant and my coat to another, and straighten the straps of my icy blue gown while I wait for her to get closer.

"I RSVPd didn't I?"

"Well, yes, but I thought...well, your father wasn't sure if you were still coming or not." She looks slightly uncomfortable and I can only imagine the irritated tirades she's had to endure from my father since I pretty much told him to fuck off.

"Well, I'm here. Not to worry."

"He'll be very happy to hear it." She nods and looks down at her tablet, quickly swiping through a few screens. "You're at table one." I raise a brow and she ducks her head. We play this little game at every single one of these things. She puts me at the main table with dad and the heads of whatever organization is benefitting from the gala, and I promptly find myself a seat elsewhere. I give her a warm smile.

"Table one. Got it." I wink and she sighs, but smiles. She thankfully has gotten used to the song and dance that is me and dad, and I think she actually sympathizes with me a bit, so she always turns a blind eye as much as possible and doesn't usually rat me out unless dad outright makes her. She likes me, but she won't jeopardize her job and lie for me, which I respect.

I head into the massive ballroom, appreciating the gorgeous decorations. The event planning staff of the Celeste are the best in all of Seattle, bar none. The ceiling is draped elegantly in white and silver and light blue silk, twinkling lights weaving throughout the fabric to give it that magical winter wonderland feel—it's the theme, after all. Everywhere I look are ice sculptures, crystal icicles, and diamond-studded snowflakes. There's even snow drifting gracefully from hidden blowers within the silk above, melting harmlessly just before they land on any party goers and ruin anyone's hair, of course. It's the perfect mix of whimsical and luxurious and I allow myself to smile, taking everything in. Mom would have loved this one, for sure. She loved the snow more than any other person on earth. Dad had even proposed in a glass igloo under the Northern Lights. I wonder if he's thinking about her tonight the way I am. I wonder why they couldn't figure out a way to work. I wonder if them not working, despite the intense love, is what has me so fucking scared of this thing with Rizzo.

Actually, scratch that. I don't need to wonder about that last one. I know that's at least part of the reason and I hate that I know it. I thought I'd gotten over letting their issues be my issues, but apparently not.

I see dad talking to a few people near the largest ice sculpture, and nod in greeting when he catches my eye. He raises his glass my way in response and I think that maybe he's going to let the whole job thing lie, at least for tonight. He gestures to the décor and a smile pulls up his lips, one of those rare, unguarded ones, and I know exactly what he's saying, the exact same thing I'd just been thinking: *she really would have loved this*. I smile back at him and nod again, my eyes burning. He turns back to greet some new important person coming to chat with him and I continue on through the room.

I stroll right past Table One, snatching up my name card on the way, and wander to a table in the far corner instead. There's an empty spot, so I slide right in, happy that I don't even have to bother switching out place cards and all of that. A server approaches quickly with a tray of themed drinks—some kind of blue concoction with sugar crystals rimming the glass to look like ice. I take one and thank the man, and he gives me a bright smile.

"You're more than welcome, ma'am," he says, eyes lingering on mine for a moment before he walks away. He's handsome enough, that's for sure. Hell, maybe that's what I need to get AJ—*Rizzo*, I tell myself with gritted teeth. I down my drink, appreciating the fruity taste, and try to get my thoughts on the right track.

Maybe that's what I need to get *Rizzo* out of my head: going home with someone else. He's on the road tonight in Denver, so lord knows he's probably got plenty of girls just waiting in the wings to jump his bones the second he walks out of the locker room. The thought makes my skin heat in irritation. I pull out my phone and decide to check the score of the game...and end up watching it live instead, apparently a glutton for punishment because I need to see him. I love watching him play. The way he moves on the ice is sexy as hell. I'm being admittedly rude and completely ignoring the other people that sit down at my table, but I don't really care. I wince when Jules takes a brutal hit against the wall...and smile when Rizzo gets into a fight.

"Oh thank God, another sane person." I look up and find an older gentleman grinning at me, warm chocolate eyes sparkling. "I would much rather be watching my Vipers than sitting in this monkey suit." He tugs at his collar and I laugh. He quickly adds, "Not that it isn't a good cause, of course, but...all of this isn't really my idea of fun." He gestures to the room.

I smile at him. "Your wife drag you along?"

"My husband, actually. He *loves* this stuff." He grimaces and I can't help but laugh. He nods to the screen. "What's the score?"

"We're up 2-0."

"Yes!" I tilt the phone so he can see and scooch my chair a little closer to his so we can share the screen. They'll start speeches and the auction and everything after dinner, so we have a while to enjoy the game. "Man, I love watching him skate. It's like he's made of smoke sometimes, I swear." Of course he's talking about Rizzo but he's right: watching him skate is a real thing of beauty.

"Yeah, he's great." After the second period, we're up by five, and I reluctantly put my phone away when dinner is served. I actually enjoy the night with my new table buddy, Kent, and his husband, Jones, the two of them cracking the whole group up nonstop.

Thankfully, dad doesn't try to have a conversation with me...and the handsome server from before keeps catching my eye. *Fuck it,* I think. After the game, Rizzo will be balls deep in a puck bunny or three, so I might as well hook up with someone too, right? I stand from the table, making sure he sees me and I give a maybe not-so-subtle nod towards the door.

"Excuse me, I'll be right back," I say to the table. I glance at the server again and Kent chuckles low.

"Oh brava, my dear. Brava, indeed." I swat him with my napkin but grin as I make my way towards a side exit. I force myself not to remember that it's the same one I escaped through with Rizzo all those weeks ago. Just as I push it open, I turn back and see if the server is still watching. He is. He smiles widely, knowing exactly what I'm saying without speaking a word. I exit and wait in the hallway beyond, pulse racing.

Part of me is saying this is a bad idea, that it isn't even what I *want*, but the other parts are telling me to just do it. Rip the band aid off with someone new. Feel something that isn't the hurt or longing or annoyance that seems to be all I've been feeling since I fucked things up with Rizzo.

The server slips through the door and smiles.

"Hey," he says in a deep, husky voice.

"Hi," I breathe.

"I'm —" I kiss him to silence him.

"No names," I whisper against his lips. He smiles and kisses me back, palming the back of my head to hold me to him, maybe a touch too hard. The kiss is...not great. Too much tongue and zero finesse with it. But I'm determined to force Rizzo from my mind and this seems like the best way at the moment. What's that old saying? The best way to get over one man is to get under another one? So, I'm determined to make myself enjoy this.

"Damn, baby, you're sexy as hell," he rasps, kissing along my neck as he backs me against the wall. I roll my eyes. His words do nothing to turn me on. In fact, it's like the fucking Sahara right now down south. *It's fine. It'll be fine.* I close my eyes and try to just relax into the moment, but then he sucks hard on one spot, like a fucking fish, and I feel myself make an absolutely disgusted face. *How in the hell is that hot?? And so help me God if this moron gives me a fucking hickey...*

I huff out a frustrated sigh and pull his head back up, kissing him again and attempting to take control of it. Maybe if I show him what I like, he'll get the hint. He palms my breasts roughly, like they're basketballs and he's Shaq, and everything about this is the most unsexy encounter of my life. He does not, in fact, take my hints and instead decides it's a competition of who can shove their tongue into the other person's mouth the hardest. This was a terrible fucking idea.

Thank God, my phone chooses that moment to buzz. Maybe Hattie had taken me seriously and is calling in a fake emergency to get me out of this event.

"One second, I need to check this," I say, pushing him away. He steps back but keeps his hands latched onto my chest until I give him a pointed look. He sighs, but releases his prizes. I pull my phone out of my clutch and see a text from Rizzo. I blink in surprise.

Rizzo: Hey, can you call and check on Mac?

I frown and straighten, and the idiot takes that as an invitation to lean in again, licking my neck. Not a sexy little lap of his tongue, either. Licks it like a cartoon dog licking a bone. *Bleh.* I push him away and maneuver away from the wall, putting some space between us.

"Uh, everything ok? I gotta get back to work soon..."

"Go ahead, something important came up. Sorry."

"We could hook up after," he says with a smile.

"I don't think so." I walk down the hallway towards the stairs and he calls after me.

"For real?"

"A thousand percent!" I call as the door slams shut behind me. I wipe saliva from my neck and feel like I might puke. "Oh, gross! God, that was a disaster." I shake my head and decide to never speak of this to anyone for as long as I live.

I quickly type back a response.

> Hey, is everything ok?

> Rizzo: I think so, but she got spooked earlier
> in the parking garage.

"What the hell?" We'd been texting in our group chat with her, me, and Bobby earlier and she hadn't mentioned anything at all. We were all joking around—Bobby told the worst dad joke of all time, I'd asked Hattie to be ready to fake the emergency, and she started adding "eh" to the end of every message since Bobby was home in Canada visiting family for the next couple of weeks for the holidays. He wasn't nearly as amused as we were, but everything had seemed fine.

> I'll call her right now.

> Rizzo: Thanks. You know how she is. She
> doesn't like to ask for help or "bother"
> people, but she was definitely freaked out.
> She's staying at Shep's place.

> I'll def check on her.

The three bubbles pop up and disappear like he's typing more but then rethinking it. I hate this.

> Good game, btw.

> Rizzo: you were watching? I thought you
> were at some event?

> I was being a terrible party guest and
> watching on my phone. Have to support my
> favorite goalie, duh.

I bite my lip, hoping he jokes back. I want that back so badly, realizing now how much I've been missing it.

> Rizzo: You don't have to lie, Nat. I know you
> wanted to watch my fine ass skate around
> all night.

I smile and sigh in relief, huffing out a soft laugh. *Baby steps.*

> You mean Roman's fine ass, right?

> Rizzo: 😬

> Rizzo: Call Mac. Text me later.

> Me: Yes, sir 🫡

That tension that's been clenching my chest ever since everything got so screwed up with Rizzo finally eases a fraction. I feel like this is the first step back in the right direction with us. And if he wants me to text him later, that means he doesn't plan to be otherwise occupied, right?...

I shake the thought away and call Hattie. She picks up on the third ring.

"Are you alright??"

"Yeah, I'm...I'm fine," she says, though she sounds seriously shaken up. But when she continues, she sounds perfectly normal and I can practically hear the fake smile she's got plastered on her face. "I got freaked out in the parking garage, but it was nothin'. I think I just watched one too many scary movies the other day, that's all." I narrow my eyes as I make my way down the stairs, heels clacking loudly.

"Are you sure?"

"I'm positive. What the heck is that sound?"

"I'm running away from this event down the stairwell," I tell her, half serious. I am ready to get the hell out of here, only partly because of my incredibly cringey make out session with the server. Hattie laughs. "Do you want me to come over? We can watch movies all night—non-scary ones. I'll stop for popcorn and candy on the way."

"Rain check? I think I'm just gonna hit the hay."

"You sure?" I ask. I don't want to push. Lord knows I'm the last person who can say anything about not being entirely forthcoming with what's going on in my head, but I get the feeling that something is definitely wrong with her.

"Yeah, I'm good, I promise. Thanks, Nat."

"Ok, call me tomorrow. Or text me later if you change your mind and want me to come over."

She promises she will and we hang up. I make my way back around to the entrance of the ballroom to grab my coat. Despite the unease about Hattie, my lips actually curl when my phone buzzes and I see Rizzo's name. I head out into the cold, feeling better than I have in weeks.

The good feeling doesn't last as long as I'd hoped. Dad asks me to a late lunch the next day and I decide that it's time to talk. I can't ignore him forever, after all. And I don't want to. As much as we clash, he's my dad and I love him. He's all I have left. I don't want us to be on opposite sides of some stupid, imaginary battlefield.

So, I meet him at one of our favorite spots and he already has my favorites ordered for me when I arrive: BLT, extra bacon, with cheese fries and ranch for dipping, of course.

I smile at him and he returns it. Maybe this will stay nice and civil. Maybe he's finally come to terms with my life choices and understands that I'm happy (complicated love life notwithstanding) and he's going to tell me that he's good with it. Hey, I can hope for a Christmas miracle, can't I?

Wrong.

We barely get through hellos and comments about the Winter Wonderland event, before he dives right in. I don't even get to take a second bite of my sandwich before my hands are clenched into fists and my appetite is gone. Ok, that's a lie. I'm starving and that makes me even more mad that he couldn't even let me enjoy my fucking lunch before ruining everything.

"I'm not doing this, dad," I say, quietly but firmly.

I can't believe he still thinks he can just make all these decisions about my life without my consent. He once again doesn't even *ask* if I would be interested in Lysander's position, it's not even a conversation. He just tells me when I'll be starting, like it was a done fucking deal.

Actually, scratch that, I can one thousand percent believe it—and it's making me see red. I'm so over this.

"Yes, you are. The discussion is over."

"What discussion?" I hiss. "There is no discussion, there never is with you! You decide and expect me to just obey. And for a long time, that's how it was, so it's my own fault for setting the precedent I guess, but not anymore." The muscle in his jaw ticks as he clenches his teeth and I can tell that he's trying his best to keep his composure.

"This little game has run its course, Natalie."

"This isn't a game." I feel like we keep having the same damn conversation over and over. I grit my teeth. He isn't the only one fighting for composure here. And I have a feeling I'm going to lose. "This isn't me acting out. This isn't me trying to get attention. This isn't even me rebelling just to piss you off like that summer in Sydney. This is my fucking *life,* the one I'm choosing for myself after all these years. And I happen to really, really love it. Why can't you see that? Why can't you accept it?" *Why can't you accept me for who I am?*

And it's like a lightbulb goes off. That's the crux of all of this, why this hurts so damn much. Him refusing to accept my life as-is means that he doesn't accept *me* as-is. He wants to change who I am. My heart cracks and my nose burns with tears, both of pain and anger.

Dad slams his hand down on the table, rattling the silverware and making me flinch. A waiter does an immediate about-face to go hide in the kitchen instead of refilling our water glasses. *Smart man.* Other patrons glance our way a little uncomfortably, but neither dad nor I give two shits what they think.

"Because this is ridiculous, Natalie! You are more than this. You're *better* than this. Working for a hockey team? Come on, you can't be serious. Your place has always been in the company with me, to continue on our family business"

"I don't want the family business, damn it! I don't want the legacy. I don't want any of it! Why the fuck do you think I changed my last name, dad?" He grinds his teeth in irritation. My choice to abandon his name for mom's has always been a sensitive subject, but I don't care right now.

"Haven't you gotten over it yet?" he spits and, to his credit, I can tell he immediately regrets it.

"Haven't I gotten over *my mother suddenly dying* and my entire world slamming into a sharp, ugly clarity revealing how fucking *miserable* I was? Is that what you mean?" I ask slowly. I glare daggers at him, hot, angry tears flooding my vision. "I might just need a little longer on that, dad." I stand and throw my napkin on the table before storming out of the place without an *I love you*. For the first time ever, there's no I love you.

Before I even make it to my car, my phone is buzzing. I pull it out of my pocket and see Rizzo's name, and while part of me wants to talk to him about everything I'm feeling right now so badly it actually kind of surprises me, the other part doesn't want to talk to anybody about jack shit. I just want to go curl up on my couch and binge watch *Supernatural* and ugly cry for hours. But I answer all the same, because I know just hearing his voice will make me feel a fraction better.

"Hey, Rizz, look now's not a good time ok, I—"

"Nat, you need to get to the hospital right now." The panic in his voice makes me freeze in my tracks, my blood turning to ice and everything with my dad vanishing into the background.

"What's wrong? What happened? Are you ok??" Why the fuck is he in the hospital?

"The short of it is Mac's crazy fucking ex found her."

"Oh my God," I breathe, terror gripping me. She'd told me about Josh and even though I don't think she told me even half of the gory details, she told me enough to know that the guy was a legitimate psycho. Like stalking her and prone to outbursts of violence kind of psycho. She had to move half way across the country basically in secret to get away from him. *And he found her. Oh God, oh God, oh God.*

"She's ok, mostly, but...ah fuck, Shep was shot, Nat. I don't know... I can't..." I can hear him spiraling and my heart twists painfully. It makes me snap out of my frozen stupor. I need to help him. I need to check on Hattie. I need to be there for Shep. *Please let him be ok. Please, please, please.*

"I'm on my way. I'll be there in fifteen minutes."

Sixteen

RIZZO

"Stop. Fucking. Doing. This. To. Me. You. Asshole," I snap at Shep, punctuating each word with a punch to the arm without the gunshot wound in it.

Gunshot.

My best friend was fucking *shot*. I still can't quite wrap my head around it. The past forty-eight hours are a blur of flashing lights, police reports, waiting rooms, and some of the greatest terror I've ever known. He chuckles lightly and grabs the front of my shirt, pulling me in for a somewhat awkward, one-armed hug.

"I love you too," he says, voice rough. I let out a long, long, *long* breath, one I feel like I've been holding since the minute he called me as he raced to Hattie's place that day. I'd immediately called Lance, one of my buddies with Seattle PD to bring in the calvary, and made like a bat out of hell for Mac's house myself. I pulled up just after Rand, the head of security at the arena, and, as stupid as it was, we both ran right inside. The scene was like something out of one of those crime shows or maybe even a horror movie. I shudder now even thinking about it: Connor collapsing to the floor, covered in blood; Hattie screaming over him; a psycho lying a few feet away with a giant gash in his side, crimson pooling all around him. I'm not even ashamed to say that I was hoping he was dead. He wasn't, but he's locked up tight and from what I hear, he's staying that way for a good long while.

I finally pull away and sit on the side of the bed.

"Can we maybe make it like a New Year's Resolution or something for you to *not* end up in the hospital next year? That would be fucking great." He huffs out a laugh, wincing a bit. The bullet went straight through and by some miracle, the damage was minimal. He'll be out for a bit, but he'll make a full recovery and be back on the ice in no time, all things considered.

"I'll see what I can do." We share a smile that says way more than words ever could and that tight fist strangling my heart over these past few days finally eases the fuck off.

He gets released the next day and even though I'm right around the corner now, I practically live at his place for the next week, helping with Ollie and trying to keep the circus at bay. Pretty much everyone in the whole damn organization ends up here at one point or another. The guy is well-loved that's for damn sure.

Right now, it's just me and Nat on Shep Watch while Mac takes a much-deserved shower and Ollie is having a play date with a friend from school. Mac has barely left Shep's side since he came home and I can't say that I blame her. I can't even imagine being in that situation. They *both* could have been killed and the thought makes my chest feel cold and hollow. If it had been Nat in trouble like that...I force the thought away, afraid to even think it.

"It makes you think about how quickly things can change, doesn't it?" Nat whispers now. We sit at the kitchen table while Shep naps on the couch.

"It does," I agree. She reaches over and places a hand on my forearm, holding my gaze. I can see the wheels turning and as much as I want it, I don't want it like this. I know she's gotta be freaked out and this whole brush with death is probably bringing up memories of the sudden loss of her mom, but I don't want that to be the reason she agrees to give this another shot.

"Rizzo, I...I mean, we..."

"Not right now, Nat. Please." I pull my arm away and run a hand through my hair. "I don't want a pity fuck and I don't want you making a decision based on this insane situation that's got everyone all keyed up." I sigh and look up again, feeling weary down to my bones. I need sleep. I need to believe that everything will be fine. I need to stop seeing Connor shot and possibly fucking dying on the floor in front of me every time I close my eyes. I keep having nightmares, each one slightly different—sometimes we don't make it in time; sometimes we get there in time to *watch* Shep get shot; other times, it isn't Shep at all, but Nat with the bullet sailing towards her. Those are the worst—but all leave me gasping for breath when I wake tangled in my sheets, covered in sweat with my heart racing.

She holds my gaze. I didn't mean for it to sound harsh or anything, but it's the truth. I don't want her to suddenly decide she wants to give us a real go just because she's having a *life is short* moment. If and when she gets over whatever made her bolt from my apartment that night, I want it to be because she actually wants it. After a few minutes of studying me, she finally nods, and I think there's a bit of respect in her eyes.

"Alright," she says, giving me a small smile. My lips curl in return and something in my chest unclenches for the first time in weeks. Mac comes back from her shower then, toweling her hair.

"Thanks, y'all. God, I needed that."

"You really did. You were starting to get a little ripe, Mac." She rolls her eyes and Nat snorts.

"Of course, Hads," Nat says, getting up from the table. "Can we do anything else to help for tonight?"

"Nah, I think we're good. Things are finally settling down a bit around here, so we should be all set." Nat wraps Hattie in a tight hug and when she steps away, I do the same. She squeezes me tight and I kiss her on the head.

"Call me if you need anything. I can be here in five minutes."

"I will. Thanks, Rizz. And tell Lance thank you for me. He's been amazing through all of this."

Nat and I head through the living room towards the front door, but I stop by the couch on the way.

I lean down and whisper, "I know you're awake, you asshole. Stop eavesdropping." He grins but keeps his eyes shut to maintain his innocence. I slap him gently on the shoulder. "See ya later, bud."

Once outside, Nat turns to me, eyes filled with determination. I quirk a brow, wondering where this is going.

"What you said in there, about us not just jumping back into bed or whatever because of everything that's happened?" I nod. "You're right."

"Well, I usually am," I say with a smirk and a smile curls her lips even as she shakes her head and rolls her eyes.

"Ya know what, I've suddenly changed my mind about what I was going to say..."

I hold up my hands in surrender.

"Ok, ok, I'm sorry. Please continue."

"So, I think you're right, but...well..." She sighs heavily. "I miss my fucking friend, Rizz." My chest twists. As much as I want more with Nat, I really miss the way things used to be between us too. I miss sending each other stupid memes. I miss laughing at inside jokes so hard that it makes everyone else around us annoyed as hell. I miss venting after a hard game or when I feel like I'm fucking up. I miss her telling me like it is even when I might not want to hear it. I miss her. I miss us.

"I miss you too, Nat. A lot."

"So, I have a proposition."

"Oh now you know I love a good proposition." She huffs out a laugh.

"Why don't we focus on being friends again—*real* friends, the way we were. None of the fake bullshit we've both been pulling lately." I can't help but smile. Guess neither of us was really doing a great job of fooling the other one. She fiddles with her key ring while she waits for my answer. Is she really worried that I'll say no? That I can't go back to being friends now? Sure, I still want more than friendship, want it so badly that it actually startled me when I first really let myself think about it, but if I can't have that, I'll take the next best thing and that's having her back in my corner again. *And maybe things will change from there...*

"I think that a true friend would want to come help me unpack a bunch of boxes. I've been really fucking slacking. We can order pizza and I have plenty of beer in the fridge." The tension eases out of her shoulders and she smiles, a real, full smile that I haven't seen in too long.

"Throw in cheesy bread and you've got yourself a deal, Thirst Trap."

Hours later, we've pretty much given up on unpacking and are lounging in the living room surrounded by bubble wrap and stacks of random shit. She's laying on her stomach on the rug in front of the fire and thumbing through an old yearbook.

"Oh my God, you were so tiny!" she exclaims, giggling as she stares at the team photo from my freshman year. "You had to have weighed like eighty pounds soaking wet here."

"I hit my growth spurt late, alright," I say, rubbing the back of my neck, but smiling. She laughs lightly, turning pages and looking more relaxed than I've seen her in a while. Her phone buzzes—again. It's like the tenth time in the last hour. Every time, she glances at her screen, clenches her jaw, and puts the phone away without answering.

"So, who are we avoiding?" I ask. I prepare myself for it to be another guy. I can handle that. Probably. She sits up and leans her back against the couch opposite the one I'm on.

"My dad," she says with a sigh, surprising me. Nat hardly ever talks about her family. "We got in a big fight the other day. The day everything happened with Hattie and Shep actually. I'd just stormed out of the restaurant when I got your call."

"Do you wanna tell me what the fight was about?"

"The utter disappointment that is me pretty much."

My brow furrows. "You can't be serious?"

"Ohh as a heart attack."

I slide off the couch to the floor so that we're eye level across from each other. I spread my legs out in front of me and ignore the stupid, stupid rush I feel when her leg settles against mine. I'm going to have to get that shit under control if we're back to just friends again.

"How is that possible? How could anyone think you're a disappointment?" She gives me a sad smile before she exhales roughly.

"He's just always wanted to dictate everything in my life: where I went to school, what I majored in, my career after graduation. And for a while, I let him, but after my mom died it was like everything just became painfully clear suddenly, like I'd been looking at my life without glasses on and then BAM—20/20 vision. I was really miserable in that life, just kind of...existing, not really living. So, I quit my job in New York and moved back home to start over doing something I actually chose for myself for once. I found the job with the Vipers and I've honestly loved every second of it."

"But dad isn't thrilled?"

She huffs out a humorless laugh.

"He thinks it's ridiculous and that it's just a phase I'm going through trying to get over losing mom." She shakes her head angrily, but there's so much pain in her eyes that my chest clenches. I want so badly to fix it somehow, to make the pain go away, but I have no idea how. She shakes herself. "Anyway, I just wish that he could understand that I'm finally happy, that he could just accept it and not care that I'm not following in his footsteps, ya know?" All because she doesn't want to be a damn realtor too? What the hell?

"I'm really sorry, Nat. That's...that's awful. I can't say that I know what it's like because I was really lucky that mom and Ray always supported me no matter what I wanted to do—even when I decided to give musical theater a try." She arches a brow and I shudder. "It did *not* end well and solidified my desire to make hockey my life. But, they were both there for me a thousand percent, Hank too as the bonus dad-like figure. So, while I can't relate, I can tell you that I think it's shitty and that he's an idiot."

She exhales roughly, as if she's been needing to hear those words for a long time.

"Thanks, Rizzo."

"You're welcome." Our gazes hold for a long moment and I try to ignore the heat that starts to simmer. *Friends, friends, friends.* She smiles and knocks my ankle with hers.

"So tell me more about this musical theater fail...

Seventeen

NAT

Things are great and shitty all at once.

I'm still pissed at dad and not even close to ready to talk to him again yet. It's more than just the jibe about not being over mom's death, it's the fact that I'm not enough for him and that he thinks he can still just bulldoze my life. I won't let it happen anymore. I won't give in or let him think it's ok, and if that means icing him out for a while, then so be it.

But things with Rizzo have been amazing. I hadn't realized just how much I'd missed him until we found our way back to how things were before. Well, not *exactly* how they were before: we're actually closer than ever now. We've been spending almost every minute that I'm not working and he's not practicing or playing together. I went with him to get his first tattoo, Hattie and Shep in tow too, and while it was really cool to share that experience with him, staring at him shirtless for hours while he got the Celtic cross inked onto his chest was a special kind of torture. I'd almost forgotten just how good he looks unclothed. Sure, I've seen it on his social media accounts since we stopped hooking up, but seeing it in person is a whole other story. The tattoo came out amazing, but I have to force myself not to imagine running my fingers and tongue over the lines more often than I'd care to admit.

We've gotten his place completely set up, including a room for Ollie which she absolutely loves.

"Just for me!?" she'd exclaimed when we'd brought her upstairs to do the big reveal. The room actually has it's own little loft space inside it and is probably the coolest room in the house.

"Just for you, Olligator," Rizzo had nodded, ruffling her hair. She'd screeched then, thrown her arms around him, and then gone full on kid tornado and torn through the room, trying to look at and play with everything all at once. Hattie had teared up at the sight and then punched Shep in the arm when he called her a big softie, but I'd be lying if seeing Rizzo climb up into the loft to play barbies, doing his best Australian accent because apparently Ken was Australian for unknown reasons, didn't do some kind of number on my heart...and ovaries. *He's going to make one hell of a dad one day*, I'd thought.

Despite him saying that he didn't want me to make any decisions because of everything that happened with Hattie and Shep, that's exactly what happened. Seeing how close they came to losing the person they love made me realize how stupid all my fears and insecurities and whatever the hell else that caused me to bolt that night really were. I know what I want and even if there's a chance that things don't work out the way I want, that Rizzo isn't really ready for a relationship and I get my heart broken, it's worth the risk.

I'm not going to tell him any of that yet, of course. I don't want him thinking it's just a knee-jerk reaction, or anything, because it's really not. The situation just made me push past the bullshit and accept what I'd been feeling for months. Even so, for now, we're just friends, but I can admit to myself that I'm already falling for him more and more each day.

"How about this one?" I call from across the Christmas tree lot. It's only a few days away, but they thankfully still have a pretty decent selection.

"Where the hell are you?" he yells back.

"Marco!" I call, running my hands over the limbs of a giant spruce.

"Polo!"

I grin. "Marco!"

He bursts out from behind a tree behind me, settling his big hands on my waist and squeezing, making me yelp and giggle as he tickles me. I whirl and dance out of his grip, smacking his arms.

"Asshole," I breathe. He smiles and winks. "What about this one?" I ask again, pointing to the beauty I found.

"You don't think it's a little...uh, gigantic?" He eyes the tree, pulling his gaze up, up, up to the very top. It's admittedly pretty damn big, but he's got the space for it now. His living room ceilings go on forever and this baby will look absolutely perfect tucked into the corner next to the fireplace.

"It's perfect," I say, staring at the tree in wonder. "It's your first Christmas in your new place. It should be perfect."

"Well how the hell can I say no to that, huh?"

"Plus, I already told Ollie we were going to get an even bigger tree than the one Shep cut down, so you kind of have to get this one." He laughs at that, his blue eyes sparkling, and fuck if my stomach doesn't do a stupid little flip.

"A chance to one-up Shep? Done and done!" He turns and scans the lot for an employee and catches someone's eye. "We'll take this one!" The kid looks to be seventeen, maybe eighteen, but exhausted and completely over working at the lot as he heads over, but once he's closer he stutter-steps and his eyes light up.

"Oh my God, are you...you are! Holy shit, you're Anthony Rizzo! I'm a huge fan, dude. I have your jersey at home and everything!"

"Oh thanks, man," Rizzo says, holding out his hand to the kid. He looks like he might pass out, but reaches out to shake it. "You can call me Rizzo."

"Holy shit. I'm Tyler."

"Nice to meet you, Tyler."

"Oh man, this is so cool. Would you, uh, would you mind taking a picture with me? My buddy Jake is never going to believe I actually met you—you're pretty much his hero."

"Psh, fuck that, give him a call right now, man," Rizz says.

"Seriously?!" The kid looks like he just got told he had free run of Disneyworld for the day. Rizzo grins and Tyler frantically FaceTimes his friend. Rizzo throws me a wink and I smile back. He's so good with his fans. I've seen him spend literal hours after games making sure every single kid who wants one gets an autograph or a picture.

Jake answers on the second ring.

"Jake! Dude, you'll never guess who's here right now."

Rizzo steps into the frame and slings an arm around Tyler's shoulder and I hear Jake sputter.

"What's up, Jake?" Rizzo says with a winning smile. "My buddy Tyler here says you're a Vipers fan."

"Holy shit! Oh my God. Is this real?? *Oh my God!*"

They chat for a few minutes about hockey and Rizzo's personal stats and records, but Rizz is great about steering the conversation back to them too, asking them about school or their own hockey accolades. It's completely obvious that both boys are in heaven and fuck if I don't fall a little more in love with him as I watch. There are so many athletes out there that don't give a shit about their fans, but Rizzo—almost all of the Vipers really—actually take the time to show them that they care. It's amazing to see.

He meets my gaze and arches a brow in question. I nod, knowing exactly what he's asking.

"Hey listen, my friend Nat here," he turns the phone so that Jake can see me and I wave, and then twists it back to his own face, "can work some magic and get you guys in the locker room before the next game if you want. You can meet all the guys, get as many autographs and pictures as you want. VIP tickets. Free food. The whole shebang. What do you say? My Christmas gift to two of our best fans."

Tyler's eyes snap to mine over the top of the phone, mouth gaping. "For real!?"

"Absolutely," I assure him. "Your families too," I add. We always keep a handful of tickets and swag set aside for stuff like this.

"Oh my God, my dad is going to lose his mind. Like, legit, I think he might cry. This is a way better Christmas gift than the socks I got him," Jake says and I can't help but laugh. They finally hang up, Rizz takes a few pics with Tyler, posting them to his own social media immediately and tagging Tyler, surely making the kid feel like Superman. I get his and Jake's information to get their VIP packages set up while Rizzo works on getting the huge tree strapped to the top of his Range Rover.

We head to find ornaments and lights next and I eye him while he drives.

"That was really cool of you."

He scoffs. "I'm always cool, Nat."

"And so humble too," I say with a roll of my eyes, turning up the radio.

"Do I get to open it now?" AJ asks—yeah, he's AJ again, what can I say? He shakes the box near his ear like he can figure out what's inside by listening to it. "Come on, I don't want to wait until tomorrow."

I laugh. "You sound like a five-year-old, you know that right?" He grins at me.

"You can open yours too if you want. Come onnn," he whines and I can't help but smile. I've been doing a lot of that this last week. It's crazy that to think that it's only been a handful of days since Hattie was almost kidnapped and God knows what else, since Shep was shot, and since my entire life shifted in front of my eyes once again. It's so cliché to not make these choices or see the truth until I'm presented with a life-altering event, but it is what it is. The important thing is that I see it and I *do* make the choice, eventually.

"Ok, ok fine," I say with a laugh. "We can open them now."

Since I'm still on the outs with dad and AJ wanted to let Hattie and Shep have family time for Christmas Eve, we decided to spend it together. As friends. Still just friends and nothing more...for now.

He rummages through the boxes under the tree. At least twenty of them have Ollie's name on them and it warms my heart all over again seeing how much he loves that little girl. He finally pulls out one with ice-skating tacos on it and I grin, wondering where in the hell he found the paper. He hands it over and settles onto the floor in front of the couch beside me. His couches are really comfy, but I've become slightly obsessed with lounging on the super plush rug in front of his giant fireplace. Our gazes meet, the twinkling lights from the tree making his baby blues sparkle, and suddenly, I can't hold the words back anymore.

"Hey, AJ I..." He quirks a brow, his body tensing when I use the name out loud.

"I'm AJ again?" he asks quietly. *Here it goes.*

"If you want to be?" He exhales slowly and the moment he waits before answering feels like an eternity. He said he didn't want me to make any rash decisions, but this isn't that. I want to tell him everything, to explain how I'm feeling, how I've felt from the beginning if I'm being completely honest with myself, but I'm going to let him decide. If he isn't ready—or, worse, doesn't even *want* this anymore—then that's ok too. I'll live with whatever he decides and we'll be fine.

"I don't think I've ever wanted anything more, Nat." I sigh in relief, a smile curling my lips.

"About that night at your apartment."

"Nat, you don't have to—"

"I do though. I'm sorry I freaked. That was more about me than you and I shouldn't have said the shit I did."

"It's alright. I'd be lying if I said I was completely sure how the fuck to even navigate this. I can't promise I'll be a good...boyfriend or whatever," he says, running his hand through his hair and shrugging the word off like it's nothing, but I can tell there's a bit of nervousness there, "but I *can* promise that I'll try, that I really fucking want to try. I'm not just after sex with you, Nat—though I've been thinking about that nonstop since that very first night, don't ever fucking doubt that." I huff out a laugh. "There's just something..." He shakes himself, seeming frustrated or afraid that he's saying too much. "I just want to try to be more. That's the only way I know to say it. I want more with you. And I would never, ever cheat on you, Nat. On anyone. I think that's fucked up and cowardly and that's not me. If my feelings ever changed, I would be a man about it and tell you. I would never go behind your back and hurt you like that."

"I know. I really do. Like I said, that was my own stuff coming out. And I want more too. So...we'll just take things slow and not put pressure on, deal?"

"Deal," he says and the absolutely devastatingly perfect smile he gives me breaks my heart a little.

"Ok, ok, back to presents."

"On three," he says with a grin, and I nod.

"One...two..." I can't say I'm surprised when he starts to tear into his box before he reaches three.

"Fucking cheater," I grumble, rolling my eyes as I start to unwrap my own gift like an actual civilized human instead of a honey badger. He throws the scraps of wrapping paper into the air and I giggle, trying to shield myself from the falling debris.

"I play to win, Nat. You should know this by now...." He trails off when he looks in the box and then busts out laughing. "Oh my God." He pulls out the gift, still cracking up. "Is this...a mistletoe belt buckle??"

I smile. "It seemed right up your alley." His eyes spark with amusement, mischief, and a touch of promise, and my stomach twists with a quick, sharp stab of desire. It's been too long since I've touched him, since I've had his lips on mine, his hands on my body. He stands and pulls his shirt up, holding the hem beneath his chin so he can fiddle with his belt unobstructed, and *fuck me*. I swear he didn't have this many abs the last time I saw him. They've multiplied in the last week since he got his tattoo. I barely stop myself from reaching out and running my fingers over those enticing dips and ridges, possibly running my tongue across those criminal fucking indentions beside his hips.

I pull my gaze away and open my own box, huffing out a laugh when I pull the sweater out.

"Santa's Favorite Ho Ho Ho?" I arch a brow at him and he grins.

"You would definitely be his favorite," he says with a wink. I laugh and pull it on over my t-shirt, leaning back to show it off. He beams, clearly proud of himself, and I love that we both got each other stupid shit. Just one more way we seem to always be on the same page with things. I'm not saying we agree on everything—in fact, some of our drunken debates about the dumbest stuff are some of my favorite memories—but we just...get each other. *Ugh. I sound so fucking corny.*

I laugh when he finishes securing the belt buckle in place, the mistle toe hanging just over his crotch. He spreads his arms, showing off his new accessory, and then he arches a sexy, teasing brow at me.

"You know the rules, Nat..."

I'd be lying if I said I hadn't imagined this exact scenario when I'd bought the damn thing, but I hadn't been sure if we'd be in this place yet or not. So, I'm all too happy to set my empty box aside and push up to my knees kneeling in front of him. He inhales sharply, like he wasn't sure if I'd be game or not. I give him a sultry grin and lean forward, tugging up his shirt to kiss his stomach just below his navel. He shudders and I meet his gaze up his body.

"Want this gone," I whisper, shoving his shirt farther up his torso and planting another kiss on his smooth, taut skin. He quickly yanks it off, so fast I can't help but chuckle lightly, but then I'm free to explore the perfect parts of him I've missed so much. I run my hands over his abs and chest, trailing my fingers over the bottom edge of the cross before he holds my palm against his heart, letting me feel the thundering. I leave it there and run the other one down his side, making him jerk and tremble.

"Fuck, I've missed this..." he rasps.

"You have no idea, AJ..." I drag my tongue across that indention, from hip bone to just above his cock, and he groans deep in his throat. He gathers my hair in one of his big hands and holds it out of my face. I love that he loves to watch. I slowly begin to undo his belt after all his hard work and ease his zipper downward, leaning in to kiss along the same path over his boxer-briefs. He's so hard already, and my heart races in anticipation. I've been dreaming about him since our last night together, thinking about him constantly. I've missed my lips on him, my tongue, my fingers. I've missed the sounds he makes and the way he talks. I've missed the way he tastes. I've missed *everything*.

"Don't make me wait, Nat. For the love of fucking God, don't make me wait..." His muscles are clenched tight and a slight tremor runs through his entire body. God is he as desperate as I am right now? *Impossible.* But he must be damn close with the way his breath hitches and his pulse races at his throat. I grin as I trail my hand down his chest where it joins my other one, poised at the hem of his jeans. I grip them and his underwear together and start to tug them down—only for the doorbell to ring.

"You have got to kidding me," he barks out, clearly annoyed as hell. "I'm going to kill whoever is at that door..."

I sigh and pull back, knowing that only a few people would be allowed through the gate, and a sharp sting of fear goes through me at the idea of something being wrong down at Hattie and Shep's place.

"Go check, what if it's—"

"Shep. I know, I know. I'm going." He eyes me for a moment, the hunger and yearning in his eyes making a shiver run through me. "Later," he promises, pinching my chin between his thumb and forefinger in that incredibly sexy way that makes almost every bit of self-control leave my body. He sighs and releases me, grumbling as he adjusts himself and puts his pants back to rights, grabbing his shirt from the floor and tugging it on. I stand and smooth my hair down. Whoever is at the door better be glad they showed up when they did because a few more seconds and there would have been no stopping this for anything, of that I am painfully aware. The heat flowing through me is like a living, breathing thing, stalking inside me and demanding release. I literally ache, and I clench my thighs tightly to try to assuage it. It does absolutely no good, of course.

To my utter delight, he grabs my hand and tugs me with him to answer the door. I lean into his side as he swings it open, trying not to think the worst. My brow furrows when I see two strangers on the doorstep...but no, not complete strangers. They look familiar...

"Mom? Dad?" AJ breathes. "What the...what are you doing here?" I drop his hand and take a step away so he can wrap his arms around his parents on the porch. "You aren't supposed to be here until after New Years." He's surprised but I can see the absolute joy in his eyes at seeing his parents here.

"With everything that's happened with Shep, we decided to postpone our trip and come out here instead. We thought it would be a nice surprise..." His mom's eyes shift to me and I give her a somewhat nervous smile. "Oh goodness, did we interrupt something...?"

"No! No, not at all." I feel my cheeks heat and AJ gives me a flirty look.

"Mom, dad, you remember my friend Nat?"

"How could we forget the first girl you've had on a FaceTime call with us in...ever?" his dad says, stepping forward and wrapping me in a big hug. I'm surprised but smile, hugging him back.

"Hello again Just A Friend Nat," his mom says with a warm smile, stepping in to give me a hug as well. We both laugh and AJ runs his hands through his hair. She pulls away and eyes my sweater and I look down. Oh God. *This* is what I'm wearing when I officially meet his parents for the first time? *Fucking hell...*

"Oh, uh..."

"Hilarious," she assures me. She glances to AJ and purses her lips. "And is that a...mistletoe belt buckle you have on, dear?" The more she speaks, the more I can hear the undertone of her accent. Ray nearly chokes on his laughter and AJ rubs a hand over the back of his neck.

"It was a gag gift," I say, scrunching my nose, suddenly worried that they're going to think I'm an awful person or something.

"Equally hilarious," Muriel laughs heartily. "I'm honestly surprised he doesn't own one already."

I let out a relieved sigh-slash-laugh and meet AJ's eyes. He winks and I feel myself relax.

"Well come in outta the cold. Let me grab your bags. I mean it, dad. Leave it and get inside," he warns and I can't help but smile. Ray holds up his hands in surrender and walks further into the foyer, Muriel on his heels. I glance back as AJ grabs the bags from the porch and he gives me an apologetic look. I shake him off, letting him know it's fine. I turn back to the others.

"Can you I get you a drink? Kitchen and living room are right this way," I say gesturing. They walk ahead of me, *ooing* and *aahing* about the house as they go and I take a deep, settling breath.

Christmas with his parents.

So much for no pressure.

Eighteen

RIZZO

WELL THIS IS...UNEXPECTED.

I'd been excited to see my parents on my doorstep, don't get me wrong, but I'd also been worried that it would be too much for Nat. I mean, we literally just said no pressure and we'd take things slow and then *BAM* she's in the middle of a family reunion not five minutes later. But she's taking it completely in stride and has assured me no less than ten times that she's totally fine. I know she's good at hiding her feelings, but I don't think she's hiding anything now. She really is totally fine. Happy even.

She and Ray were instant friends from the second she made him a perfect Manhattan and they figured out they share a love of old Westerns, and mom can't stop grinning like she knows some big secret. They seem to really like her and the feeling of utter joy of all of us being here together, playing Pictionary beside a beautiful Christmas tree in my first real home...well, it's not something I'm taking lightly.

"Ok, ma, I need you to focus, alright? We *cannot* let them beat us."

"You mean beat you worse than we already are?" Nat chimes in and I cut a murderous look her way. I'm trying really fucking hard to keep my competitiveness in check, but it's not easy. Ray laughs and they bump fists. They are, admittedly, killing us. I turn back to mom and point to my eyes.

"Focus on me. Right here. You got this."

She nods and stands at the dry erase board that Nat had insisted I get for Ollie's room. Turns out it was a great buy and works perfectly for game night. Mom looks at her card and nods again, perfectly confident.

"Ok...ready...go!" Nat calls, starting the timer.

Mom draws...a blob.

"Uhh, a ball? A globe? A pond...ma! Do more! I need more!" She adds smaller blobs to the bigger blob and I shake my head. "Are you serious?"

"It's obvious, AJ! Just look at it..." Mom taps her marker on the blobs, as if that will help me suddenly see what it's supposed to be, and I throw up my hands.

"Ma, those are fucking blobs of nothing! This isn't a Rorschach test, come on!" Ray and Nat burst out laughing from their couch and I flip them off, which only makes them laugh harder.

"They most certainly are not just fecking blobs. It's not my fault you're shit at Pictionary!"

"*I'm* shit?" I ask incredulously.

"Five...four...three..."

"Maaaaa," I groan as Ray and Nat finish the countdown in unison. I collapse back into the couch behind me and pull a pillow over my face. Ray and Nat whoop and cheer and despite my competitiveness frothing at the fucking mouth in irritation, I can't help but smile.

"It was an airplane!" mom says defensively. "How could you not see that?"

I remove the pillow and stare at her wordlessly. She stares back but then her lips curl upwards, clearly amused with herself.

"I need another drink," I gripe and push off the couch, heading into the kitchen. I rummage in the fridge for a beer and when I straighten Nat is there, grinning, her cheeks flushed. I narrow my eyes at her.

"Are you here to gloat?"

"A bit," she says with a cocky quirk of her brow. I can't help but huff out a laugh. I also can't stop myself from reaching out and wrapping a hand around her waist and tugging her towards me. She gasps quietly and I lean in, brushing my lips softly against hers. She melts into me, draping her arms over my shoulders and tunneling her fingers into my hair. I kiss her deep and slow, gently rolling my tongue against hers when she parts her lips eagerly. I pull away after a few seconds that feel like hours and smile when she speaks, a little breathless.

"What was that for?"

"For being you."

She smiles widely and I lean in to kiss her again. I can't seem to fucking stop. I really hope this thing with us works out because I'm not sure I can go back to being friends again now. I don't know that I can give up kissing Natalie Morgan for the rest of my life. I'm fully aware that this puts me in a precarious position and sets me up for...heartbreak of all things. I don't want to think too much about that now though. I'm trying very hard to just live in the moment and be grateful for every second I have. I'd told Nat not to jump into bed with me that night at Shep's just because she was freaked out over what happened, but I'd be lying if I said it didn't affect me in that exact same way. Seeing how close the two of them had come to losing everything hit me much harder than I expected. I've never been unhappy with my lifestyle, or even close to ashamed of it, but now I have a feeling of...I don't know, wasted time? Or at the very least, the need for change.

And that need for change centers directly on this beautiful woman currently wrapped in my arms.

"I think we're going to hit the hay," Ray calls from the living room. We pull apart and head back that direction.

"You sure, dad?"

"Yeah, airports always make me tired. Plus, gotta go to bed early so Santa can come." He winks at Nat and she giggles. She pulls away and gives him a hug while Mom comes around the corner and wraps her arms around me.

"Do you need anything?" I'd already showed them the whole house and gotten them settled in one of the guestrooms upstairs before we'd eaten dinner and started our Pictionary war. Mom pulls back and puts a hand on my cheek, eyes sparkling with joy.

"No, sweetheart, we have everything we need. I think you just might too," she adds with a knowing look, gently patting the pendant that she knows is below my shirt. I haven't taken it off since she gave it to me my freshman year of college. *It'll will keep you safe, my boy. It'll bring you the luck you deserve.*

"It's very new, mom. Like literally I'm talking fifteen minutes before you got here kind of new, so…just don't go reading too much into everything yet."

"Hmm," she says with that look that says she knows I'm completely bullshitting her. Not about the newness, but about being unsure of what everything means yet. And ok, she's right. I already know how I feel about Nat. I have for months. But I'm not ready to voice that yet and need time to wrap my head around it more, *really* understand it because fuck if I know how to deal with…being in love with someone. Even though I know that I love her, I still need to make sure that I can really do this whole relationship thing and not fuck things up before I go dropping L bombs all over the place. I know for a fact from listening to Nat talk about her parents that two people can love each other so damn passionately and still not be together.

Mom pulls away and wraps Nat in a hug, and I don't miss the way Nat seems to break a little, squeezing mom tightly and closing her eyes. I know she's missing her own mom so badly in this moment and I wish there was something I could do. Mom seems to understand without having any reason to—it's not like she has any idea that Nat lost her own mother just before Christmas last year—just one of those magical mom superpowers I guess, and she holds Nat a little tighter, stroking her hair.

Ray slaps me on the back and I grin. He may not have been the one to bring me into this world, but he's the one who taught me how to be a man in it, and for that I will be forever grateful.

"She's a keeper, son. Hell, I think I might like her better than I like you." He winks at me and I laugh.

"I can't blame you there, dad. Not one damn bit." He smiles and squeezes my shoulder once before stepping away to join mom where she's finally let Nat go. She still holds one of Nat's hands though and reaches out to gently cup her jaw in that mom way of hers and I swear the gesture heals a bit of Nat's broken heart.

"We'll see you two kids in the morning," mom says, dropping her hands, and my parents head up the stairs. When they're gone, I lean back against the counter and pull Nat to me again, settling her between my legs and resting my hands on her hips.

"You don't have to stay if you don't want to. If it's…too much. I won't be upset or anything, I promise. I can drive you home—" She pushes up onto her tiptoes and cups my face, running her palms over my two-day stubble. She presses her lips to mine to shut me up. I tug her more fully against me and she moans quietly, slowly sweeping her tongue against mine.

"I want to stay," she says before biting gently on my lower lip, making me groan. "Besides, I do believe we have…*things* to continue. Things that were interrupted earlier…" She curls her fingers into the top of my jeans and tugs me even closer with her grip on my belt buckle, making her point crystal fucking clear.

"Mmmm," I rumble against her mouth, sliding my hands up her back and deepening the kiss. I can feel her heart hammering against my chest and my cock is suddenly very, very interested in the conversation. "Think you can be quiet, Natalie?" I whisper against her skin as I kiss along her jaw and down her throat. She gasps and shivers.

"I…make…no promises," she pants, holding me to her, silently begging me not to stop. I better or I'll fuck her right here in the middle of the kitchen—which I plan to do at some point, but maybe not when my parents are upstairs on Christmas Eve. I laugh against her throat and drag her earlobe through my teeth before pulling away and picking her up quickly, making her yelp.

I throw her over my shoulder, give her ass a playful swat that makes her giggle, and head to my room. I shut the door behind us and slide her down my body. She's panting, eyes wide and hungry, and fuck if she's ever looked so beautiful. I grip the bottom of her sweater and tug it up, and she immediately raises her arms to let me pull it off of her. The t-shirt comes next and I take a minute to groan in approval of the sexy, red lace bra she has on. She reaches out and pushes my shirt up roughly and I chuckle at her greediness as I reach back and grip the neck, pulling it off and tossing it to the floor. She runs her hands over my chest, lingering on my new tattoo that I know damn well she thinks is sexy, and down my stomach. My muscles flex under her touch, greedy for more. *God I've fucking missed this.*

"I can't decide where I want you first," I say quietly as she unhooks my belt and unbuttons my jeans. She reaches inside the fly and runs her palm over my aching shaft. I groan roughly and grip her nape with one hand, settling the other on her hip.

"What are your options?" she breathes, slowly moving her hand, stroking and driving me to near insanity.

"Well, there's the bed...the wall..." I gnash my teeth and tear her own jeans open, shoving them down her thighs and tunneling my hand beneath her lace panties. She cries out when I sink a finger inside. "*Fuck, Nat. So wet already.*" She makes a sexy little whimpering sound and I pump my finger in and out in time with her strokes up and down my cock. I don't think I've ever been so hard, it's verging on painful already.

"Then there's the other wall...or the other...the floor...the bench... the shower...*Dear God* do I have plans for you in this room—*this whole fucking house*—Natalie."

"Don't write checks your ass can't cash, Thirst Trap," she rasps, rocking her hips onto my hand, begging for more. I oblige, sliding in a second finger and making her groan loudly. She strokes faster, harder, and I really wonder for a second if we're both just going to finish like this. Hell, I'd be fine with it—it's hot as hell. But, no, on second thought, there are other things I want to do right now instead.

I grin and push the heel of my hand against her clit, making her buck her hips and gasp loudly.

"Is that a challenge, Nat? You know how I deal with challenges..."

Her eyes flutter open and she meets my gaze. Her lips slowly curl upwards and I know the answer. I slam my lips to hers then, my control completely frayed and the intensity of my need burning like fire in my blood. I shove her panties down her thighs and she steps out of her jeans, kicking them away. I pick her up again, claiming her mouth as I walk her across the room. Her back hits the dresser and I lift, setting her atop it. She spreads her thighs and I settle my hips between them. Thank God this thing is the perfect fucking height. I *might* have eyeballed it for that very reason in mind when we were in the store. Sue me.

I reach behind her to unclasp her bra and she throws it to the floor after she tugs the straps down her arms. I immediately dip my head and latch my lips around one nipple, swirling my tongue before sucking hard.

"Ah, fuck!" she cries, burying her fingers in my hair and holding me exactly where she wants me. I've missed this so damn much. The feel of her. The way she isn't shy to demand what she needs. How my entire body craves hers in a way I've never experienced before. I would normally draw this out, play and tease and make her come at least twice before I sank my cock deep inside her, but I don't think I can do any of that right now. The desire clawing inside me is like an animal, frenzied and feral, and it won't remain caged for long. We've had sex before, *amazing* sex, but this is something more now. We're together. We're starting something here, or at least trying to, and that makes this differ-ent. It makes it important. It ignites a fiery, desperate passion in my chest that I think might consume me completely if I'm not careful.

"Need you," I pant, moving to kiss her again and running my hands over her breasts and down her sides, palming her ass. "Can't wait much longer."

"Good, me either. I'll cash in the belt buckle later," she says, a smile in her voice. "Fuck me, AJ. *NOW*." Her words send a shudder down my spine and turn the blood in my veins to pure fire. No, not even fire. Lava. Molten and unstoppable.

"So demanding, Natalie…"

She groans in annoyed impatience against my lips and I chuckle.

"Hang on, gotta grab a rubber—"

"You don't have to," she says quickly and I freeze, quirking a brow. She chews on her lip. "Well, I'm on the shot and you said you haven't been with anyone else since we started hooking up, right?"

"Swear to God. And I get tested regularly. Kind of a requirement of being a responsible man-whore and all." She laughs lightly. I don't want to ask but I do.

"And you haven't either?" If she has, it's fine. It was her right. We weren't anything to each other but friends. Still, I hold my fucking breath while I wait for her to answer.

"Yes," she admits and even though I said it would be fine, my heart sinks. "I mean, no. No!" she quickly corrects. "I tried, once. I thought maybe if I just bit the bullet and hooked up with someone else it would get you out of my mind. We kissed for all of twenty seconds and it was horrible." She shudders and curls her lip up and I can't help but laugh at her expression. "I'm serious. It was like kissing a gorilla. I bolted."

I reach out and brush the hair from her temple, sliding my palm along her cheek.

"And did it?" I ask in a low, husky voice, "get me out of your mind?"

"Not even close," she says with a sigh. "I don't think anything could do that, AJ." I lean in and kiss her then, my heart thundering in my chest. She pulls back and holds my gaze. "So, with all that said...I want you with nothing between us."

"*Fuck me*," I say quietly.

"That's the plan," she says with a sexy little grin. I press her knees farther apart and shift her ass closer to the edge. I grip my cock and position the head in the right spot, hissing in a quick breath between clenched teeth when I meet wet heat. I never, ever have unprotected sex. Ever. This is a first and dear God I think I might not be able to last. No. Absolutely not. Anthony Fucking Rizzo is no two-pump chump. I'll last if it fucking kills me. I take a deep breath to ready myself, mentally preparing just like I would for a game. Everything is just a matter of focus, whether it's sex or handling a puck.

"You might want to hold the fuck on, Nat."

She bites her lip and I shove my hips forward, filling her in one long, deep thrust. *Fucking hell* the feel of her all around me with nothing in the way this time is unreal. She leans forward and cries out into my shoulder, digging her nails into my lower back with one hand and gripping the edge of the dresser with the other. I laugh when I realize what she's doing: trying to be quiet.

"I hate to break it to you, baby, but there's no way I'm letting you be quiet tonight."

With that promise, I begin to move, thrusting my hips and pounding into her hard and fast, the way I know that she loves. She holds on to me, scratching and biting and arching her hips to meet mine. The drawers rattle but thankfully the thing doesn't bang too loudly against the wall, but honestly, at this point I couldn't care less. I hook my elbows beneath her knees, tilting her back and spreading her wider, hitting an even deeper angle. She braces herself but with the sounds she's making, I don't dare let up.

"AJ, oh God, don't stop...right there..." She throws her head back and cries out as she tumbles over the edge.

"Ah, fuck, can feel you coming..." I grit my teeth, not ready to be done yet. I pick her up again and sink to the floor, settling her over my lap, still feeling her spasming gently around my cock. She wraps her arms around my neck and pulls my face to hers for a deep, searing kiss. She grazes her palm over my cheek, rolling her tongue against mine in a slow, sexy rhythm as she starts rock her hips.

"That feels so good," she moans against my lips, and I wrap the length of her hair around my fist, pulling gently to tilt her head back so I have better access to her throat. I lick and kiss and nip as she rides me, slow at first but then building speed. I use my other hand to help wrench her back and forth harder, needing everything she can give me.

"God I missed this. I missed how good you feel, how good we feel together," she says between gasping breaths. I kiss my way back to her lips, sucking her bottom one between my own.

"I missed you too, Nat. I missed *every. Last. Inch*," I croak, punctuating each word with a tug on her hips. She pants, digging her nails into my shoulders with one hand but sliding her other to brush her fingers over my pendant. She settles her palm over it, right over my heart. I cover her hand with mine for a second, and then meet her eyes. "Show me how much you missed me, baby. Remind me how much you love riding this cock."

"AJ," she groans, half plea, half prayer, entirely sexy. She whips her hips faster and I rock mine as I wrench her downward. "Almost...don't stop...fuck, fuck, fuck..."

She comes apart again and this time I capture her scream with my mouth on hers, kissing her like I've dreamed of these weeks without her. She doesn't stop rocking her hips, thank fucking God, and I'm about two seconds from letting myself go completely.

"Nat," I manage to bite out, "do you want me...to pull out..." God, I'm so close. I focus all of my energy on holding out a few more seconds. I need her answer, I need her to tell me.

"No," she breathes. "No, AJ. I want you to come *just like this*."

"FUCK!" I call out as that tight shiver runs up my spine and I come hard and fast, buried deep inside her, giving her everything I have. It's fucking ecstasy. After a few more seconds, I collapse backwards onto the floor, pulling her with me to lie against my chest. We're both slicked with sweat and breathing like we just ran a marathon.

"Holy shit," she pants as I run my hands up and down her back. "That was...holy shit." My lips curl upwards.

"You said that already."

She laughs lightly before rolling off of me to sprawl on her back beside me. She reaches over and grips my hand, squeezing gently.

"What are the odds that your parents are mostly deaf and didn't hear any of that?"

"Not good," I tell her honestly, and chuckle when she covers her face with her hands, groaning. I somehow manage to stand and tug her hands away, pulling her up beside me. "Come on, you. It's time for a shower."

Her eyes light up at that and she goes up on her tiptoes to kiss me again before sauntering towards the bathroom door, putting an extra little roll in her hips just to drive me crazy, I know it.

The shower turned into her finishing what she started in the living room and me returning the favor while she sat on the built-in tiled bench. Now, we're snuggled up in my bed, her back to my chest and my arms wrapped tightly around her. If she's nervous about sleeping together for the first time—like *literally* sleeping—she's doing a damn good job of hiding it. I should probably be freaking out a bit too, honestly, but I'm not. I feel perfectly content at the thought of going to sleep with Nat in my arms and waking up the same way. *See*, I tell myself. *This relationship thing isn't that scary after all.*

I kiss her temple and she sighs, leaning down to kiss my forearm where it's wrapped around her chest and my lips quirk.

"You freaking out?" she asks, reading my thoughts from just a moment ago.

"Nope," I assure her. "I wouldn't let you leave now for a million bucks, Nat. But *you* were the one that flipped last time I suggested a slumber party, if you recall. So...how are you feeling?"

"Ok, that's fair. But you couldn't *make* me leave for a million bucks," she says sleepily, and I can hear the smile in her voice.

"Good night, Nat."

"Night, AJ," she says with a big yawn.

I glance at the clock and smile. It's after midnight. I lean in and kiss her once more before whispering in her ear, "Merry Christmas."

With that, I drift off to sleep happier than I can ever remember being.

Nineteen

RIZZO

I wake to empty arms in an empty bed. I frown, sitting up and rubbing my eyes as I glance around the room. No sign of Nat. I hadn't dreamed all of that, had I? No, there's no way in hell even my wildest dreams could have come up with the utter perfection that was last night. Shit, she hadn't freaked out again and bailed early this morning, had she?

I run my hands through my hair, worry worming its way inside my mind, but then I hear faint laughter coming from down the hall and relax, recognizing Nat's voice. I realize then that this was the first night in weeks that I haven't had that damned nightmare about Mac's place. Am I over them finally or...was it having Nat here with me somehow eased my mind, even in sleep? I sigh, assuming the latter because that just makes sense. She soothes my soul in too many ways to count just by being near me.

God, I'm a fucking sap.

It takes me a second to remember that it's Christmas morning, and the thought makes me smile widely. The first Christmas in my first house, with my first...girlfriend, surrounded by the people I love. It's a lot, but not in a *going to freak the fuck out* kind of way. In a good way. In the best way.

I rummage in the closet and pull on one of my old Viper sweatshirts before padding down the hall. Delicious smells waft towards me and my stomach rumbles loudly as my mouth waters. The best part of having mom in town is always the home-cooked meals, but I didn't expect her to get up this morning and make breakfast. There's already a fire roaring in the hearth and soft Christmas music plays from the Bluetooth speakers installed throughout the house. The sight before me sends a swift, unexpected jolt through my chest: mom and Nat cooking together in the kitchen, laughing and smiling like they've done it a thousand times, and Ray seated at the island drinking coffee, looking on like he's never been happier. *My family.*

Fuck.

And not fuck as in I'm ready to cut and run, but fuck as in I'm done for. This is it for me. I already know it and while that should absolutely scare the shit out of me, it doesn't. It excites me and makes my chest feel all warm and fuzzy and *fuck, who the hell am I even right now?* I should be running for the hills. I should be afraid of all of this happening so fast. I should be apprehensive about diving so deep in my first real adult relationship. But I'm not. I'm all fucking in and it feels one thousand percent right.

But I can't even imagine saying something so insane to Nat yet. So, I'll just keep that ridiculous little nugget of crazy tucked way down deep for now, and run to Shep for advice later like I do with just about everything. He always knows the right answer and never sugar coats shit. If I'm being an idiot, he tells me. If I'm being an asshole, he tells me. And if I'm being completely fucking nuts by feeling this much for Nat already then he'll tell me that too.

Nat looks up and catches my eye across the open space as I make my way through the living room. She gives me a warm, secret smile, and a *you doing ok with all this?* look. I smile back and nod, telling her that I'm doing just fine. Mom glances up then and smiles widely.

"Merry Christmas, sweetheart!" she says, sheer joy shining in her blue eyes that she passed down to me. This is the first Christmas morning we've spent together in a long time. Once I got older, she and Ray started a tradition of taking little trips for Christmas. They've been all over the world together. Sometimes it's a cozy cabin deep in the

Canadian mountains. Others it's a ritzy resort in the Swedish Alps. Sometimes the beach, sometimes a ranch. I can't believe they postponed this one, but I can't deny that I'm grateful as hell. And I know Shep will eat it up since mom said the reason was mostly due to him.

"Merry Christmas," I say, slapping Ray on the shoulder as I pass and coming around the counter. Mom wraps me in a tight hug, kissing my cheek when I pull away.

"Morning. Merry Christmas," I say, leaning in to kiss Nat softly on the temple, making her blush ever so slightly. She's in a pair of old pajama pants that Shep had gotten me for my birthday a few years back with flying pigs on them, and an old Cornell Hockey t-shirt. Her hair is up in one of those messy buns that look so damn good on her and it takes a whole lot of effort to keep my hands to myself. I love the fact that she helped herself to my clothes and felt comfortable enough to come out here and cook with mom on her own. Is all of this real? Is this some kind of dream? This is all too fucking perfect, right? Doesn't something awful have to happen now, like someone gets shot or kidnapped or we break up over some stupid miscommunication?

"Merry Christmas to you too, sleepy head." I roll my eyes at her but lean in to check out all the plates and platters and bowls full of enough food to feed a small army they have laid out across the black marble countertop.

"It smells amazing in here."

"We've got pancakes, bacon, eggs, French toast, and biscuits."

I blink. "I really had all that shit in here?"

"I stocked the kitchen the other day when you were playing in the garage with Jax," Nat says with a laugh. "I thought we should probably have some supplies on hand on the very good chance half the damn team ended up here at some point this week." I smile at her, knowing she's probably right.

"Oh, who is Jax?" mom asks, pulling finished biscuits off of the baking sheet and onto the platter.

"He used to work security at the apartment—you met him last year when you came out for Fourth of July I think. Anyway, he's kind of a jack of all trades and I figured I could use the help around here, and I really like the kid, so." I shrug a shoulder.

I'd offered Jax a job working for me directly when I'd moved out of the complex, and he'd jumped at the chance. He's a good kid and a hard worker, and knows a shit ton about a shit ton, but especially cars. His dad owned a garage when he was a kid and it's his dream to open his own one day too. So, I figure I can help get him closer to that dream because God knows I'm paying him more than the apartment was, and he can help keep my cars running and take care of stuff around here, especially when we're traveling. I trust him to take care of the place and I know he'd much rather be out here than sitting at that desk in a suit. So, it's a win-win.

"The Mustang is looking really good, son," Ray says, taking a sip of his coffee. I grin at the mug—it's a giant Stitch head and one of my favorites. Mac has a weird obsession with coffee cups (though she hardly ever actually *uses* any of them, she just likes to collect and display them), and has found random ones for each of the Sin Bin members. I fucking love that little blue alien and I don't even care if it's a kid's movie. *This is my family. I found it all on my own. It's little and broken, but still good—*get the fuck outta here. I cry like a baby every damn time. Memories flare up in my mind of mom and me in our tiny little apartment watching that movie over and over because it was one of the very few DVDs we had and we couldn't afford cable. *We* were little and broken, but still really fucking good. To say it's a sentimental attachment is an understatement.

I clear my throat and focus back on the conversation.

"Thanks, I just got the paint touched up a few months ago, and Jax is obsessed with washing and waxing the damn thing." Ray laughs and then mom claps her hands.

"Alright everyone: dig in!"

We all eat breakfast, open gifts, and spend the rest of the day just enjoying our time together. Nat texts her dad to tell him Merry Christmas, and though I know she isn't ready to get back to whatever their version of normal is, I'm happy when his reply makes a soft smile pull her lips upward. We all go over and visit with Shep, and mom frets over him like he's a baby bird who fell out of the nest. He doesn't even try to pretend that he doesn't love it. Mom basically adopted him as her second son after he lost his parents, and we've all been family for the better part of my life.

The fact that Mac and Nat are now part of it as well feels like everything is exactly how it's supposed to be.

"So, uh, I did a thing..." I say, walking to the edge of the ice with a four-legged fluff ball at my side, tail wagging like crazy as he eyes the ice with a mix of mistrust and excitement.

"Is that a dog??" Jules yells, skating over.

"No, it's a fucking goldfish," I say with a roll of my eyes and he gives me a level look, but it doesn't last long. A smile splits his face as he leans down to give the expected pets.

"What the hell, Rizzo?" Shep says, shaking his head. It's not an official practice, but a few of us showed up to just fuck around a bit. Shep has been dying being sidelined because of his injury, and while he isn't ready to suit up and get in the net quite yet—well, *he's* more than ready, but the doctors haven't given him the green light yet—he can skate around for a while with us at least. I was out for a month with a torn rotator cuff a few years back and had felt utterly homesick not being out there with my guys. So, I understand what he's going through and how much it sucks.

"Well, I came extremely close to telling Nat that I fucking loved her, so instead of doing that, I freaked out and got a dog. It seemed perfectly logical at the time, I swear to God."

They both start busting out laughing as a few more guys make their way to the ice from the locker room. Nat and I are keeping things somewhat quiet for now—most of the team knows, of course, but we aren't blasting it on social media or anything yet—but the Sin Bin know *all* the details and just how bad I've got it already.

Jules continues to pet the dog, and gets a goofy puppy smile in return, tongue lolling out of the side of his mouth. He's a cute fucker, that's for sure.

I'd *just* stopped myself from saying the words to Nat before we hung up the phone yesterday afternoon, and I don't know if it was the enormity of that, the fact that I felt it so damn strongly, the fear of her reaction if I did let it slip, or a combination of all three, but I'd somehow decided that a dog would be the perfect thing to put all of that love into until I was ready to say it to Nat. It made sense at the time somehow, though looking back now, it's stupid as hell. I can't say I regret it though.

Jax had come in while I was scrolling through the local animal shelter's website for adoptable dogs.

"Hey, Mr. Rizzo, how's it going?"

"Jax I swear to God if you don't stop calling me *Mr. Rizzo*, we're going to throw down." He'd smiled widely, his pearly whites sparkling almost as brightly as the diamond stud in his ear.

"Sorry, old habits. Hey *Rizzo*, how's it going?"

"Better. And, uh, good. Mostly. I think. Hey do you know anything about dogs?"

"Dogs?" His brow furrowed as he washed his hands in the kitchen.

"Yeah, I'm thinking about getting one..."

"Oh, nice. I love dogs, had 'em all my life. I actually helped train search and rescue dogs with my cousin for a while after high school."

"Soooo, you're saying you could be persuaded to add dog trainer to your list of job titles here? For extra compensation, of course," I'd asked with a grin.

"Mr.—" He'd stopped himself when I shot him a look. "Rizzo," he corrected with a smile, "you're already paying me way too much. I'm happy to help with the dog—and actually I know of one who needs a home if you're interested. A guy in my building is getting stationed overseas and can't take his golden with him. He's about six months old and already crate and potty trained and everything. Crazy as hell, but a really good dog."

One thing led to another, and first thing this morning, I was picking up a dog. I'd fallen in love with the goofy boy the minute I laid eyes on him and he'd immediately jumped into my arms, resting his paws on my shoulders like a child.

"So, uh, yeah, I guess I was having a mini-freak out and decided the dog made more sense than scaring Nat off or saying the words out loud or fuck if I know, really, but anyway: everyone meet Zamboni."

He barks and wags his tail even faster. I know there's no way in hell he actually knows that's his new name yet, but I'll pretend that's a sign that he likes the sound of it and is totally on board with the change. No offense to the guy I got him from, but Buckley was a horrible name.

Zamboni leans his head out over the ice, sniffing, and then reaches out one tentative paw. He scratches experimentally at the ice, and then looks up at me, smiling again. I swear to God he seriously fucking *smiles*. It's crazy.

"Well come on, buddy. You're the new unofficial Vipers mascot—better get used to the ice." I move to step out onto the rink and coax him to follow. He's a little unsure at first, but then the idiot goes absolutely wild, running and sliding and falling and having the time of his damn life. Everyone laughs and plays with him and I make a mental note to see if Mac and Nat can find a dog-sized Vipers jersey for him. Maybe my social media feed will be filled with Zamboni pics and vids from now on instead of thirst traps. It feels weird to keep doing those when I'm dating someone, though Nat hasn't said anything about it.

"Ollie is going to flip," Shep says, leaning back against the wall as we watch Howey and Jules play chase with the dog. We both laugh when Zamboni runs and throws himself down, sliding on his stomach across half the ice before jumping up and doing it over again and again.

"I thought as much. I'll bring him over tonight if you want."

"Sounds good, we'll order pizza." He turns his head and gives me one of those looks. "So, you almost dropped the L bomb, huh?"

"Shut up," I grumble.

"Nah, man, it's great. I'm just still in shock I think. I mean, if you'd asked me a couple of months ago if Anthony Rizzo would ever be caught dead in a relationship, let alone completely in love and ready to start playing house—don't even act like you haven't thought about moving her into your place, I know you fucking have." He's right, I have. Yet another thing I'm not bringing up yet because—*crazy*. "I would have told you that you'd taken one too many hits to the dome."

"I know. It really is fucking crazy. I one thousand percent thought I'd have freaked out about all of this commitment stuff at least twenty times by now or royally fucked up somehow, but I'm good. Really good. I mean, we shouldn't be surprised that I'm excelling at this like I excel in everything," I add with a cocky grin and Shep punches me in the shoulder. I rub the spot but laugh. Despite my initial apprehension about dating, it's been amazing. There have been zero doubts or regrets. I don't miss the random hookups at all—even tossed my Slut Cell as Jules calls it into the lake—and having someone to actually *share* my life with is hitting more harder than I would have thought. My life was fine before, great even, but this is so much better than I could have imagined. I realize now that it wasn't a matter of being afraid to date, it was waiting for the right person to do it with, and that is one thousand percent Nat.

"I'm really happy for you, man."

"Thanks, Con," I say, a little more seriously than before. "Seeing you with Mac...well, it kind of changed the way I look at all this shit, honestly. So, you're part of the reason I finally grew up and wanted something more than one-night stands and back-room hookups."

He grins. "Those are fun, but," he shakes his head and I can see in his eyes how much he fucking loves Mac, "having something more with someone who really *gets* you like no one else, who loves you for all the good and the bad and everything in between—who loves you *through* the good and the bad—well, it's pretty fucking life-altering."

"Life-altering is right." He reaches over and grips my shoulder, squeezing tightly. We share a very manly bromance moment, and then I pull out my phone. "Wanna torture the girls with videos of an adorable puppy that they can't immediately pet?"

Shep laughs and rubs his hands together like a villain.

"Oh, absolutely."

Twenty

NAT

"I'M PRETTY SURE ZAMBONI'S POSTS ARE GETTING EVEN MORE attention than your shirtless ones!" I call from the couch, grinning while I scroll through the Clipper app. Everyone is completely in love with the Vipers' newest little mascot and the videos of him running around the ice or pretending to run concessions or up in the broadcast booth with a headset on are getting mega views. I reach out and pet the lump of fur currently snoozing on my feet. He thumps his tail happily in his sleep and I grin.

AJ comes back into the room and hands me a beer, eyeing the couch where there's no room left for him thanks to the way Zamboni is sprawled out, and settling into the chair to my left instead.

"Speaking of: you haven't been posting those so much lately." I quirk a brow in question.

"Oh, yeah. Well...I kind of thought you'd be upset if I did?" I laugh at that and his brow furrows.

"I won't be upset," I assure him. He gives me a very dubious look. "I swear. For one, it's like your thing, you can't stop that now just because we're together. You're extremely sexy and that should be shared with the world," I shrug. "Plus, well...I dunno, it's kind of hot to see all these people out there thirsting over you but knowing that you're in *my* bed.

Or, well, I'm in yours technically I suppose since we usually stay here, but, yeah."

He narrows his eyes at me.

"What?" I ask, throwing up my hands.

"I'm trying to figure out if you're fucking with me or if this is some kind of test. Like a boyfriend test that I really don't want to fail." I laugh at that and ease out from beneath Zamboni's head. He opens one eye to squint at me, but I scratch his ear and he lays back down happy enough. I set my beer down on the side table and slide into AJ's lap, straddling his waist while I drape my arms over his shoulders. He gives me a low, appreciative hum, running his free hand over one thigh.

"No tests. No tricks. I'm serious. If you want to keep posting them, do it. Every like and comment just fuels my little ego knowing that I have what they want. What they get to fantasize about, I get to touch and taste. It's probably a fucked up way to look at it, but it's the truth." I shrug. It's true. I mean, it's human nature to have what other people covet, right? It's why we buy expensive cars and watches and purses.

He sets his beer to the side and slides his hand to my nape, pulling me to him for a slow, lazy kiss that makes my pulse race and my toes curl. There's a promise of pure fire beneath that kiss, the vow that it will burn out of control soon enough. We've honestly been fucking like rabbits since we started this thing and I can't say that I'm mad about it. He wasn't kidding when he said he had plans for me all over the house. We even made a legit list one night—alcohol may have been involved—and have it taped up beside the dresser in the bedroom. We've marked off about a third of it and though there are a few that I'm really not quite sure are even physically possible, it's a hell of a sexy, fun game making our way through the list.

He runs his hand up my thigh and over my side, slipping his fingers beneath my shirt as he moves his hand higher over my bare back. I shiver at his touch, little sparks of desire dancing over every inch that his skin touches mine. He tilts his head and deepens the kiss, still keeping things slow and measured, but there's command and dominance in the way he controls the kiss. *It's going to be one of those nights then*, I think with a grin. Sometimes, he's in complete control and I'm all too happy to surrender to him, letting him do anything and everything he wants.

Others, he wants to relax and let me call the shots. Sometimes it's hot and heavy and frenzied. Others slow and sweet and passionate. He's showed me new tricks that make me wet just to think about, and there are times when the way he looks at me, I would swear it's like I'm the only woman he's ever seen or can remember.

He kisses down my neck and I tilt my head back to give him better access. He knows exactly where to flick his tongue or graze his teeth to drive me wild.

"We...haven't hit the garage yet..." I gasp when he sucks gently at the spot where my neck meets my shoulder, the sensation sending ripples of pleasure through every inch of me.

"Mmm, I could be persuaded..."

My phone rings then and I groan. I glance over and see that dad is calling me. I haven't spoken to him since our fight at the restaurant, though we did exchange *Merry Christmas* texts. I've been trying really hard to find it in me to forgive him, and I think I mostly have, but that doesn't mean that we're on good terms. I sigh and turn my head back to meet AJ's eyes.

"I should answer," I sigh.

He kisses me quickly. "Go head, babe. We've got all night..."

The promise sends a little shiver down my spine but I reluctantly ease off of him and grab my phone.

"Hello."

"Oh, hello, Natalie. I wasn't expecting you to answer."

"Well, I did," I say. I wander towards the back of the room to the wall-to-wall glass doors and stare out into the woods, the mountains far in the distance just hulking shadows right now in the darkness. "Look, dad, I'm tired of being mad at you. I know you didn't mean to say what you did about mom."

"I didn't and I'm sorry, Natalie. I was frustrated and it didn't come out right at all." I nod to myself, knowing that if dad is apologizing he actually means it. It doesn't happen often.

"I know. And I'm over it now but I need to know if you're past the rest of that conversation. I need to know if you're ready to accept that my life is my own, and stop belittling the things that make me happy for fuck's sake. I need to know if you're ready to drop this job thing."

"I'm...not, no. Not entirely." I sigh and see in the reflection that AJ standing in the middle of the living room behind me, arms crossed and looking tense.

"Then I'm not ready to have a relationship with you right now. I'm not mad. I don't hate you. I love you, dad, despite all of our bullshit, I do, but I'm not going to have a relationship with you if you can't accept me and my life as they are, if you can't...love me for who I am instead of who you want me to be. And I'm not sorry for that. I'm happier than I have ever been, and if you can't see that and be ok with it, then I'm ok not having you be a part of that happiness." Tears prick my eyes, but I won't back down from this. I've given it way too much thought in these weeks since our fight, since Shep and Hattie almost died, since I started things with AJ and I've been so fucking happy that I feel like my heart may literally break from it.

And I knew that this might be his answer. I prepared myself to have this conversation, but that doesn't mean it doesn't hurt like hell to have him actively *choose* not to be a part of my life. I don't think he's doing it out of malice or spite, it's just the way he is. He's used to getting what he wants and knowing more than anyone else in the room. He's one of the top guys in the industry for a reason. He's confident and sure and isn't used to being told no or not having his requests—or demands—met. So, I don't blame him, exactly, but I won't just roll over or look past it. Not this time. Not anymore.

"Natalie," he says, and I can hear exasperation in his voice, but a bit of pain too. He knows I'm not joking and I guess it counts for something that he cares enough to be wounded by it, but it doesn't bother him enough to just swallow his pride and let this notion that I'm going to follow in his footsteps and carry on the family legacy go. So, this is where we are.

"Let me know when you're ready and I'll be here dad. Love you." With that I hang up, not waiting to hear if he says it back. I close my eyes and lean my forehead against the cool glass. A second later, strong arms wrap around me from behind and AJ rests his chin on my head.

"You alright?"

I sigh and turn in his arms, snaking my hands up his chest and around the back of his neck.

"I am, actually. I've thought through all of this a lot and until he can accept my life as-is and understand that he doesn't get to make decisions for me anymore, then we aren't going to have a real relationship. It sucks since he's all I have left, but this is what's right for me. Sometimes you have to draw lines even when they fucking hurt."

"Well, I'm proud of you," he says. "That has to be hard as hell and I don't know if I'd have the balls to do it if I were you, honestly."

"Lucky for you, you'll never have to. Your parents are proud of you no matter what you decide to do." I start a list. "Fail miserably at musical theater, become a star hockey player, reign as Seattle's biggest slut for what is it now? Almost ten years running?" I squeal when he starts to tickle me. I try to break free from his grip but all those hours at the gym have done him good and I'm powerless.

"Think you're soooo funny, don't you, Natalie..." He freezes and cocks his head. "I just realized I don't know your middle name. I can't scold you properly without a middle name."

"Celeste," I say breathless. "Natalie Celeste."

"Pretty," he says before that wicked gleam shines in his blue eyes again and the torture resumes. "Think you're soooo funny, don't you, Natalie Celeste Morgan?" I can hardly breathe around the laughter, tears running down my cheeks, and finally he stops, sweeping me up in one smooth motion. He tosses me over his shoulder in that weirdly attractive semi-caveman kind of way.

"Time to teach you some manners."

"Ok, we have a problem. Def Con One. Or Five. Whatever the bad one is, I don't fucking know."

Bobby snorts into his beer and Hattie grins, biting into another onion ring. The guys are gone for a three-city string of away games, and though I'll admit that I miss AJ more than I thought I would after just a couple of days, the sexting and videos have kept things very entertaining.

"Both of you shut up and help me please."

"Ok, ok, what's the problem?" Bobby asks. "Is your insanely attractive boyfriend giving you too many orgasms with his giant di—" Hattie busts out laughing, cutting off the end of his sentence.

"Why am I friends with you again?" I ask, throwing an onion ring at him. "And don't be jealous that I'm getting some finally." His face falls for the briefest of seconds and a swift jolt of guilt punches me right in the gut. I knew that he and Mystery Guy from a couple of months back didn't turn into anything, but he'd said it was fine, that he didn't care and it was just a stupid fling anyway. So, why the flash of hurt in his eyes? I don't want to pry, but if it was more than that and he's been upset all this time, I hate that he didn't think he could tell us. We'll be diving more into that soon, maybe after a few more drinks.

"Ok, seriously, what's the problem?" Hattie asks, regaining her composure.

"The V word is the problem."

Bobby purses his lips.

"Venereal Disease? Do you need to go to the doctor?" I press my lips into a thin line and he grins widely. "Ok, I'm done, I promise. V word... ohhhh, Valentine's Day?"

"Yes, that one. I'm not sure how to handle it?"

"What do you mean?" Hattie asks, brow furrowed.

"Did you already forget that until very recently, a certain star center was allergic to relationships and all things love-related? And I haven't told him yet, but I am already very much in love with the idiot..."

Hattie gasps and jumps up and down in her seat. I smile but roll my eyes.

"As if you couldn't tell already."

"Well, yeah, it's pretty damn obvious actually," Bobby agrees, "but it's nice to hear you admit it out loud." I kick him in the shin under the table and he grunts before laughing.

"Well even without admitting it to *him* out loud yet, I don't want him to feel pressure or freak out about Valentine's or anything."

"Have you talked to him about it?" Bobby asks, taking another sip of his beer. He seems tense and I worry again that whatever happened with him and Mystery Guy left him feeling some sort of way, and talk of the holiday centered around love isn't helping.

"He brought it up the other day and it was adorably awkward. Out of nowhere he just goes "Valentine's. We…do that, right?" I had no idea how to take that so I just said "sure" but then he got his concentration face on and I'm worried he's thinking he has to go all out or something. And he so doesn't. I don't even really care about the stupid holiday other than the half-priced candy the day after. I mean, no hate to anyone who likes it. In theory, it's nice that there's a day dedicated to love and all of that, but…I dunno. Maybe I'm just cynical."

Hattie gives me a crooked smirk.

"You're talking to the girl who hated Christmas up until a month ago. I'm the queen of cynical when it comes to holidays and expectations that go with them. But that being said, it's actually nice as hell to put all that stuff aside and just enjoy the days for what they are: a time to be with the people you care about and be grateful that they exist. Or, ya know, didn't get murdered by a psychopath in my living room when said psychopath tried to kidnap me." She hikes a shoulder when Bobby and I both give her level looks. "What!? I can't joke about it?"

"Too soon, Hads. Too fucking soon," Bobby says shaking his head. He'd been so upset that he hadn't been here for all of the crazy and to help out afterwards. He'd felt like he let us all down or something even though we assured him a thousand times that he was where he was supposed to be: visiting his family for Christmas. Which is literally the point Hattie is making right now.

"So ignoring that totally fucked up comment," I say, giving her a pointed look that only makes her smile bigger, showing off her damn dimples that I'm only a little bit jealous of, "I'll make sure he knows there's no pressure but will go with the flow on whatever he decides to do. But, uh, any suggestions on what to get a guy for Valentine's Day?"

"You in lingerie," Hattie and Bobby both say at the same time. They look at each other and crack up and I take a long drink, though my wheels are turning. AJ *is* particularly fond of lingerie…

Twenty-One

RIZZO

"ARE YOU SURE YOU WANT TO GO OUT?" NAT ASKS FOR THE third time. We've been kind of laying low with our relationship as far as being in the public eye, so we haven't had many nights out on the town, just the two of us. I'm not some mega celebrity or anything, but I am pretty recognizable around Seattle and there are plenty of paparazzi and news outlets that like to lurk around and catch the local athletes and musicians whenever they can. I don't particularly care if the whole fucking planet knows that I'm seeing Nat, but she didn't choose a life in any kind of spotlight. It's not fair of me to shove her into one until she's ready.

"I swear to God if you ask me again, I'm going to introduce you to one of my favorite words, Natalie."

"And what would that be?" she asks, half challenge, half intrigue.

I turn and hold her gaze when we stop at a red light. I slowly inch my hand upward from where it rests on her leg just above the top of her thigh-high boot. The combination of the tall boots and short skirt made my pulse and cock both jump when she'd opened the door. We almost hadn't left the house at all and spent the entire night in bed instead, but knowing what I had planned for the evening I'd forced myself to behave. Mostly.

She moans quietly when my fingers brush the silk of her panties, stroking gently.

"*Edging*," I whisper, that simple word holding the promise of so much. She gasps, her pupils dilating.

"Is that supposed to be a threat?" she asks as I continue moving my fingers. I chuckle low.

"Oh sweetheart, you have no idea..." I start to pull my hand away and she arches her hips forward, silently begging for more. My lips curl. Oh this is going to be fun.

"Are you sure you don't just want to go home right now..." She bites her lip, her voice full of a nervous hope. I settle my hand on her knee and squeeze gently.

"Patience, baby. *Patience*." She squirms a little and I laugh, my nerves forgotten for a moment. But all too soon, my heart is galloping like a fucking Clydesdale inside my chest again. *It'll be fine*. I'd admittedly been a little worried about the whole Valentine's Day thing. I mean, it's not like I have any experience being a boyfriend on this particular holiday or anything and I wasn't sure if Nat had big expectations, but, as usual, Shep helped me figure my shit out.

"I don't know what the fuck to do here, Shep," I'd said, running my hands through my hair in frustration while we sat on two benches in the gym. "Do I go super huge? Or intimate? Do I just do something stupid like a stuffed animal and some candy? Or maybe jewelry?"

"I think you need to chill before you hyperventilate." He'd grinned and I'd scowled.

"What's so fucking funny?"

"It's just nice seeing Mr. Cool and Collected, Always Knows What Women Want freaking out about Valentine's Day."

"Fuck off, asshole." He chuckled and I'd thrown a towel at his face. "Help, damn it."

"Ok, ok, here's what you need to do: stop focusing on the holiday and the pressures of it, and just think about what you would want to do for Nat on a random Tuesday in the middle of September to show her you love her. Big. Small. Whatever. Just do that and stop worrying about all the extra shit just because of the day."

He'd made it seem so fucking simple, and the plan started to form almost immediately. Now I pull into a parking spot around the corner from the bar and cut the engine, quickly hopping out and coming around to her door to open it for her.

"Well, aren't you the gentleman?" she says with a smile as she takes my hand and I help her up. I don't even try to hide my attempt to catch a glimpse up her skirt and she swats at my chest playfully as she stands and tugs her skirt down. Her hair is pulled half up, the rest down in loose, sexy waves that cascade down her back like a waterfall of gold. I reach out and push a few strands away from her temple, grazing my knuckles softly down her cheek before stepping back onto the sidewalk.

"Gentleman in the streets. Freak in the sheets," I confirm with a grin.

"Oh don't I know it," she says quietly. She glances at my hand but quickly pulls her gaze back up to look around. I shake my head in exasperation and grab her hand, interlacing our fingers and bringing the back of her hand to my lips. "You sure?" she asks again and I give her a look that promises she'll regret that. She bites her lip, not seeming too upset about it whatsoever.

We head down the sidewalk and a light snow begins to fall. Nat leans her head back and smiles, and all I can do is stare. I know it sounds cliché as hell, but she literally steals the breath from my lungs.

We round the corner and I usher her to the front of Delaney's. She seems to relax when she sees where we're going and confirms that I hadn't been lying about our casual night out. Then recognition flashes in her eyes and she gives me a sly smile.

"I remember this place."

"Oh really? Hmm, hot date with an even hotter guy, perhaps?"

I reach the door first and meet her gaze before I pull it open. She smirks and hikes a shoulder.

"Eh, he turned out alright, I guess." I narrow my eyes and she chuckles. I lean in to give her a quick kiss and let the feel of her lips on mine calm my racing heart.

Here goes nothing.

I pull the door open and step aside, gesturing for her to go in first. She keeps her eyes on me for a moment as she walks through the door, but then she turns to look inside and freezes.

"AJ, what…"

I put a hand on the small of her back and usher her further inside so we can close the door against the chill outside. The entire place is empty, save Sean behind the bar who inclines his head to us in greeting, and Erica, who's standing in the middle of the room and gesturing to the small table along the back wall. Almost every other surface is covered in arrangements of lilies and roses and peonies—her favorite flowers—and twinkling lights.

I usher her to the table while she stares around the bar, speechless. My heart is thundering my chest, but I feel good. Better than good. I help Nat out of her coat and Erica takes it with a warm smile, holding her hand out for mine next. Nat settles into her chair and I slide into the one across from her.

"Drinks?" Erica asks.

"I'll, uh, have a rum and coke please," Nat says, still very much confused.

"Guinness. Thanks, Erica."

She nods and heads off to hang up our coats and grab our drinks.

"Ok, what exactly is happening here?" Nat asks, leaning towards me.

"This is our Valentine's Day, Nat." She blinks and I lean my elbows on the table. "There's so much pressure to do a big thing on the fourteenth, but I didn't want to wait until then to—" I stop talking when Erica comes back, leaning away a bit so she can set down our drinks and a basket of cheese curds. Nat smiles and I grin. I know my girl and her love of all things fried cheese. She grabs one and pops it into her mouth, lips curling up while she waits for me to finish. I take a long sip of my drink and then a deep breath. I let it out slowly.

"I didn't want to wait until then to bring you back to the place that it happened."

"The place that what happened?"

"The place that I fell in love with you." Her lips part as she inhales sharply. "In this bar, at this table, I knew I was done for, Natalie. I knew that night, before we even went back to my place, that I was a goner." Her eyes water but I don't stop. I don't think I can now that I've started. "You've been one of my best friends, you know me better than almost anyone else in the world and aren't afraid to call me on my bullshit when I need it most." She huffs out a laugh as a tear escapes from the corner of one eye, slowly rolling down her cheek. I'm really fucking hoping that's a tear of joy. I reach over and grip her hand, running my thumb in slow circles over her smooth skin. "You make me laugh even when I don't want to. You make me feel like I'm more than just a name on the back of a jersey. You...you're everything, Nat. *Everything*. I love you. I'm *in* love with you. And I really fucking hope you love me back because I've never done this before and I'm admittedly feeling a little vulnerable."

She laughs again, smiling through the tears. She reaches across the small table and grips the front of my shirt, pulling me into a kiss that makes my heart stutter and my blood turn to straight fire.

"I love you too," she whispers against my lips. I feel like my chest may crack in two from the eruption of pure fucking joy that her words send through me. My lips curl upward and I kiss her again, cradling her cheek with my hand. I really wish there wasn't a table between us right now and that we weren't in a fucking bar. Maybe this was a terrible plan after all.

Nat pulls away first and when I meet her gaze, we both smile like idiots.

"I can't believe you planned all this. Did you practice that speech?"

"Not at all. I had a whole other one written that quoted Shakespeare and Celine Dion and shit, but I decided to just go off script instead." She snorts and tosses a cheese curd at me. I catch it and pop it in my mouth, giving her a huge smile. God this might be the best day of my life.

We eat and drink and laugh and dance...and possibly hook up in the storage room. It's all fucking perfect, every single minute of it. Jax picked up the Maserati not long after we'd gotten here and Jerry is waiting outside for us when we finally stumble back out into the snow. We barely keep our hands to ourselves in the car, but don't make it past the entry way once we're finally back at my place. What feels like hours later, we're sprawled out in front of the fire place in the living room. I'm not exactly sure when or how we made it from the foyer to here, but this is where we're spending the night because I don't think either of us can move a muscle.

Shep and the crew have Zamboni, thank God, so the only thing I have to worry about for the rest of the night is finding the strength to grab pillows and a blanket from the couch a few feet away. I grunt as I heave myself up, grab the goods, and settle back down beside a nearly comatose Natalie. I throw the blanket over us and maneuver the pillow under my head, tucking Nat's against my chest.

"That sounded like it was difficult," she mutters.

"It was a Herculean effort, I'm not gonna lie. I think you fucked me into near immobility, Natalie Morgan." She snorts and snuggles in closer to my side.

"I think this might just be the greatest night of my life, Thirst Trap." My lips curl at the corners and I sigh in pure, utter contentment.

"Ditto, Nat. Ditto."

Twenty-Two

NAT

Everything is still a little surreal but I'm leaning into it full force. That night at Delaney's had been...perfect. Absolutely fucking perfect. I never would have thought that Anthony Rizzo would be the king of grand gestures but my God, he aced his first attempt with flying colors. The fact that he'd done it days *before* Valentine's Day instead of *on* it and avoided the cliché of it all made it all that much better. Our first official Valentine's together was a nice, lowkey affair of pizza, beer, and a fun new set of restraints that attach to the bed. It had been one hell of a night.

I'll hand it to him. He's really rocking this whole relationship thing like a pro seeing as it's his first one. I know that it's all a bit crazy and fast, but I can't quite make myself care. It feels too right to worry about if anyone else thinks we're moving too quickly or thinks we're insane.

"You remember when you called me and Connor disgusting?" Hattie says as we make our way down to the ice for the game. She has a shit-eating grin on her face and I narrow my eyes in mock annoyance.

"Shut it," I tell her. "We aren't nearly as bad as you two."

"Lies. You're worse," Bobby says, falling into step beside us.

"I hate you both, have I mentioned that lately?" They both laugh and we stop and grab beers and snacks before we had down to our customary spot at the glass. We settle in and watch as the guys stretch on the ice. AJ meets my eyes across the rink and gives me a cocky smile and a wink. Shep does the same to Hattie and...I follow Bobby's gaze where it locks with Jules' in a weirdly tense moment before they both look off in other directions, as if pretending they didn't see each other. *Hmm...*

"Did you and Jules get in a fight or something?" I ask.

"What? No...well, kind of yeah. It's nothing though, just stupid stuff. So, how are things on the dad front?" he asks, quickly changing the subject. *We'll be circling back to that later. No way it's nothing...I wonder...*

"No real change. He's not ready to accept my life and stop trying to control it, so I'm not ready for us to have a relationship." I shrug. "Simple as that."

Hattie reaches over and squeezes my forearm.

"I know that's gotta be rough though, even if y'all weren't super close to begin with."

"It is what it is," I sigh. It does suck but I'm not going to budge.

"So when are you guys gonna go official official?" I give Bobby a confused look and he clarifies, "Like social media and magazine covers and the whole nine yards?"

"I don't know, I feel like that'll jinx us or something."

"Oh please," Hattie says, rolling her eyes. "Y'all are end game, I know it."

I feel like even thinking it really will somehow ruin everything, but I can see myself with AJ forever. I can see a life, a family, all of it. I laugh her off and we chat about other things while we wait for the game to start.

When the second period ends, we're up five-one.

"Damn, Nat, you must be his good luck charm because Rizzo is on fucking fire!" Bobby yells when the crowd erupts as Rosie, the goalie filling in for Shep until he's greenlit to come back, makes a save. He's pretty good, but he's no Connor Shepherd. The doctors are telling him it'll be another month, at least, but knowing him, he'll be back in another two weeks, tops. He's stubborn as hell and looks like he's coming out of his skin watching the game from the bench.

I grin before cupping my hands around my mouth and yelling with everyone else. He skates backwards by us then, grinning and gliding his glove over the glass. I shake my head and mouth *showoff* before he turns and skates off again. He really has been killing it these past few weeks, even breaking the Vipers' all-time goals scored record. AJ said the same thing, that I was his lucky charm, but I won't give these two the satisfaction of agreeing with them.

"He's Irish—he's just got good luck in his veins," I call back and they both give me looks that say I'm full of shit. I stick out my tongue at them and then grab everyone nachos, feeling like I'm on top of the world.

As soon as he walks out of the locker room after the game, I can't help but leap into his waiting arms and slam my lips to his. Watching him play has always been hot, but watching him play like *that*, like a fucking rock star who met my eyes across the ice at every possible second? It's sexy as hell. His hair is wet from the shower and little droplets of water drip over my fingers as I tangle my hands through it.

"Mmm, a man could get used to this kind of post-game greeting," he murmurs against my lips. I laugh and reluctantly let him put me down so we can walk out to the parking garage. Most everyone else has left already since AJ stayed after to get patched up a bit—nothing major, just a small split over one eyebrow—and do an ice bath, so it's almost deserted. I hop in the passenger seat of the Range Rover while he tosses his stuff in the back. He slides into the driver's seat and I immediately throw myself over the center console and pull his face to mine again. He tangles his hand into my hair, groaning into the kiss that spirals out of control almost immediately.

"Nat?" he asks, half excited, half confused.

"I can't wait until we get back to the house. I want you *now*." The sound he makes is a near growl and then he's got my leggings and panties yanked down faster than I would have thought possible. I kick off my boots and shove the material down the rest of the way, whimpering into his mouth as he thrusts his tongue at the same time he thrusts two fingers exactly where I need him. He pumps them in a deep, hard rhythm and I'm already soaked and ready. Desperate.

"Then get your ass over here, baby," he rasps as he grips my hip and yanks me over his lap. I settle my knees on either side of his hips and I'm so thankful that he didn't decide to bring the Maserati today. That thing is almost impossible to fuck inside. *Almost.* We made it work, but admittedly laughed more than anything trying to figure out the logistics, and that was just in the garage at his house. Now, we don't have that problem and there is no fucking laughing, there's just a fiery, carnal desire that's about to consume me like wildfire burning completely out of control.

I reach down and fumble with the button and zipper of his jeans and he tugs my sweater off, leaving me in just my black lacy bra. I free his cock and he makes a choking-groaning sound as I stroke once, twice, and then quickly position him beneath me. This isn't a slow, sweet bout of sex. This is feral and frenzied and hot as fuck.

I sink down his shaft and cry out, the sound muffled against his lips.

"Ah, fuck Nat! You feel so fucking good." He grips my hips and guides me to start riding him, hard and deep. I grip his shoulders, digging my nails in and holding on for dear life as he starts to buck his hips upward as he wrenches me down. *Fuck, fuck, fuck.* I kiss him again, thrusting and rolling my tongue, demanding and taking what I want. He gives me everything, knowing exactly how to make me so drunk with pleasure that I barely even perceive the world around me. There is no world around me. There's just me and him and our bodies fitting so perfectly together.

"Just like that, baby. God, I love when you ride me..." He sucks on my lower lip and I moan, whipping my hips faster. This angle is sublime. I don't care that we're in public. I don't care that this is ridiculous. I don't care about anything but the man below me and his lips on mine and the thundering of our hearts as we climb and climb and—

Bright flashes of light nearly blind me. I stop moving, frozen in shock.

"What the fuck?" AJ barks.

I blink, trying to force the white spots from my vision. When they clear, my heart sinks. Three guys with cameras surround the outside of the car, snapping picture after picture of us. *Of me fucking riding Anthony Rizzo in the front seat of his car. Shit, shit, shit.* I guess it's a good thing he hadn't taken my bra off or this would have been really, really bad, but it's still not great. I throw an arm over my breasts to cover myself anyway and lean close into AJ's chest.

"Back the fuck up!" he yells at the paparazzi, sounding pissed as hell. The fury in his eyes startles me and I think he might really kill these guys if he gets his hands on them. "So help me God if you're still standing there when I get out of this car..."

We're kind of stuck. If I pull myself off of him *everything* will be on display for the cameras.

"AJ, I can't move...I don't know what to do..." This is beyond mortifying. I've never been caught hooking up in public before. I feel like a stupid teenager caught under the bleachers by the principal.

"Here," he says quietly, and I can tell he's trying to keep his voice level. He grabs my sweater from the other seat and drapes it around me as he hoists me up, effectively shielding me from a *Britney circa 2006* moment, and sets me in the passenger seat. He's all but shaking with anger and irritation, but when he meets my gaze as he shoves his cock back into his pants, there's also fear there. Is he worried that I'll be upset? That I'll blame him? *I* was the one who said I couldn't wait until we got home. He runs his fingers through his hair and then turns to open the door, yelling at the paparazzi some more. They're smart enough to scatter before he even makes it out of the car and I quickly yank up my pants while he chases after them. My heart is beating out of my chest and my arms and legs feel almost numb from the shock of it, but it's slowly starting to wear off. I'm mostly just embarrassed I think.

AJ comes back to the car, slamming the door behind him.

"Fuck!" he yells, starling me as he punches the steering wheel. He squeezes his eyes shut and I reach over and lay a hand on his arm.

"Hey," I say gently. He sighs heavily and opens his eyes, turning to meet my gaze. He looks...distraught.

"I'm so fucking sorry, Nat."

"It's alright. It's not your fault."

"It is though. This shit is my life, not yours. You didn't ask for that."

"I asked for you, and all of this comes with it. It's a small price to pay." He looks like he's trying to gauge if I'm serious or not. "I knew I'd get photographed with you at some point, I just thought I might have my top on when it happened." I smile at him and he huffs out a small laugh. "We'll just have to be more careful next time we decide to fuck in public like horny teenagers, that's all." He slowly relaxes, a small smile curling his own lips.

"So, there's going to be a next time?"

"Oh you better believe it, Thirst Trap…"

"So, do you want Annie's or The Lighthouse?" I ask as I unlock my front door. I need to grab a change of clothes and start some laundry before we head to get some breakfast.

"Hmm, I'm thinking Annie's—they have the best waffles and I'm definitely feeling waffles."

I laugh as we walk through the doorway, rummaging in my purse for my phone. It's been buzzing all morning but I haven't checked my messages yet. AJ and I were…distracted before we left the house. Twice. I look up and scream when I see a man standing at my kitchen island. AJ immediately steps in front of me, pushing me behind him with a sweep of his arm.

"What the fuck?"

"It's fine, AJ. This is my dad." I roll my eyes and step around him. He doesn't completely relax his posture, still eyeing dad mistrustfully. "By all means, let yourself in, dad. Jesus Christ." It takes me a minute to notice how tense he is, almost shaking with…anger? His gray eyes, so like mine, are practically burning with it. What the hell? He ignores my comment about barging in.

"Wonderful, the hockey player is here too," he spits.

"What the hell? What are you doing here?"

"What am I doing here? *What am I doing here??*" He slams a tabloid down on the counter, followed by three more. I stare in horror when I see…me. Me in AJ's lap, half naked in his car, to be exact. *Oh God, the paparazzi from last night.* I don't know why, but I hadn't even considered this as a consequence of being caught in the parking garage. I just thought "oh, well I guess people will know we're dating now, no big deal." I feel so fucking stupid now.

"Oh God," I whisper.

"I wake up this morning to see this shit plastered on every tabloid in the newsstands." I want to point out that hardly anyone actually buys stuff from the newsstands anymore, but I know that doesn't matter. Sure enough, he holds up his phone, open to one of his social media apps. "All over every fucking social media platform." He turns the phone back to him so he can read the caption on one of the posts. "Natalie Morgan, aka Natalie Harrington, daughter of real estate and hospitality mogul and well-known philanthropist, Charles Harrington—"

"Harrington...?" AJ asks, trailing off as realization hits. "Holy shit," he breathes. My stomach knots. I didn't exactly lie to him, but I haven't been completely truthful and he has every right to be upset right now. I give him a look that says we'll talk about it later and can only hope he's fine with that. I turn back to face dad before I can read his face.

"—was seen getting up close and *extremely* personal with Seattle Vipers' star center and notorious playboy in a parking garage after last night's game."

"Dad, stop, it's not—" He cuts me off, looking more furious than I've ever seen him, even when I nearly burned down the lake house when I was sixteen and threw a party without permission, and I swallow hard. There's a dull ringing in my ears and there's a somewhat dream-like quality to everything. This can't possibly be real.

"*This* is what you're so hellbent on doing with your life? Why you refuse to give up this bullshit career," he doesn't need to use air quotes for me to know exactly what he thinks of my job. I clench my jaw, but he's not done yet. He shakes his head in...disgust, and despite every-thing, it fucking *hurts*. "Your mother would be so disappointed in you, giving up the life you should have at the company to be his whore of the month." He sneers in AJ's direction and it feels as if he's slapped me in the face. To bring mom into this, to say that she would be ashamed...and a small, sad, broken voice in the back of my head wonders if he's right. Tears well and I feel like I can't breathe.

"Hey, that's enough!" AJ says firmly, stepping forward. "You can say whatever you want about me, I don't give a shit, but you will *not* speak to her like that. I don't give a fuck if you're her father, or the richest man in Seattle, or the Queen of fucking England. You will not disrespect her again, or we're going to have a big problem, do you understand me?" he says, his voice scarily calm. He squares up to dad, pulling himself up to his full, impressive height and I think for a second he might really clock my father right in the jaw. His hands are loose at his sides, but I know his stance is deceptively casual. AJ knows how to fight. Hell, in a way, he gets fucking *paid* to do it.

Dad isn't used to not being regarded as the most intimidating man in the room, but he's smart enough to know that AJ would destroy him if he pushes his luck. It's not like I *want* a fight to break out but I'd be lying if the fact that AJ is willing to go there for me is one of the only things keeping me from spiraling and completely breaking down right now. Dad clenches his jaw over and over, but takes a very small step backwards before turning back to me. I can tell he's trying very hard to keep his voice even when he speaks again.

"You either stop this now, all of this," he cuts a glare at AJ before looking back to me again, "or I'm cutting you off."

I push past the hurt and shame and embarrassment, and snort in disbelief.

"I haven't taken any money from you in years, my *salary* in New York notwithstanding seeing as how I fucking earned that. What the hell are you talking about cutting me off?" I had a trust fund from mom, plus everything from her estate which was substantial, and everything I had saved from my job before I moved back here. I make decent money from the Vipers. So, I've been just fine on my own for quite a while.

"This house," he says, steam practically coming out of his ears in irritation.

"This house was mom's and then became mine," I say, brow furrowing. What the fuck is he talking about?

"This house was never your mother's. It's always been mine, Natalie." I blink, then blink again. He half-ass explains, "We kept it in my name for myriad reasons that don't matter now, and just never got around to changing it." My heart sinks. All this time, I thought I was out from under his thumb completely, but apparently not. My eyes fill with tears of anger.

"When I moved back here, you said...you said everything was taken care of with the house, that I didn't need to worry about it."

"Because you didn't. You were grieving and didn't need to be bothered with details of whose name was on a fucking deed, Natalie."

"But...but you knew what I was really asking. You know I hate taking your handouts! I always have. You let me believe it was mine," I say, shock making my voice sound thin.

"Yes, I did." There is no remorse in his eyes, not a single fucking shred of it. I huff out a humorless laugh.

"You just had to have me under your control in some way, didn't you?" I don't know if what he's saying is true, that he just didn't want me to worry about the house while I was trying to handle losing mom, or if my own conclusion is closer to the truth, but right now, it doesn't fucking matter. I see red and my heart splinters. Either way, he lied, knowing full well that I would have wanted to know the truth of it after the initial shock of mom's death wore off. I shake my head.

"If that's your ultimatum, then I choose my life as it is. I choose *him*, dad." I throw out a hand towards AJ. "He is my choice, always. So, I'll be out of the house in two weeks and then you can do with it what you will."

He blinks in shock, like he didn't really believe I'd give up the house so easily. It's not easy at all. It's fucking torture. This is the house I'd grown up in, the one seeped in so many memories of mom, and even dad too, that it feels as if it's a living, breathing part of me. Birthday parties and sleepovers, celebrating victories and letting tears fall with defeats, joy, pain, laughter, love, sorrow—all of it happened within these walls. My height is marked on the door frame upstairs. My handprints are in the concrete of the patio. My childhood dog, Marbles, is buried in the backyard beside the rosebushes. My first kiss, my big fallout with my best friend, Michelle when we were in tenth grade, my prom pictures senior and junior year—it was all here. I can't imagine just...leaving it.

But I will. I'm going to remove myself completely from my father's control and if that means I have to sever a part of me to do it, then so be it. Give me the fucking scalpel.

He grinds his teeth.

"Have it your way, Natalie." I force the tears not to fall and keep my shoulders back, my spine straight. I swear I see the tiniest hint of pride in those gray eyes when he sees that, but it's gone too quickly to be sure. He moves towards the door when AJ shifts to the side to let him pass. He lets the door slam shut behind him and all of the air rushes out of me, my legs threatening to give out. AJ is there in a heartbeat, gathering me in his arms. I cling to him, so grateful that he isn't pissed that I was less than forthcoming about who I really am. He just holds me until I've got enough of a handle on myself and the situation to step away. I look at the tabloids strewn across the counter again and shake my head.

"I didn't even think about this last night," I admit quietly. "I don't know why, but I didn't even think about them plastering those pictures all over the place."

"I'm so sorry, Nat."

"I guess we're officially official now," I mutter, thinking about the conversation I had with Hattie and Bobby at the game yesterday. I sigh and lean my elbows on the cool granite of the countertop, putting my head in my hands. I feel him shift beside me, leaning against the counter.

"So...you're really a Harrington, huh?" I look up and meet his gaze. There's not anger there, but there's some disappointment and confusion, and a touch of hurt. I don't blame him. If he told me he was hiding a whole part of himself from me, I'd honestly probably be storming out right about now.

"Legally, no. My name really is Natalie Morgan. I took my mom's name after they divorced to separate myself from him, from...all of it." I wave my hand, encompassing the entirety of the Harrington name. The hotels and apartment buildings, the foundations, the scholarships, the stadiums, the hospital wings—the list goes on and on. "But...yes. I'm a Harrington."

His eyes bulge and I know he's putting pieces together.

"The fucking Celeste...the hotel is named after you." I nod and he runs his hands through his hair, shaking his head slowly. "And you were there that night for his fundraiser because you're a part of the foundation too, whether you like it or not, right?" I don't answer because he already knows the truth. He begins to pace through the area between the living room and kitchen and I just watch, feeling helpless and honestly a little terrified. What is he really thinking? Is he pissed? Will he...end this?

"Jesus, Nat, you said your dad worked in real estate."

"Technically he does..." It sounds weak even in my own ears and he gives me a level look.

"I thought he was a fucking *realtor*, not the guy who owns half of Seattle for fuck's sake. And not just Seattle from what I understand..." I can see the wheels turning. Everyone thinks that Anthony Rizzo is just a hot, dumb jock, but really, he's smart as hell and sees way more than anyone realizes. "I'm assuming that's who you were working for in New York, then? The east coast branch of Harrington Group?" I nod again.

"Do the others know? Mac and Bobby?"

"No, you're the first to find out the whole truth. I'm sorry I didn't tell you. I just...I've never wanted to be in that shadow, but especially since I came back after my mom's death. I didn't want any of you to know who I really was, or who my family was, I guess, because I was trying to start over. I didn't want the name to be the first thing anyone saw." I chew on my lip, worry opening up a pit in my stomach the size of the Grand Canyon. *Oh God...what if he leaves?* It's a real possibility and he would have every right to but fuck, I really don't know if I can take it if he does. And to think, I'd been convinced that *he'd* be the reason this didn't work out, that he'd be the one to ruin it.

"Are you mad? You have every right to be, I'm just...asking," I finish lamely, my throat feeling thick.

"Mad?" He studies me and I hold his gaze, too afraid to look away. He sighs. "No, I'm not mad, Nat. I'm...I don't know, hurt I guess that you didn't think you could share this part of your life with me. I understand that you didn't want to when you were first starting with the Vipers, or even when we were all just starting to hang out as friends, but now that we're more, I...well, I just thought that you felt like you could share anything and everything with me, Nat. I thought we were both in the same place."

"We are," I say, desperate. "I do. I just...it just never seemed like the right time to bring it up. I wasn't trying to hide it from you now, I promise, I just kind of forgot, honestly." He snorts and I push on. "I'm serious. I've been so fucking happy since we started this that I haven't thought about anything else, especially the things that try to blotch out even a tiny bit of this happiness with their darkness, and my dad and our relationship and that whole part of my life is a huge ball of fucking dark. So, I pushed it all away and didn't even think about the fact that you didn't know about it. Because it didn't matter. You know me better than anyone else in the world ever has, the real me down to my bones, regardless of my last name, regardless of who my parents are, regardless of the front I've put on for almost everyone else in my life. You know me, AJ. All of me. I need you to believe that. Please believe that."

I let out a shuddering breath, realizing that I just kind of word vomited all of that at him. A tear escapes down my cheek and I wipe it away quickly. He takes a step towards me and cups my face between his big hands. I take a deep breath at the touch, needing it more than I even realized. He traces his thumbs over my cheeks and I reach out to splay my hands on his chest.

"I do believe that, Nat. I know you, baby. Trust me, I know who you are no matter what name you use, I just want you to share all the pieces of you with me, even the ones you may not like very much. None of them can change the way I feel about you. I fucking love you more than I thought any person could love someone else and it makes me want to know every little thing about you. Good, bad, ugly. *All* of it, Nat." I sigh, his words making the pit in my stomach close up and my heart swell inside my chest.

"I love you too." He leans in and kisses me then, soft and slow. We finally pull away and he leans his forehead against mine.

"You seem...relieved," he says.

"I am. I thought...well, I thought you might leave."

"Would you have?"

"Probably," I tell him honestly and he pulls away, brows clear up to his hairline in surprise. I give him a small smile. "I would have stormed out and then realized I was overreacting and we'd have really great make-up sex afterwards." His lips curl.

"Oh, that's a much better plan, actually. Hang on." He makes as if he's going to bolt out the door, taking a few quick steps away from me. I laugh and grab onto the hem of his shirt as soon as he's close enough again, tugging him towards me. He grips my waist and picks me up to set me on the edge of the counter, moving to put his hips between my thighs. I wrap my arms around him and lean into his chest as he rubs my back in slow, soothing circles.

"Thank you," I whisper. *For not leaving. For understanding. For loving me.* He kisses the top of my head and I squeeze him harder.

"So...are you loaded then?" he asks after a few minutes and I can't help but laugh.

"Uh, yeah, pretty much," I admit into his chest. He steps away and arches a brow at me.

"Ya know, I kinda thought you were just a big ole gold digger this whole time."

I smack him in the chest and he grins.

"No more secrets, at least not big ones like a whole secret life, deal?"

"Deal," I promise him, and then I sigh, knowing I've got a shit ton of stuff to figure out in a very short amount of time, but right now, all I want to do is crawl back into bed with the man that I love.

"How about—"

"Annie's to-go and you make up for being a lying hussy with hours upon hours of stupid hot sex in my bed since you're now a homeless street urchin?" he finishes, giving me *that* smile, the one that I fell so fucking hard for even when I tried like hell not to, and I laugh, knowing that no matter what's coming down the pike, I'll be fine as long as he's with me.

"That sounds a hell of a plan."

Twenty-Three

RIZZO

"So, on a scale of one to send-me-sexy-nudes, how much do you miss me already?" I ask over the FaceTime video. We'd had to leave for another string of away games the day after everything had gone down with Nat's dad and it's honestly been a bit of a whirlwind. The media attention was…a lot, but I convinced her to let us become "official official" as she puts it, on our own terms after the stupid paparazzi photos were posted everywhere. I didn't want the world thinking that Nat is just another in my admittedly lengthy list of hookups. She's so much more than that and the thought of people putting her in that box made me want to start punching things.

So, I'd posted a bunch of pics of us from the last few months with the caption "when you fall in love with one of your best friends, life just makes sense," and I think it made her feel better about the whole thing. She'd even teared up when she saw it and then promptly threw a pillow at me when I started to tease her about it.

Despite the whole Harrington secret identity bombshell, things with us are solid. Yeah, I'd been a little hurt, I won't lie, and that had thrown me a bit—I've never been hurt by a woman before, so I wasn't really sure how to navigate it—but I understand why she kept that part of herself and her life hidden, and at the end of the day, she's still the same Natalie to me. She's the same girl I fell in love with and can't imagine my life without. So, yeah, things are good with us. Great. Fucking perfect.

"Hmm," she says, tapping her chin. "I'd say send-you-sexy-videos-of-me-doing-very-naughty-things-to-myself level."

I groan and wipe my hand over my mouth.

"You're killing me, woman." She grins and I have to adjust myself. Just the mere thought of seeing her playing with herself because she misses me makes me hard as hell.

"There's an apartment open in your old building," she says. "Not the penthouse like *some* people," she gives me a pointed look and a grin, "but it looks pretty nice."

"Oh, that's cool," I say noncommittally. Neither have us have brought up the obvious answer to her housing predicament which is for her to move in with me. I think she thinks asking me will test the limits of my relationship skills a little too hard. And I haven't brought it up because...reasons. So, for now, she's house hunting. "I bet Jax knows who's place it was. He knows all the dirt on everyone in that building."

"Oh, noted. I'll ask him when I go to pick up the hyena." I laugh at her description of Zamboni. He's a great dog, but he really is crazy as hell, especially when he gets the zoomies. He literally ran in a circle around the living room thirty-seven times in a row the other night. Thirty-seven. In a row. Without stopping. It was nuts and of course hilarious, and the video has gotten over a million views.

"So, are you ready for my big St. Patrick's Day Blow Out? It's going to be epic. *Beyond* epic. I'm still waiting to hear back from the city officials about dying the whole lake green, but I have high hopes. I'm *very* charming and usually get what I want..."

"You are so ridiculous, but I'm definitely ready to see one of these parties for myself." My annual St. Patrick's Day parties are pretty legendary around Seattle and this one is sure to top them all. "Are you sure I can't help you set up or take care of anything for it?"

"Nope, it's all taken care of. Jax's girlfriend is a fantastic event planner. Her people are doing all of the work. We just get to show up, drink an unhealthy amount of green alcohol, and have fun."

"Well, I guess I better find something special to wear then. Something green and...crotchless, perhaps?"

I groan loudly at that particular visual.

"It's bad form to get me hard as fuck right before game time, Natalie," I scold. She gives me one of those sultry, challenging looks and my cock throbs. I'm already dying to get back between her thighs, to have her nails digging into my back and her breathy moans caressing my skin. It's crazy that we're still so fucking feral for each other, but I honestly hope it never fades.

"Mmm, I guess I might need to be punished when you get back. What was that word you love so much again?...*Edging*?"

I lick my lips, memories of the last time we'd played out this little game flashing in my mind and making me hard as fuck. Natalie, strapped to my bed, body soaked with sweat and trembling as I brought her to the brink over and over and over but never let her fall, not until hours later. God it had been the sexiest thing I'd ever experienced in my life and the thought of a repeat makes me want to hop a plane back to Seattle right this second. They can play the game without me, right?

"I think that can be arranged," I say in a low, gruff voice.

"Rizzo! Stop dirty talking with your girlfriend and get the fuck out here already!" Jules calls and Natalie giggles. I grin and sigh.

"Alright baby, I gotta go."

"Good luck. You may just have a video waiting for you when you get done..."

"You are an evil, beautiful, perfect woman. Love you."

She bites her lip and smiles. "Love you too."

"I was thinking about our next Ireland trip," mom says the next morning as we chat while we wait for our flight back to Seattle.

"Oh yeah? Anything special in mind this time?" We're set to go in just a few months again and she's in full planning mode already.

"I was thinking that a certain pretty blonde might want to come with us..."

"Hmm, yeah, I can ask Gronski if he wants to join." Mom laughs.

"I'm serious. I know this is still new but...well, I've never seen you so serious about anyone, AJ." *You have no idea, ma*, I think. "So, she should come with us. It'll be fun and I promise to be on my best behavior."

I snort.

"You and Natalie will be causing mayhem at the earliest opportunity, I have zero doubts."

"Alright, that's probably true, but I still think it's an excellent idea. Just float it to her and see what she thinks."

"Alright, I will."

"Oh good! I'll wait until after you ask before I bring it up." I shake my head, grinning. She and Nat are regular texting buddies and Ray told me that mom has been overjoyed with my new relationship. She never shamed me for my playboy lifestyle, of course, but I know she always worried that I was lonely.

My phone buzzes at my ear and I pull it away to check the screen. It's a text from Jax's girlfriend, Lucy, with planning questions.

"Hey, ma, I gotta run. I'll talk to you later, alright? Love you."

"Ok, sweetheart. I love you too."

I grin as I scroll through the picture options Lucy sent. I text back my answers. This night is going to be amazing. Shep settles into the chair beside me, offering up one of the two bottles of water he snagged.

"Thanks, man."

"So, how's the planning going?" he asks with a grin.

"I think it's safe to say it'll be a night no one will forget any time soon."

"Hell yeah," he says, clamping me on the shoulder. "Can't wait. Anything else I can do to help?"

"Nah, man, thanks. I've got one more thing to take care of myself, and Lucy's got the rest covered."

He smiles wider and squeezes my shoulder before dropping his hand.

"This is going to be a night for the books, my friend."

"Even better than Drunk Hunt sophomore year?" Shep and I had orchestrated a huge drunken scavenger hunt that year. We had fifty people split up into teams of five, each team had a video camera, and a list of over two hundred different challenges to complete or things to find spanning all over campus, each one worth a varying number of points. Most things involved alcohol, or nudity, or both. More than one team had been chased by police and the videos that each team took would make fantastic blackmail tools for a few of our classmates who went on to become congressmen and senators. It was one hell of a fucking good time and one of the best nights of my life.

"That night will live in infamy, it's true, but...this one may just top it." He winks at me and my lips curl.

It's going to put Drunk Hunt to shame.

Twenty-Four

NAT

"Oh you know what, I heard there was a, um...big drug ring operating out of that neighborhood, actually," Hattie says about another rental I'd found. I would rather just buy something, but I'm short on time, so I figure I'll grab a rental for a few months and then really figure everything out. Dad hasn't given me a date certain to be out by or anything, but I want to get this done and over with. In fact, we haven't spoken at all. I guess when I move out I'll just have the keys delivered to his office via courier and that'll be that. My whole relationship with my dad down to a stranger delivering keys. I try not to think about that too hard or I'll start crying and maybe never stop. Despite everything, he's my fucking *dad*. I don't what this to be how we end up.

I narrow my eyes at her. She seems to be trying to find things wrong with every single listing I've shown her and I don't really understand why. I think maybe she's trying to protect me, like if she stalls me long enough, I'll change my mind and try to work things out with my dad and not have to leave this house that she knows holds such a big place in my heart. I love her for it, but I'm not going back. My decision has been made. I've had a few really good cries about it and I've come to realize that a house is just a house. It's the memories that matter and nothing can take those away. So, I'm ok with it. Really.

"Drug ring, huh?"

"Oh yeah. Huge. Tons of meth." I arch a brow and give a look that makes it clear I'm not buying a word of that, but she merely grins a dimply grin at me and I can't help but laugh. "So, what about this one?" she asks, changing the subject and holding up a gorgeous emerald green satin cocktail dress with beading along the sweetheart neckline.

"Oohhh," I say, reaching out to run my hands over the material. "But are we sure this isn't too fancy for a St. Patrick's Day party?" I realized when we set out to go shopping that I never confirmed with AJ on dress code—well, the dress code everyone else sees anyway. I'm all good on the one that only he gets to ogle after everyone else leaves—and he's in some important meeting right now, so I'll have to rely on Hattie and Shep's word for it.

"Nah, Connor said it's always like New Years Eve Party attire, but just, ya know, in March." AJ throws his famed St. Patrick's Day party every year, this just happens to be the first year he gets to host it as his own place. I know he's really excited about it, but stressed too. He's really thrown himself into the planning, talking and texting with Lucy constantly to get all the preparations done just right. It's kind of adorable actually and my heart twists a little remembering what he told me about St. Patrick's Day when he was a kid, how special it was for him and his mom and their little celebration they'd do every year. I love that his love for the holiday has stayed with him over the years and though the way he celebrates now is quite a bit different, the fact that it's still so important is really sweet when you think about it.

And I've got green Kool Aid, shamrock cookies, and decorations made out of construction paper (thanks to some help from Ollie, of course) ready for a little celebration of our own that morning. I think he's going to love it. Might even cry a little. Ray and I are betting on that actually.

"Hmm, well I think I have the perfect heels to go with this, then."

I pull down AJ's long drive, marveling at the thousands of green and white twinkling lights hanging in all of the trees lining the road on either side all the way down the quarter-mile stretch. I pull around the circular part of the driveway that wraps in front of the house, and Jax is waiting with a giant smile. He opens my door for me and helps me out.

"Wow, you look beautiful, Nat." It had taken weeks for me to finally get him to stop calling me *Ms. Morgan.*

"Thanks, Jax. Everything looks amazing. Lucy did fantastic!" More lights are tucked within huge, elegant flower arrangements lining the wide stairs leading up to the front porch. It's like something out of a fairy tale. Not quite what I'd envisioned for a St. Patty's Day rager, but still gorgeous. AJ had loved our little celebration this morning and though I lost the bet and he didn't end up crying, there were definitely some unshed tears in his eyes, so Ray decided we could call it a draw.

But as much as he loved that, I know he's so excited for tonight. He was practically vibrating with it all day and could barely sit still. I take in the decorations again, ready to get this thing started...but I frown. Something is off. Shouldn't there be music blaring from inside already? Voices raised in cheers and debauchery? It may be semi-formal attire, but the vibes are most definitely going to be frat party on steroids. As they should be. I'm ready to kick Jules' and Bobby's asses in beer pong and later do drunken, unholy things to AJ.

My brow furrows a bit.

"Am I the first one here?"

"Nah, I've parked a dozen cars down at Mr. Shepherd's already." I know he got a couple of other guys to help run the valets back and forth from Shep's place to here with the golf cart, but I don't see any of them. They must be down at the other end. He gives me a winning smile and gestures for me to head inside, his honey eyes sparking with...something. Maybe just excitement for the party. I smile back and head around the car while he slides into the driver's seat.

My heels clack loudly against the stone porch and when I push open the door, I'm...confused.

It's dark in the entry. The overhead lights are off and the only illumination is provided by candles burning on small pillars lining the hallway, draped with more flowers. Now I hear that there is music playing, but not at all the music I expect. It's Michael Bublé crooning softly instead of the *Best of 2000s Club Mix* that we'd spent hours coming up with yesterday. There are no other voices, no drunken singing, or people toasting, or hell, even someone puking already.

"Uh, hello?" I call as I take a few slow steps through the foyer. *What in the hell is going on?*

"In here," AJ says from around the corner in the living room. I take the last steps past the wall and freeze.

AJ is standing in the middle of the living room in a sharp deep gray suit with a green tie. All of the furniture had been moved out for the party—or what I'd thought was a party—and now the entire giant room is filled with flowers and more of those soft, twinkling lights. Zamboni sits at AJ's side, a green bowtie on and smiling that golden smile. He wags his tail and barks at me in greeting, pushing back on his hind legs and pawing at the air like he's waving. I smile, though my heart is galloping like a racehorse.

"AJ, what's happening?" My eyes are already watering at what I *think* is happening, but...no, it can't be...that's crazy, isn't it?

He smiles and he looks so damn gorgeous that it takes my breath away.

"You look absolutely beautiful, Nat," he says in a low voice as his eyes travel down my body and up again. He traces his tongue over his bottom lip, biting it gently before grinning. He arches a brow and cocks his head, clearly asking me why I'm still all the way across the room. I walk towards him on somewhat numb legs, my heart in my throat, and when I'm just a foot or so away, he sinks down to one knee.

"Oh my God," I whisper.

He pulls out a box and holds it out towards me. I hold my breath as he slowly opens the lid—

"*Holy shit,*" I gasp when I see the stunning ring within and he huffs out a quiet laugh. It's an absolutely massive solitary cushion cut diamond in the center, with smaller diamonds lining the two thin bands that split to cradle the larger stone. I can't even begin to guess how big the thing is or how much it cost. It's the most beautiful ring I've ever seen. This has to be a dream. I *have* to be dreaming...right?

"I know that this is crazy fast and that we haven't been dating all that long, but they always say when you know, you know. And I *know*, Nat. Deep in my soul and beyond a shadow of a doubt, I know that you are the only one for me. From the second I heard you squeak when you first met me..." My eyes fly wide for a second.

"Oh God *you heard that??*" He's never brought it up before, so I always assumed he didn't notice. His smile somehow gets even broader and I groan, covering my face.

"Of course I did and it was fucking adorable. Even in that moment, I knew that you had me. I'm not going to lie and say it was love at first sight, but you caught my eye in every possible way that day, caught my attention like no one else ever had, and when we all started hanging out, everything in my life just shifted without me even realizing it. Everything was pointing me to you, Nat. You became one of my best friends, and now, I love you more than I ever thought I could love anyone. You make me feel like *me* in a way no one else can, like I'm more than just a hockey player or a thirst trap or whatever else. To you, I'm just AJ and it feels so fucking good to have that in my life. I never knew how much I needed it until you. And, yeah, it's a little scary, but if there's anyone that I want on this crazy, terrifying, amazing ride with me, it's you. You're my best friend and the love of my fucking life, and I can't imagine not spending every second of every day of forever with you. So, will you marry me?"

Tears track down my cheeks and I hold his gaze.

"You're serious?"

"As a fucking heart attack, baby." He grins and waits. "So, is that a yes, or..."

"Yes," I say, laughing through the tears. "Yes, yes, yes!" Zamboni barks again and spins around in circles when AJ slides the ring on my finger. He stands and cups my face between his hands, leaning in and kissing me like there's no tomorrow. I wrap my arms around him and he picks me up, spinning me around and I can feel him smile against my lips. He sets me down and then voices erupt from behind us.

I turn to see our friends pouring into the room, all smiling and clapping and, in Hattie's case, crying.

"You knew??" I ask. "You all knew!?"

"We did," Howey confirms.

"*I* didn't until about 5 minutes ago," Jules complains.

"That's because you can't keep a secret for shit," Shep says, tugging

AJ into a bear hug while Hattie strangles me in one of her own. I catch Jules and Bobby sharing a quick look before they both tear their gazes away and join in the congratulations.

I eye Hattie with a narrowed gaze. "So this is why you were deliberately shooting down every housing option I found?" She smiles a little sheepishly.

"Well, I didn't want you to lose out on a deposit and first months' when you already had a place waitin' for you—assuming you said yes, of course. If you hadn't, or if you aren't ready to live with this knucklehead, I'll really start helping you look for places tomorrow." I look over at AJ, laughing and smiling with the guys, and my heart just can't fucking take it.

"I think I'm just fine here." She squeals and jumps up and down.

"Wait, so there was never any St. Patrick's Day party? But it's your tradition."

"Oh there's still a party. A huge one. But this was more important to do first."

I wrap my arms around him again while Hattie pours everyone champagne.

"I'm more important than St. Paddy's Day? Wow."

"It's a close second." He kisses me and then grasps my hand, bringing it to his lips as well. He kisses my finger, just above the diamond. "I'd planned to give you a Claddagh ring, actually, but, well, I couldn't find one with a big enough rock attached to it to be honest."

I throw my head back and laugh at that, kissing him again and assuring him that I would have been happy with a piece of string tied around my finger if it meant I got to be engaged to him.

"Oh in that case, we'll just take this baby back tomorrow then..." I yank my hand away, cradling it to my chest protectively and he grins.

"I said I *would* have been happy with the string. You chose otherwise and well, no take backs, sucker."

"Alright y'all, hush!" Hattie calls over the din. It's a small group, but the Sin Bin—plus Jax, who has become a new honorary member in recent weeks—aren't known for our inside voices. We all quiet down. "Ok, everyone got their champagne?" We all nod and she raises her glass, all of us mirroring the motion. AJ slides one arm around the small of my back, holding me close to his side, and I snuggle in just a bit closer. Her eyes water as she meets his eyes and then mine. *The big softie*, I think as I blink away my own tears.

"To two of the best people I know. I'm so happy you both got over being complete idiots and figured your shit out." Everyone laughs and Shep leans in to kiss her on the temple. I know one day they'll be where we are and I'll be giving the toast to them. "I cannot wait to see you spend forever together. We love you. Sláinte!"

"Sláinte!" we all echo, and hearing the word first in Hattie's southern twang and then in Jules' thick Bostonian accent, has us all dying laughing.

"Murphy MacManus said it best: It's St. Paddy's Day—everyone's Irish tonight! Drink up, assholes!"

We all cheers again, chugging the rest of our drinks.

"So, where's this other party?"

"At The Bowery," AJ says, wrapping his arms around me from behind. "But it's up to you if you want to go, or if you'd rather celebrate...*privately*." He leans in and whispers the last word directly into my ear and I shiver violently.

Just when I'm about to tell him that the answer is definitely Option B, I notice someone else standing just inside the room from the foyer and I freeze. The surprises just keep on coming tonight apparently.

"Dad?"

RIZZO

THIS IS THE BEST NIGHT OF MY FUCKING LIFE. I HADN'T BEEN worried exactly, but I'd been nervous as hell. It's batshit crazy but, well, what about Nat and me hasn't been? It may be insane, but I know it's completely and totally *right*. I spent most of my adult life loving the freedom of not being tied down. But now, all I want is to be tied to Nat in every possible way for the rest of my life. When you know you want forever, why wouldn't you want forever to start as soon as fucking possible? So, yeah, I don't give a shit if anyone else thinks it's too fast or too crazy or too whatever else.

Knowing I was going to do this is the reason I hadn't asked Nat to move in the second that she had the fight with her dad that day. I figured it would be way smoother to ask my *fiancé* to move in. I have a flare for the dramatic, what can I say?

Everything had gone perfectly to plan—even this newest development was a contingency I'd planned on, just in case.

Charles Harrington stands on the other side of the room, looking only the tiniest bit flustered. Nat stiffens in my arms when she sees him and I straighten. He meets my gaze and gives me a nod of understanding and a bit of respect, and I return it.

Nat turns to me, confusion in her eyes.

"What's going on? Did you call him?"

"I...just laid out some facts and let him do with that information what he would. But I think you two should go talk now that he's here. He doesn't completely deserve it, but...olive branches and all that." I shrug. "Use the office." I give her what I hope is an encouraging look and kiss on the forehead. She looks a little skeptical, but there's a bit of hope there too. Despite everything, I know she doesn't want to cut her dad out of her life. They may not have the easiest relationship, but he's still her dad and I know she loves him. She nods and walks towards her father. He tenses but follows when she gestures down the hall.

I let out a long breath. I hope to God this doesn't turn out to ruin this entire fucking night. If it does, at least maybe I'll have a good excuse to punch the guy.

I think back to my meeting with him yesterday.

I'd gone to his office and to his credit, he hadn't just had security toss me out immediately. His office is on the top floor of one of the tallest buildings in Seattle and the room itself and the view very much give *Master of the Universe*. He'd been seated behind his massive mahogany desk and looked stoic as hell when I'd walked in. He probably intimidates most people, but my hands had clenched into fists as I'd stalked inside, remembering the shit he'd said to Nat that day at her place, and he didn't look intimidating to me. He looked small and pathetic, but I forced myself to keep my cool. I had things to say and decking the guy probably wouldn't help matters.

"And to what do I owe this pleasure?" he'd asked, the sarcasm so sharp it could cut through steel.

I held up a hand.

"That'll be the last bit of talking you do for the next few minutes or I swear to God I'll put you through a wall for the way you spoke to Natalie last time I saw you." He'd narrowed his eyes, his jaw clenching, but I'd given him a look that told him I was dead fucking serious and he apparently believed me, so I continued on when he remained quiet.

"I'm here to talk, not to have a conversation. I'm asking Natalie to marry me tomorrow night." His eyes widened a fraction in surprise, but he didn't try to comment. Smart man. "I'm not here to ask you for permission—you don't have any right to have a say in her life after how you've treated her, and I'm pretty sure Nat would kick my ass if I actually asked you anyway—I'm just here to tell you to your face that I'm going to marry your daughter. I love her more than anything else on this earth and I'm going to give her the best possible life that I can. I will use every single breath that I have making sure she knows how fucking amazing and beautiful and smart and talented and special she is, making sure she knows how loved she is. You don't deserve to know, but I'm telling you anyway, because if I'm ever lucky enough to have a daughter of my own, I sure as shit would want to hear this from the man who wanted to marry her."

His jaw worked beneath his short beard as he clenched and unclenched his teeth, but there was more than just anger in those gray eyes then, the eyes that are so much like Nat's that it's startling. There was...regret. Hurt. Maybe even a little shame.

I'd leaned forward and thrown a piece of paper on his desk—my address and a time.

"If you decide to get over your bullshit, there you go. If not, well, it's your loss, honestly, not hers. But I know what it's like to have a parent *choose* to walk out of your life and she deserves better than that. Make the better choice. Just because her life may not be the one you pictured for her doesn't mean it's not a damn good one."

With that, I'd turned and walked out of his office without a backwards glance.

"Damn, I still can't believe Nat is really a Harrington," Bobby says taking a sip of his champagne and wrinkling his nose, pulling me out of the memory. I laugh.

"Want a beer instead? I've got plenty."

"Oh God yes, please. I've never liked this stuff. Probably stems from projectile vomiting after drinking too much of it at my cousin's wedding when I was like fourteen."

"Same here," Jules says, sidling up to us. "I mean about not loving champagne, not the puking thing. Come on, Bobby, I'll grab a beer with you." Bobby thins his lips for a heartbeat before putting on a very convincing, but very fake, smile. Jules said that the two of them got in a pretty heated argument over "something stupid" and they're apparently still working on getting past it. I have a feeling I know what it is, but that isn't my secret to tell, so I'm keeping my trap shut.

"Want anything?" he asks before they walk away.

"Nah, I'm good."

Mac comes up after they walk away and throws her arms around me, kissing my cheek.

"If you had told me five months ago that Anthony Fucking Rizzo would not only be in a real, monogamous relationship, but *engaged*, I woulda said you were smokin' the good stuff."

"I know, I know." She wipes the lipstick off of my cheek and the sheer joy I see shining in her eyes makes my throat feel thick. My best friend really did get the best girl. Well, aside from mine, of course. "Thank you for the help scheming."

"Our pleasure," Shep says, walking up behind Mac and pulling her back into his chest. He leans down and kisses her cheek before rubbing his scruff against her, making her squeal and giggle.

"So, uh, what's the story with her dad showing up?" Mac asks quietly.

"I went to see him." Her brows fly up.

"No shit?"

"No shit," I confirm. "There were some things he needed to hear and I guess he listened to them. Or, I'm hoping that's why he's here. I guess we'll see." My phone buzzes and I pull it out. "Oh, lemme grab this. One sec." They nod and walk away to talk to the rest of the group.

"Hey, guys," I say, answering the video call.

"Well??" mom asks, practically jumping up and down in her excitement. I'd only told her it was happening right before Nat was supposed to arrive because God love her, mom is worse at keeping secrets than Jules. She wouldn't have spilled the beans on purpose, but she somehow would have found a way, I just know it.

"She said yes." My cheeks are throbbing from the dumb ass grin I can't seem to wipe from my face. Mom screams so loudly I wince and Ray covers his ears. "Ma. Ma! You're going supersonic here," I say with a laugh.

"I'm sorry, I'm sorry. I'm just so happy, sweetheart!" Her eyes water and Ray beams.

"Congratulations, son."

"Thanks, dad."

"Well, where is my soon-to-be daughter in law? I want to see that ring."

"She's...talking to her dad, actually." Their expressions of shock are so nearly identical that I want to laugh.

"Wow, so your big pep talk worked, huh?" Ray asks.

"Only time will tell."

Twenty-Six

NAT

I don't know why in the hell my dad is here, but I refuse to let him ruin this night. We walk into AJ's office and my lips curl at the sight of all of his old trophies and framed jerseys lining the walls. But the smile fades quickly as I close the door and cross my arms.

"What are you doing here?" I ask, jumping right to the heart of it. I have celebrating to do and I don't want to waste a single second of this night. It's AJ's favorite holiday and my new favorite too.

"I found an old letter from your mom," he says, completely throwing me for a loop. Of all the things I thought he'd open with, this wasn't even close to making the list. "We used to send each other letters and notes, from the time we first started dating up until the day she died."

"I had no idea," I tell him honestly. She'd never said a word about them. He nods and there's something different about him, a heaviness that I've never seen before.

"You know that we were...too combustible to be together in the conventional sense, but we loved each other every second of every day for over half our lives." My eyes prick with tears, and I don't even know why. Talking about mom? Hearing dad talk about how much he loved her? Residual emotions built up from everything else that's happened tonight? Who knows.

"Your fiancé came to see me," he says, making me blink in confusion once again.

"He came to ask your *permission*?" I ask, incredulous.

His lips actually curl up at the edges. "Not even close, actually. He came to *tell* me that he was marrying you and essentially to get my head out of my ass." I can't help but huff out a laugh at that and his smile grows ever so slightly before he turns serious once more. "After he left, I grew a bit...introspective, I guess you could say. He made some compelling arguments, I'll admit. I ended up going through my box of letters from your mom—it's what I do when I need a bit of grounding, to get lost in the conversations with the love of my life and the greatest friend I ever had—and I found an unopened one. It was from a few months before she died and I somehow missed it. I swear it was like she meant for it to happen, like she hid it until the moment I needed it most..." He shakes himself, a small smile pulling his lips upward. I've never heard him talk about mom—or life in general—this way. There's something different about him I realize now, like I'm seeing him for the first time or like he's taken his armor completely off for once.

"In it, she told me how unhappy you were in New York and that if I didn't stop trying to push my own vision of your life on you, one day I would push too far, that I'd push too fucking far and I'd lose you forever and it would be the worst mistake of my life. And as usual, she was right. She thought she would be there to help us find our way through it, of course, but...well, the world is cruel sometimes."

I swallow hard, my eyes burning with tears now. He clears his throat and takes a deep breath.

"I'm sorry, Natalie. I shouldn't have tried to force this life on you when you so clearly didn't want it. I had a vision for how I thought your future would be, our future, together, and you know how hard it is for me to let go of a goal once I set my eyes on it. I wouldn't be here, wouldn't be the person I am or have the empire we do if I wasn't this way. But, I shouldn't have pushed so hard, especially not after you told me it wasn't what you wanted. And I never should have said those things that day at the house. That was entirely out of line, and I apologize."

I stare at him, not sure I'm really hearing him right at all.

"What the hell did AJ say to you?" What could possibly have brought this on?

"He reminded me that I have a choice here, and I don't want to choose to walk away. I don't want to choose to not have my only daughter in my life. Willow would be disappointed if she was here, but not in you, Natalie. Never you. She'd be beyond disappointed in *me* and the way I've been acting. I think..." He exhales roughly and rubs the back of his neck. "I think that I've been so focused on your future and getting you back at the company because it helped me cope with losing her. Like if I just kept blinders on to everything but the future I was so damned determined to control, then I wouldn't have to think about what we lost, about how much I miss her every single day. It wouldn't be real..." His voice cracks at the end and so does my heart. I knew he was hurting but I never realized how much and how alone he was in his grief. I should have known, shouldn't I? I should have tried harder.

"Dad," I whisper, tears falling slowly down. He clears his throat and meets my eyes.

"I can't promise that I'll do everything right all the time, but I am going to try, Natalie. I promise you I'm going to try if you're willing to try with me."

"I..." I dare to let myself believe his words, dare to let myself imagine a life with dad in it without us at each other's throats over every little thing. I see a future of all of us spending holidays together, of him playing with his grandkids one day, and I want it. It's all that I've ever wanted. "I would really like that, dad."

He lets out a long, shuddering breath, and the weight of the world seems to have been lifted from his shoulders. He smiles then, a real, soft smile that crinkles the skin around his gray eyes. It's a smile that I rarely see but that warms my entire heart.

"Well let me see the damn ring," he says, and I can tell he's trying very, very hard not to cry. I huff out a laugh and walk forward holding up my hand so he can see the ring. He lets out a low whistle. "I'm impressed." He meets my eyes again. "I'm impressed with the man, too."

"He's a pretty damn good one, shirtless selfies notwithstanding." He laughs at that, and it's been so long since I've heard him laugh like this that I think I must be dreaming.

"Come here, kiddo." He holds his arms out and I sink into them, wrapping my dad in a hug, the first real hug we've had in too long to remember. I really hope that this is the start to a new beginning for us. And it's all thanks to AJ. God, if I wasn't already completely in love with the man, I sure as hell would be now.

As if reading my thoughts, dad adds quietly, "Now, I'm not giving him all of the credit, mind you. I was already trying to find a way to swallow my pride and fix this, but...well, he gets the win for giving me the push I needed." I laugh lightly and Dad squeezes me so damn tightly. We both hold on for a long, long time. It's the most cathartic hug in the history of the world, I think.

We eventually pull away and I smile.

"Come on. I want to introduce you to my friends."

Hours later, AJ and I lay tangled up together in his—*our*—bed. We'd celebrated both our engagement and St. Patrick's Day *hard*, starting with entirely too much green beer and ending with an accidental flash mob rendition of *From Now On* from *The Greatest Showman* in the middle of downtown. It was epic and the best night of my entire life for so many reasons. I'm engaged to the man I love more than anything in the world. I have amazing friends who have turned into family, who love me and all my crazy choices. I really feel good about the place dad and I are in for the first time in my adult life. No one ended up kidnapped or shot or in the hospital.

Best. Night. Ever.

"So, mom wanted me to invite you on our next Ireland trip before I even told her I was going to propose." AJ runs his fingers lazily through my hair and I want to purr like a cat.

"Really?" I can't help but grin. The immediate acceptance and love both of his parents showed me since the very beginning makes my chest clench every time I think about it. They're seriously amazing and though I wish so badly that my mom was here with me, I'm so grateful that Muriel is already a willing substitute.

"And I was thinking...there's this castle in Belfast that I've always loved..."

"Are we buying a castle now??" I ask with a smile and he huffs out a laugh.

"If you want a castle, baby, I'll buy you a fucking castle, just say the word. But actually I was thinking it would be a perfect place for a wedding."

I press myself up onto my elbows and look down at him. He's so damned handsome that I could cry. His hair is a tousled mess, his lips a touch swollen from our kisses, his five o'clock shadow looking incredibly sexy in the low light. He reaches out and pinches my chin gently between his thumb and forefinger.

"What do you say?"

I know how special Ireland is to him, the deep connection to family that it's always meant to him, and the fact that he wants to marry me there and make me a part of that makes my chest twist from pure happiness. My lips curl upward.

"I think I could be persuaded to marry my Irish thirst trap in an Irish castle." He smiles that heartbreakingly perfect smile and shifts his hand, sliding his palm over my cheek and pulling me down to kiss me softly.

"Have I mentioned how fucking lucky I am lately?"

"Hmm, not in the last five minutes, no." I say with a smirk. He rolls so fast that I can't even yelp, pinning my body with his. My hands run up his sides and across his lower back, and he makes a low, appreciative sound that rumbles through his chest. He leans down and kisses me slowly, the deep deliberate sweeps of his tongue making my pulse race and my toes curl. His St. Christopher pendant rests gently on my chest, just above my heart, and the cool metal and familiar weight has become a comfort in these months.

"I love you, Natalie Morgan."

I wrap my hands around his nape, tangling my fingers into his hair.

"I love you more, Anthony Rizzo."

He kisses me once more and grins against my lips.

"Not possible," he argues. "But one thing's for sure: I am one lucky bastard."

Acknowledgments

As always, this book wouldn't exist without the help and support of a bunch of people, so this is the part where I scream big, giant, huge, enormous THANK YOUS! to:

- My awesome husband, Dennis, for always supporting me in this weird hobby.
- Kayleigh, Lexie, and Kala (still funny) for being members of the best group chat in the world, for nonstop cheerleading, support, fan-girling, hype-girling, bullying, and love. Jeff Beans. Get the pudding. I love you all so hard.
- My amazing PA, Nancy for being a rock star and never thinking I'm crazy—or, well, that's probably not entirely accurate, but at least not running for the hills when I get these insane ideas to release books with practically no warning 😄
- All of my amazing ARC readers - you mean more to little indie authors like me than you can possibly realize.
- All of my equally amazing regular readers. Yeah, you, the one reading this right now. THANK YOU. I wouldn't still be doing this without you.

Also by K.D. Miller

<u>YA SCI-FI AND FANTASY</u>

- The Outliers Series (Titan Rising; Titan Unleashed; Titan Reckoning)
- Evansfire

<u>ADULT PARANORMAL ROMANCE</u>

- Veracity of the Gods Series (Dark Burning; Sweet Tempest)
- Red
- Vows Forged in Blood

<u>ADULT CONTEMPORARY ROMANCE</u>

- Carpe F*cking Diem
- Puck the Holidays (Vipers Sin Bin - Book #1)
- Wrong Place. Wrong Time. Right Viscount.